ISBN 13-978-0-578-22187-8
www.becomethemachine.net

3010
BECOME THE MACHINE

HERMAN JENKINS

TABLE OF CONTENTS

PROLOGUE

In the year 2995, infighting sets in among the Shell Dwellers, a lineage of digital travelers scattered across space and time, and descendants of the first hybrid machines who visited earth and seeded the planet with life. The Shell Dwellers are sworn to protect the earth and the spirit and purpose of the games they hold sacred. The Shell Dwellers are the keepers of the living keys and the secrets of human kinetic code sequencing, ultimately possessing the ability to manipulate DNA code to enhance human abilities

In the Shell Dwellers' dispute, a living key is lost. This unforeseen happening causes a ripple effect through time that creates a new dimensional reality where sport is no more. In this new world, sport has been unseated by virtual gaming technology integrated with artificial intelligence.

The only way to unravel this alternate reality is if the lost living key finds its way. If the Shell Dwellers fail, the world of sport will be forever lost in time and forgotten.

I hate my brother. I say it, but I don't think I really mean it. But I do. I hate my brother. I don't know who died and made him think he is God, but he certainly believes himself to be. I mean, not in a literal sense, but he is a jerk.

That may not be the most appropriate way for an eleven-year old to describe her brother, but all I can say is, I've got to call a spade a spade.

This summer day began like any other. Jason came downstairs brushing his hair and went straight for the mailbox. He came back in the door with a stack of mail folded under his arm that looked like two Sunday papers. There were two bills for my mama, and a postcard from our cousin Jen who lives in China. He didn't bother reading the postcard. He gave it to me. The rest of the mail was his. All from coaches that want him to play basketball, football, or both at their school. "Blue chip scholar athlete," "five star recruit," "generational talent," ESPN and the newspapers use these words to preface his name like I use "Mr." and "Mrs." to address my teachers. They worship him.

"Mama, can we get some breakfast up in the pride land?" He yelled up the stairs.

"Boy don't talk to me like that. I will be downstairs in a second!" Mama roared back.

I could have mouthed right along with those words to mock her. She says the same thing to him all the time. I mean, the first part is right, but I'm still waiting for the day she tells him to fix his own damn breakfast.

As I do every morning, I was sitting in the study on the computer. I love coding. You know, scratch code, the building blocks of software, apps, basically, everything we do on our computers and phones. I can't get enough. I was finishing code for an app I was building for summer camp, and that's when my brother walks in.

"Hey, what's that over there in the corner?" He said.

I looked to the corner. I knew there was nothing there, but I looked anyway. My brother grabbed the mouse and clicked the refresh button. He erased hours of work, and now, I was pissed.

"Mama!" I screamed at the top of my lungs, but of course she dismisses me. I punched him in the arm and he just stood there like a block of stone. Everyone seemed big to me, but Jason was really big.

"Girl, quit all that hollering, and loud talking. You see I'm cooking breakfast." Mama said. I so badly wanted to say, "No, you're cooking Jason's breakfast." That would only get me slapped and add injury to the insult. I know that's not how the saying goes, but in this instance, it works.

A text popped up on my phone in all caps. It was from my friend Shawnee, and it said:

NINJA IS STREAMING LIVE ON TWITCH!

"What!" I shouted anxiously as if Shawnee was in the room.

"Ninja is streaming on twitch!" I eagerly texted back:

When?

"Who the hell is Ninja?" Mama said, looking at me like I was speaking Farsi.

"What? He is only like the greatest gamer of all time Mama! This guy has more hits online than LeBron James, the President, and any rapper you can think of. He's like a gamer god. Forte Night legend!"

"She doesn't care about your little video game world, Mesi." Jason said, waving the stack of mail in my face. "When you start getting letters for playing those stupid games, and she can see the return on her investment, then she might start paying attention."

He was waving envelopes back and forth in my face. Each addressed to him from Notre Dame, Michigan, Alabama, Duke, UCLA, USC, Detroit, and so on. The list doesn't end. A text came back from Shawnee, but my phone battery died as soon as I unlocked the screen. I wanted to scream.

"Whatever! You act like you don't play video games or use the computer." I said. "E-gaming has taken off!"

"Yeah, I'll play, but you are in the school shooter training program. There is a difference. I play real games, real sports. You play with toys. You play them baby games. They're two completely different things," Jason said, "and that coding garbage is even stupider. Looks like you are trying to write the alphabet backwards."

"Shut up Jason! Just leave me alone." That's why you ain't going to Michigan. You're going end up right here in Detroit going to U of D! Who are they, the Tartars?" I snickered. "When that lame band plays their fight song, it sounds like they're letting air out of a balloon!"

"Detroit is the Titans and Wayne State ain't been the Tartars since Tupac was alive, Dummy. Wayne State was the Tartars now they're the Warriors. Detroit is the Titans. You don't even know what a Tartar is." Jason said.

"I do know what it is. It's a Mongolian warrior. You didn't know what it was," I said, "and that's why you ain't going to Michigan."

7

Jason didn't like that. It was a crime against humanity to tell Jason what he wasn't going to do. He swiftly folded up his mail and bumped my chair angrily as he reached over me to grab the envelope opener off the desk. He walked toward the door, and I said nothing as he bopped on by looking like George Jefferson.

Don't get me wrong. I love George Jefferson. He don't take no mess, but he still walks funny. Mama would let me watch *The Jeffersons*. She says they are no different than us. They did what we were trying to do, and that was move on up to the east side. But *Good Times*, she won't let me watch that because she says J.J. is a coon. Mama can't stand a black man playing a fool, unless it's Jason.

"Can you come sit near the window Mesi? I want to listen to the radio and catch the morning sports talk. You know we get best signal through them braces Magneto." Jason said, laughing. I mean he was cracking himself up.

"Leave me alone, Jason." I said. He is still laughing at his own jokes. Who does this? Oh, yeah, my brother does.

"My name is J-Squared. Jason Joshua. Two "J"s. Two sports. My name is J-Squared."

"Mama named you Jason!" I said. "Just like daddy!"

Out of the corner of the living room I hear the rustle of the newspaper and the most warm and welcoming voice.

"Quit pestering that girl."

It was Grandpa. He had been living with us for a few years now, and even he has noticed how Jason has changed over the years. I get tired of Grandpa preaching to me and I'm only 11, but that doesn't stop me from listening. Most of what he is saying is true, except the parts about him hunting down dragons, and playing in the Negro Leagues. I know Grandpa is old, but Mama says, just because you were black, born in the 1930's, and played on the sand lot, doesn't mean you played in the Negro Leagues. She says Grandpa played baseball like I bowl, which isn't very good.

"C'mon old man I'm just messing with Mesi." Jason said.

"My name is Missy."

"I just like calling you Mesi because nobody cares about soccer, or anything else you do."

"That's enough!" Grandpa yelled. Coughing, he crumpled his newspaper to cover his mouth. He struggled to catch his breath and regain his composure.

Mama came over to him to check on Grandpa. She brought a glass of water.

"Jason, go eat so we can get you to work," You two have gotten your grandfather all worked up." Mama said.

"You *two*? What did I do?" I said.

"Girl, shut-up! Fix yourself some cereal." Mama yelled.

I made oatmeal just because she commanded cereal. Jason was cleaning the syrup off his plate with the last few waffles on his fork. He tossed the sticky plate into the sink and walked out of the kitchen. The microwave beeped, my breakfast was done, and for a few minutes, it was quiet.

Jason crept past Grandpa in the den. He was sneaking because he didn't want to disturb Grandpa. He knew he had a lecture coming. I could see him get to the second stair, and Grandpa flipped the page of the paper.

"If I had a few more sentences left to read you would've made it upstairs." Grandpa quipped.

"Ta-dow! How you like me now!" I said laughing from the kitchen.

"Shut-up, Mesi!" Jason said, annoyed.

Grandpa folded his paper up neatly and sat it on the den coffee table, which was actually an old footlocker that he will not allow anyone to open under any circumstances. That's why it's just a table.

"Come here son and sit down. I want to talk to you," Grandpa said, calmly. Jason walked back into the den and sat down as defiantly as he could.

"You represent this family and our name out there in this world son, and you have no shame." Grandpa said. "Quit cheating yourself with this selfish behavior. Cheaters never win. If you cheat in one area of your life, you'll cheat the others. We are creatures of habit."

Jason was silent, but not curiously quiet. He was looking at the mail in his lap and ignoring Grandpa.

"You really think you're the man don't you? Listen to me, son," Grandpa said, as he whacked the wood floor with his cane. The sound startled Jason a bit and gathered his attention. He looked at Grandpa, annoyed.

"There is no future without respect for the past. Have you no respect for your elders, those who made a way for you?" Grandpa asked.

"There ain't no road that was paved by my so called ancestors that can take me up out this hood," Jason said. "All I got is J-Squared, and that's all I'm going to need, old man."

"Call me old man one more time, ok." Grandpa said. **"Don't be so ungrateful son. There are a lot of places you could live in this city. Your mother has worked hard to give you this life.

9

Nothing good comes from kicking everybody while you climb up the ladder." Grandpa stuttered as if he was trying to recall an old friend, "Fake hype, ain't that what you call it? You might really think that you're alone, and that *you* is all you got. But let me be the first to tell you that *you* ain't all *you* need."

Jason rolled his eyes.

"Everything you have can be taken away, son. It can be more easily taken away if you don't respect it, if you don't have respect for yourself. It is a privilege to play the games you love and to be acknowledged and respected for it, but the real essence of sport is found in maximizing your gifts. You are using your gifts to pursue the full greatness of what this shell of a body can accomplish by competing. To do this, it requires your whole person. When you think about it that way son, you can allow your whole person to grow. Not just Jason the ball player."

I could tell that Grandpa was just getting started. He took off his glasses and leaned back in his chair. Jason was twiddling his thumbs and tapping his toes, looking off in the distance at the photos on the wall, studying for any detail that he had missed in the pictures over the years. The pictures have been there since before he and I were born.

"You should learn from your sister and recognize her gifts. Don't be so close-minded. It's good to have your thing, but that doesn't make the rest of us insignificant. That attitude cost you a championship. I watched that state final last year, and you blew it trying to be the man. You don't pass because you don't respect what your teammates can do, and you are not willing to give them a chance to show what they can do. Everybody in college was the man on their high school team."

"Seriously Grandpa. I gotta go to work soon." Jason said.

"You've got time." Grandpa said. "I'm going to tell you the truth because I'm old, and you don't get old being no fool. Until your mother comes downstairs, you and I ain't got nothing else to do."

Jason didn't like Grandpa chastising him about his game. Grandpa didn't play in the Negro Leagues, but he was a playground basketball legend. He never played professionally because he was injured in the war. But when he came home, he became one of the most successful high school basketball coaches in Michigan. Whenever Jason sees the old school ballers at St. Cecelia's Gym, Detroit's historic temple of basketball, they know who Grandpa is, and Jason wants nothing more than to bury the comparisons and expectations. In Jason's mind, the only way to erase Grandpa's legacy was to do what

Grandpa never did; make it to the League, make it to the NBA or the NFL.

"Look at what's happening to the game son? All this doping, the greed, these kids taking money from boosters, you can't blame them. They should be paid. Most of them need it. But the coaches and corporations conspiring around these kid's futures are grown men. Jason, you already know what we have had to say no to through this process of your recruitment alone. I could go on and on." Grandpa said.

"You are going on and on." Jason said annoyed.

Grandpa paused and looked at Jason.

"So, I see. You want to be the fourth fool in the Bewick four." Grandpa said.

It was quiet for a beat. Grandpa says this all the time. It's a story about three boys who decided to rob a liquor store. The police got a tip, and as soon as the boys came out of the store, they were met with warning shots and surrendered. But a fourth boy came out of the store, and he was shot and killed. He had nothing to do with the crime. I guess the lesson is to pay attention – know and understand the situation. Grandpa only invoked this parable when he wanted it to be clear and evident that the "situation" was making him upset.

Then, unabated by Jason's flippant attitude, Grandpa continued with his slow, deliberate cadence.

"I know sports and these aren't the games I remember. This is crazy, and they are all on their way to hell in a hand basket if you ask me. People are starting not to care. Is it about money son, or is it about the spirit of the game? Are you a person or a battery? Money comes and goes, but the spirit of the game is infinite and eternal. If I were you son, I would embrace my opportunities with a little more grace and humility."

"I ain't got time for no riddles old man!" Jason said as he stood up and turned to walk out of the den. He heard mama walking down the stairs with her keys jingling in her hands.

Out of nowhere, Grandpa's cane whacked Jason right in the back of the head. If Grandpa had any of the strength of his youth it would have left a knot on Jason's big head. It happened so fast, that if I had blinked, I would have missed it. I laughed hysterically!

"C'mon Grandpa. You're messing up the haircut," Jason said, fixing his hair. "I'm still the man!"

"I see you ain't call me old man again, you knuckle head!" Grandpa said.

"I love you Grandpa!" Jason said, laughing as he cut in front of me to get out the door and into the car.

Those were the words out of Jason's mouth that always caught me off guard – "I love you," – because I knew he meant it. I think Jason loved us all. But I swear, when we dropped Jason off at the park that day for work, I wished he would never come home. I just didn't think it would really happen.

Mama pulled up to the park to drop me off for work and through the fence, I could see crowds brewing for the pick-up games on the far side of the park. Mama managed to get me here early despite having to sit through philosophy class with Grandpa. Mesi was in the back seat, where she's supposed to be. Her face was glued to the screen of her phone as usual. I stretched between the bucket seats, and gave her a kiss on the forehead while I was trying to hide from Mama that I was pushing buttons on Missy's phone to reset the game she was playing.

"Quit playing, Jason!" she said, squirming.

"Get out and get to work Jason. I rushed to get you here on time." Mama said giggling.

I kissed Mama on the cheek and walked to the courts where a few other camp counselors had arrived early. I got a text message. It was from Mia. We had been dating since sophomore year. We were friends since middle school and everyone has the fairytale dream about us getting married but I don't know about all that.

Hey.

I texted back a little annoyed. I'm not sure why, but I was annoyed.

Hey. How are you?

Her reply came instantly, like she had already typed it or something.

I'm pregnant.

Instantly I went from annoyed, to feeling angry, and then denial all at the same time. This cannot be true. This is terrible timing. Is she crazy! I'm not trying to be nobody's daddy right now. I texted Mia back.

You what?

I waited anxiously for her response and this time it couldn't come fast enough. Ten seconds passed and it felt like an hour. The phone beeped.

WE NEED TO TALK...

I noticed my friends walking over toward me. I messaged back quickly.

I can't right now. It's not mine anyway, why are you telling me?

"You good bro?" Mark asked, interrupting my private rage. "You look like you just saw a ghost."

"I'm cool," I said.

Mark was with Chris and Steve. I knew Mark and Chris. We grew up together, and they are my high school teammates.

13

Steve Cain plays for a rival school, Southeastern. This moment was not going to be a debriefing session about how I was feeling. I didn't trust Steve, and the last thing I need is to get the gossip mill churning.

Steve and Chris live on the same block about a mile from our house near Alter Rd. Their hood is crazy. Gunshots all day, drugs running in and out, police and ambulance sirens, I can still hear them faintly at night from where we live. Grandpa might think I'm not, but I was glad Mama moved us off the block. At least the people around here seem to care about the hood. They cut the grass, keep the houses up, and they keep an eye out for the kids. Only bad thing about that, the neighbors are always snitching, especially them old people, and these new people. And then there are the clowns who come over here and break in Mama's car thinking we got money. That's just stupid. Mama hustles off the Bridge Card and these fools think we are rich because the lawn is cut. Cut your own grass if you want to feel rich. That's how I feel. We are one check from being broke and then have to spend money to replace the car window. I know the new people ain't do that.

"Whatupdoe J!" Chris said.

"What's good?" I asked.

"I texted you earlier. They've got the three-on-three going on later at the far side courts. We were thinking about skipping out on work to enter the tournament," Chris said, as he was spraying himself with cheap cologne trying to cover up the smell of the cigarette he had just squished underneath his new Jordan's.

Chris was one of those kids that thought drinking and smoking made him cool. I thought that was dumb. I didn't drink or smoke. He would steal from his father's stash in the basement. It was nothing for him to get liquor or beer, and he was always up on a hustle.

"Not just thinking about it, I already put the money down to enter!" The grand prize is $2500. Between the four of us, that's more than we will make all week working this camp," Chris said.

"Ooh, that's easy money," I said

Then I had a flashback to that time my mother caught me at the park swinging on the monkey bars when I was supposed to be at work caddying at the golf course. It did not end well. To this day I think she had a homing device in my sock or something, because who just shows up at Joe random park to find their kid playing hooky from work? Trust me, I was not trying to be found.

"I think I'm good though, fellas. These camp checks ain't that bad."

"Dude, you trying to work hard or you trying to be stupid? There ain't a team in the tourney that can beat us. That's light work for a couple racks of cash!" Chris said.

Steve was quiet up to this point. I don't know what his deal was, but he seemed more pissed that I wasn't going to do it than my "real" homeboys.

"If he don't want to do it, we can win it without him. We don't need him to win," Steve said defiantly.

"No dude, we need J!" Mark said, pushing back the blonde hair from his face. "If J plays, we win hands down."

"If I play we win hands down. I carry SE, I can carry us in a three on three," Steve quipped.

I don't know if this was reverse psychology on his part or not but I was not about to let nobody from SE stake claim that he can replace me and take my spot. I was definitely in at this point. The only thing I was thinking about was how to skip out on the job.

"Whatever bro. I'll play," I said.

I gave Mark and Chris our secret handshake. Steve felt left out. If I wanted him to feel different, I would have given everybody fist bumps or went for the bro hug. It was intentional.

"What's the plan to get out of work?" One of us has to punch in and give the alibi for the rest of us."

"I'll go," Mark said. "What do I tell them?"

"Tell them that we were all supposed to car pool together, but J had a dentist appointment, and Steve and I got sick form lunch yesterday," Chris said. "Then, maybe an hour into camp, there's so much going on, you can peel off and come join us."

We packed up our things and headed over to the far side courts. The Camp Director was pulling up by the time we were well on our way. There was no way he could recognize us in the distance. The only thing I could think about now was how I am I going to spend this money.

It was hot, and the afternoon was sweating itself away. The whole scene is everything I love about home. The bees were chasing kids running around with sticky Faygo bottles in their hands. Charcoal was smoldering from a few public grills, and the court was packed. Old school whips with the big chrome wheels parked in the lot. Music bumping in the trunk, with all the hit songs that I like that mama doesn't want me listening to.

The street hustlers organized the tournament. Besides the Twin's Deli and Skully's Barbershop, there aren't too many businesses sponsoring programs for the kids in our hood. The hustlers show up to bet on the games and sell raffle tickets and ribs to collect the championship pot. So today, we weren't getting a check. We were getting paid straight up cash. Steve, Chris, and I were whizzing through the tournament by the time Mark was able to join us. We had already reached the semi-final round. This was good because there was only about an hour left and my mother would be picking me up.

"Mark, what's good? You finally made it," said Chris.

"Yep, they bought the whole story. We had a car pool SNAFU. Took a while to break out though, longer than I expected. I'm supposed to be on trash duty. That's a do and disappear job anyway. I'm clear."

"You're in this game, you can take my spot," I said.

Out of the corner of my eye I checked out the crowd and it was growing, buzzing.

"Young Jay is playing. He's out there on fire!" I heard someone in the crowd saying.

Another girl screamed. "He is on fire. That boy is hot!" The girls standing around were all giggling.

I love home, but I couldn't help but think that these people ain't got nothing else to do in the middle of the day in the middle of the week but come see me play on this dirty playground. I got to get out of here.

I could see Steve grinning as if this was his time to carry the team and show just how good he could play.

"Cool. We got this." Steve said. "I've been carrying us all day anyway."

"Man, whatever," I said.

"Yo! Are we on the same team or what?" Chris exclaimed, trying to settle down the beef between us.

"No!" Steve and I said at the same time.

I looked at his shoes and he had "BEAR" written on the back of his shoes.

"Dude, you got "BEAR" written on your shoes. Is that your nickname? Teddy Bear?" Mark and Chris laughed. "You soft bro." I said.

"That's for my sister!" Steve yelled. "It ain't funny. She's sick."

The fellas paused awkwardly looking at me, like I should feel sorry or something.

"Just because she sick, don't mean it ain't funny!" I said.

Mark and Chris, started laughing again, but noticed there was a serious undertone to the exchange.

"For today we're on the same team. Let's get this money," Mark said.

"Ball game!" the referee shouted. "Blue shirts have it out."

The blue team was our team. Mark wiped the bits of loose blacktop from his shoes with his hands, and inbounded to Steve from half-court. There were so many people around the court that I don't know how people standing in the back could see the action. It's three-on-three so we're only playing at one basket. Steve took the ball, dribbled into traffic and forced a shot. The redshirts took the rebound and scored. We were down and these games can get ugly quickly. The first team to 8 points wins.

Since the redshirts scored, they kept the ball, and inbounded from half-court. One of the redshirts took a shot from deep behind the two-point line. The ball swished right through the net. I thought, 'How long do I let this go on?'

"C'mon let's go!" I yelled.

Redshirts scored again, and again before we scored our first basket and Chris called a time out.

"We got to get J in the game. Steve you sit," Chris said.

"You sit. I ain't no dog!" Steve quipped.

"I paid the entry fee! I ain't sitting!" Chris said.

"Ain't nobody getting paid if I don't check in the game," I said.

I walked over to the table and alerted the scorekeeper that I was checking in for Steve. He sat down angrily and threw his towel into the bench. He only scored one point.

I looked over at Steve and said, "At least you got that basket for "Baby Bear." I looked back at Mark and Chris and wiped the bottoms of my sneakers clean with my hands.

"Let's go!" I said.

Mark passed me the ball and the redshirt defender took my shot-fake. I dribbled around him with ease and slam-dunked one home.

"Wash, rinse, repeat!" I said. "C'mon!"

Mark passed to me again. I made another shot-fake. The crowd gasped as the helpless defender leaped in the air. He was now at my mercy, suspended in animation. I took a step-back dribble, and pulled up for two points. "Splash!" I said while the shot was still in flight towards the hoop. I turned away to look at the crowd and gave a quick mean mug to Steve, who was sulking on the bench. The ball came down through the nets with a crisp snapping sound, and the crowd erupted.

I only did this two more times and finished the game off with a sick dunk. It was on to the finals, but the clock was ticking. Mama was going to be pulling up soon. At this point, even if I got

18

caught, I'll take getting punished if I can put this money in my pocket to go with the camp check for the week!

Chris decided to take a break and sit out for the final game. He had played in each of the games with no breather. He was gassed.

"Chris you're tired from smoking them squares." I said.

"Whatever," Chris said, coughing.

If we were going to win it all with Chris out, I was going to have to make it work with Steve. That was not going to happen. I walked over to Mark and whispered in his ear before he inbounded.

"Don't pass it to Steve. Get me the rock." I said.

Mark smacked his lips in disapproval, "That ain't cool J."

"We need to win!" I said.

I could tell throughout the game that Mark was upset, but he didn't decline the request. He went out of his way to get me the ball, even if Steve was wide open. We essentially froze him out.

"Pass the ball!" Steve yelled at Mark.

"Right here, Mark," I said.

Mark passed me the ball, and Steve threw his hands up, visibly frustrated. He kept looking into the stands at a group of goons from the old block that were looking just as pissed off as he was. But by that time the game was nearly over and it was almost time to collect the cash.

I dribbled over to his side of the court and passed Steve the ball. He caught it, but he was so worked up and anxious to prove that he deserved the ball, that he dribbled right into two defenders and forced an off balance shot. His shot clanked off the back of the iron.

Mark was there to grab the rebound. He shot it up off the glass and the game was over. We had won.

Chris rushed the floor and Mark and I hit our secret handshake. We looked over at Steve and he seemed defeated even though we had won. I don't know which was more satisfying, winning or making Steve look like the bum I thought he was.

"C'mon Bear, we got you!" Chris said. " Let's go get this money."

"Yeah, let's go get this money," Steve said bitterly.

Hook, one of the streets' most respected hustlers always did the count out. While Hook was counting the money, out of the corner of my eye, I saw my mother pulling up in the parking lot on the other side of the park.

"300, 400..." Hook stopped counting. "By the way, Jay did you get the shoe boxes I left for you at the house? They want you bad bro. You need to think about that as you make that decision about school."

"If they wearing those shoes where I can play both sports then it might work, but you know what it is."

Hook paused and looked at me like I was out of pocket.

"That's how you feel? He asked. "You need to think about how many pairs of shoes was in them boxes." Hook said. He continued to count out the money. "500, 600..."

"I've got to go!" I said, stopping the exchange abruptly.

I took my $600 share, and I started to run as fast as I could across the park. I could see my mother and the Camp Director talking. They both turned and saw me running toward them. This was not good. Then I heard gunshots.

BOOM! BOOM! BOOM!

I felt something burning in my back and then my leg, and all of a sudden I fell to the ground. The money that was in my hand came raining down on me softly. I sat up and there was blood all in my shirt. People were scattering about. Cars were burning rubber. I saw this dark figure walking toward me. I couldn't really see who it was because of the glare of the sunlight. The sky was spinning. I slumped back to the ground and rolled onto my stomach. I could feel someone rip my bag off my back. In the distance I could hear my mother screaming. The thief's shoes were rustling away in the grass and on the back of the shoes I could see the word "BEAR," fading off into the distance. My eyes closed and there was darkness.

Then I felt as if I was being pulled into a soda bottle. My mind began to race with thoughts that were not my own, as if I was in another person's head. I was wallowing in a whimsy of places, and worlds I had never seen. What I knew was slipping away and being replaced, as if my mind was being reprogrammed. But I could still hear my mother.

"Get an ambulance! Somebody help my baby!" she screamed.

By the sound of her voice, I could tell she was crying hysterically. I couldn't open my eyes. I couldn't move.

Suddenly, I was engulfed in this fast approaching brightness and then I came crashing through a glass ceiling. People were running and screaming. I smashed into three floating tables that were now mangled and smoking. Racks of metal parts tumbled to the ground. Alarms were ringing. Glass and debris were scattered about. I could feel a metal suit attached to my body, but it was damaged. It would not respond to my thought commands and I could not free my arms or legs. The fixed hologram monitor inside the mask was flickering in and out. My peripheral sound was spotty at best. I could see three machine-like beings hovering over me.

"We should remove him from the exo-shell," the gray metallic ominous orb said while hovering over me.

I heard a random voice.

"He just fell from the sky right after the explosion! They're calling for an evacuation!" The voice said.

"Help me! Help me!" I screamed! "Get this thing off of me, I'm still alive!"

The droids were ignoring me, talking about me as if I wasn't even there.

"Hey! Can't you hear me! Get me out of here!" I yelled.

The three droids zoomed abruptly towards me; one of them was trying to peer through the cracked glass in the facemask of my metal suit. Another inserted a needle in between the bars of the metal frame and into my thigh. The needle pierced my skin injecting me with a tranquilizer. I screamed in pain. The medicine immediately made me feel drowsy.

"It appears that the shell is permanently affixed to the human," I heard the second Droid say. "There is no registered serial number for this droid, and no record of it in our catalog."

One of the robots stammered as it turned toward me, "Our protocol is to inform the Locksmiths, and he is to be examined and purged."

"Wait! No, you can't send me back to him," I slurred.

A small door opened from the side of the droid and a long arm with three plugs at the tip extended towards me. It was trying to access and override the metal suit's power system. I was still trying to free myself. The other droids circled behind me extending large vices to restrain my arms. I was thinking that maybe the droid is right. Maybe I am stuck in this machine. I mean, maybe I am a machine, and if that's the case these droids have agreed that it's best if I'm destroyed. Sparks were flying from the suit as I resisted with the last bit of my strength. The droid's plugs rammed into my chest and everything went dark again.

Am I dead? Was this a dream? Was this the future? Was I in another dimension? Again, I could see a light flickering in the distance, approaching rapidly, and as it engulfed me, I felt as if I was running. My feet were moving, but I couldn't feel the ground, until I tripped and fell, in a muddy puddle. At that moment, I felt everything. I was soiled all over and I scraped my knee. Everything about this place was now suddenly familiar as if I had been here all along. I heard a faint voice, slowly getting louder calling my name.

"Jason, let's go!"

I tried to stand to run and I stumbled to my feet, like my legs didn't seem attached to my body. But I got up anyway.

"Who are you?" I asked.

"Dude, did you hit your head or something? It's me, Tone, the one and only Anthony Fargus. What is wrong with you?" Tone asked.

I didn't answer. I just tried to shake off the cloudiness I was feeling in my head, and we started running. I could hear our feet echoing off the walls of the cavernous metal tunnels. Thick pipes lined the walls and the ceiling. We could hear water gushing through the tubes. Every so often we passed by a blinking control panel. The florescent green lights flashed "all systems in good working order."

"This place smells awful. "What are we doing here? How far are we away?" I asked.

"Waste harbor, what did you expect?" Tone said as he was holding his little contraption that looked like a simple magnifying glass. He pressed the tool close to the wall. "We are looking for digital markers on the walls that can only be read with this little gadget"

As he looked through the glass lens, Images started to appear in the lens that we could not see in plain sight. He dropped the lens, which hung from his neck on a small metal chain. The gadget rustled against his jacket that had a small patch with the words "Game On". He looked down at his jacket logo proudly as if seeing it for the first time.

"Third straight day for this jacket. It's like my superhero uniform."

"Is that what I smell?" I said.

Tone laughed.

"Let's go. The elevator is just down this way," he said.

"You've got to be kidding me, I said. "That's what you said ten minutes ago!"

A beam of light gleamed over our heads from down the hall. There was a loud click-clack sound that echoed the sound of a marching army.

"Get down!" Tone said.

I ducked down quickly, my face flat on the floor. I could taste trash in my mouth from the thick stench of the ground. The beam of light continued to scan the space over our heads.

"What is going on?" I whispered.

"Shhh!" Tone said in a panic. "Locksmith security droids."

The light shifted suddenly. I was ready to vomit, and then, the light went out.

"Don't move," Tone whispered.

The click-clack of the Locksmiths' gait was fading further off into the distance. Tone stood up, and with a stiff pace, he started walking down the dark hall.

"Come on. Let's go!" Tone said with urgency.

Again, I lifted myself off the floor and started to run after him. I couldn't take it anymore, and whatever it was I had to eat and possibly a few organs came flying out of my mouth. I threw up all over the wall.

"What are you doing?" Tone said. "We've got to get out of here. Those Locksmiths would have our parents picking us up from a holding cell. It's past curfew."

Tone walked over, opened his backpack and handed me a pill.

"Drink this," Tone said.

"What is this?" I asked.

"It's a water pill you idiot," Tone said.

He looked at me confused. I was out of it, but I knew we had to keep going. We couldn't come this far and turn back. I wiped my face with my sleeve and tried to gather my composure. The water capsule was working, and my mind began to settle.

"I had a towel in my bag you could've used. I mean, you didn't have to wipe that on the sleeve," Tone said.

"That's not very funny," I said.

"And don't worry about the smell. We've got active film coating on all our gear that peels away like a snake shedding skin. It only takes a few seconds," Tone said. He paused and asked, "Are you good Jason? You just don't seem like yourself today."

I took a deep breath, and Tone started walking ahead.

"Let's get going." Tone said.

CHAPTER 3 – FRIENDS

Jason is a good friend. My mother named me Anthony, but Jason is the only friend she allows to use the nickname Tone. Jason likes it that way, but my mother cannot stand for anyone else to do it. "I named the boy Anthony!" She will say to my other friends whenever they come to visit. Jason and I are a bit of an odd couple. He's interested in the gadgets I build, but most everything else about us is different. I mean he's always clean. I'm a bit disheveled. I never comb my hair. It's a waste of time. I get teased about tackling the oral hygiene, and since I was a kid, my wrist unit has never fit. It looks more like a woman's bracelet than a fixed hologram ID communicator. But I'm still smart. No, not smart, I'm a genius. A true "jack of all trades," but an apparent "master of none," because at this moment, my looking glass has us lost in the belly of the largest space station human kind ever fixed its will to construct.

After the impact, that's right, impact, humans were forced to leave earth. There were many prophecies about the end of the world. The planet seemed to have nine lives as predictions of earth's demise would come and go. Then it finally happened. A devastating asteroid - over a mile long - split in two over the Great Lakes, vaporized the landscape, and smashed into the earth.

I don't know if this is heaven, but we surely live in the heavens. Two space stations wrap completely around the earth like stacked metallic rings of Saturn. They call it the Life Ring. My friends and I call it the "Double Bagel."

The Life Ring was designed and built by Tronics Inc., a corporation owned by Dr. Damon Raven. The scale of the project was immense and could not have possibly been done without machine intelligence. As the legend is told, the machines that built this place were half-human – cyborgs. But the machines had major defects. Now, the defective machines are being hunted down and rounded up by the Locksmiths, the private security force for Tronics Inc. If I let my father tell the story, he would say rogue droids are hiding down here in the gutters of the Life Ring where we are headed to play lacrosse.

So, why we are sneaking into the belly of a space station to play lacrosse, you wonder? Well, it's illegal.

It's a long complicated story, but according to SCAM literature, the Societal Coalition Against Machines, it all started very early in the age of information. Humans were just learning to unlock the mysteries of the universe. Technology was king and the people were lost in it, growing more and more reliant on machines. It was never more evident than in how people were spending their time. People felt technology was shrinking the world. They believed that technology brought people together, but it was actually pulling people apart. People became compartmentalized in silos of their own interest. Their primitive video games had children captivated, and game makers seemed to have only one goal – to make the games seem more and more life-like, to immerse the player into a real life experience. Eventually, they succeeded.

That's when sport and real athletics met its death. People stopped going to the arenas, stadiums, and gladiator fights. People stopped tuning in to television. Sport was reduced to something that only poor children would indulge. Virtual games leveled the playing field because anyone could play. But as time went on it became more exclusive and costly. If you were poor or an outcast, it was impossible to afford ultra-speed virtual gaming networks or gain access to the culture. Eventually, only the brave, stupid, or some combination of the two would even dare play sports. For those left out, it was the only thing left to do.

Before humans could live in the Life Ring, they had to establish the order of law, and define our new way of life in space. Every aspect of human behavior was examined, and the "Leaders" deliberated what was "human." Sport was long ago judged as deviant behavior and a breeding ground for disease. We were taught that the greed and corruption in sport planted the seeds of its own fate.

"Evolution is competition so you better be up for it." My mother says this all the time, along with a lot of other things that I've grown tired of her repeating. Things like, "Now, that you've qualified for the amateur circuit, the game is all that matters." She is right. The G.R.I.D. is the Life Ring's Gaming Recreation Immersion Dock, and everyone in their noon years participates. Only a few are selected to compete in elite competitions. Being one of those few selected from the Lowland Sector where I live would be like a dream come true, atari.

The GRID's challenges are strange, and the massive crowds help create the game in real-time. Each time we play, the game is different, and anyone can affect the outcome of a match, even the spectators. Hacker codes can be tracked. Encryption can be deciphered. Good luck to those trying to cheat the system. It is believed that the GRID is the system of checks and balances that has purified recreation and eliminated cheating and corruption from human competition.

But scattered and hidden throughout the Rings are secret chambers that unlock the sports of the ancient past. We don't know who built them or why, but I've discovered almost all of them in our sector. Before my father was taken from us, he mapped the Life Ring Gutters for SCAM outcast cells operating in our Sector. I deciphered the lost simulators from his prints. How many more are hidden in the Rings is a mystery.

"Jason, let's go. This way." I said. I don't know what his problem is today.

I could see the transport elevator off in the distance. We passed a sign on the wall that read, "Off Limits: No Trespassing." We entered a glass shell corridor with panoramic windows through which we could see a clear view of earth and transport ships floating by through the dark silent vacuum of space. The walls quickly turned back to sheet metal and tubes as we reached the elevator door. I pushed the button

"So why did you guys move the game here?" Jason asked.

"This is an active fitness simulator. It's really cool. You'll see. There are dozens of them, and each one of them is different, but this is the only one we've been able to activate without being detected. They were never approved for construction, and no one knows how or why they were built. I am sure Raven would do just about anything to put the Droid who did it in the crusher." I said.

The jerky elevator had Jason looking like he would vomit again. "Hold it together Jay," I said. "It's a long trip from Tier 1 of the Life Ring to Tier 2."

The pressure was popping my ears and it felt like we were dropping from the top hill of a roller coaster with no end in sight.

"Raven's got money to lose," Jason said. "What's the big deal?"

"The Societal Coalition Against Machines, which would be us." I said, pointing to the small script on my jacket lapel.

"No, that would be YOU," Jason interrupted. "I'm not claiming any of this."

The elevator beeped and the door opened.

"Anyway, SCAM still thinks Raven is using humans as the core processor to manufacture robots. Raven is leading the hunt to have them all destroyed. If it gets out Tronics could be ruined. What happened to the thousands of people who went missing without explanation and then poof, Raven just magically appears with a droid army that could build the Life Ring in less than 15 years!"

"It's not like it's 1992, Tone. It's 3010. We have the technology to do these things. We're here and we're safe. It just sounds like a witch-hunt to me. How can we hate any machine, when we live in one?" Jason said.

"That's just it, Jason. Don't you see? Machines control us, and it wasn't always like this. We are naturally drawn to the earth like magnets."

"We call that gravity," Jason interrupted.

"No Jay, what's keeping us on the ground is some designed code of zeros and ones. That's not life. It's code. Don't you want to go back?"

I scoured through my bag and pulled out something I'm sure Jason had only seen in a museum. His crazy father would have a fit. It was a book. "Sports Illustrated" was written on the cover. The colors in the pictures were faded and disrupted by aged water stains.

"I have actually never touched real paper." Jason said. "It's very brittle."

I heard a sound in the distance. I looked back and didn't see anything. We kept walking.

"Put that away." Jason said nervously. "We're goosed if we get caught with that."

"Quit acting like a wus, you lame. My Dad has had these in the family for generations. They're kept in a climate-controlled digisafe, but I cracked the code. Finally."

Jason looked like he stopped listening after the word lame. I'm sure he thought being called a lame by the nerd with bad breath stings a little bit. Maybe I should lighten up. After all, he is a little out of it today.

"Look at these pictures. Humans climbing huge rocks, running, and jumping being free." Jason said. "This is real, I mean, it's not a simulation or a hologram like the GRID?" He asked. "I can't believe it."

"If SCAM is out to figure out how we can get back to spaceship earth, then I'm with them," I said. "No matter how much they want this place to look like earth, it's still a lie. No matter how real the GRID feels, I know it's not. We're just pushing buttons. I want to feel something Jay. I want to feel something real."

Jason's face and eyes were serious. Then he smiled.

"Ok, well I can't help you with that." He said giggling. "But maybe Kara can." He teased.

"Kara wouldn't help me call for help." I said. "Now that's the Jay I know. I knew he was in there somewhere!"

We both secretly liked Kara, and we weren't the only two either. We laughed and could hear the rest of the group around the bin. It sounded as if they had already started a game without us.

I was upstairs brushing my teeth, and I heard Mama calling my name. Her voice was burdened by a heavy cough.

"Missy!" Mama said.

I came running down the stairs.

"You ok Mama?" I asked.

Mama was sick. Physically sick. It had been weeks since Jason was shot and robbed at the playground. Her cough was getting worse, and I could tell she was losing weight. She was scrambling around the kitchen, looking for her keys.

"You need to eat something Mama." I said.

She ignored my plea.

"Right now we have to go see your brother and get an update on his condition." She said. "I'm going to be fine."

I would have been there with Mama the day it happened, but I stayed behind to keep an eye on Grandpa. Mama saw it happen. She watched him fall to the ground. She saw the smoke from the barrel of the gun. She saw the boys take his bag, but there was nothing she could do. The police asked around, and of course, no one knew anything. It was better if Jason was dead, than for anyone to snitch and tell who pulled the trigger. But Jason wasn't dead.

After an ambulance arrived on the scene, Jason was rushed to the hospital. The ER doctors were able to stabilize him, but he is still in a coma. He just lies there, with the machines doing most of the work to keep him alive. Grandpa can't bear to see it, but today he has mustered up the strength to come with us. Honestly, there are moments these last few days where I've felt like whispering 'I told you so' in his ear. But that would be bitter.

"That boy had it coming." Grandpa said as he plopped down into the car seat and situated his cane between his legs.

"Daddy, do you have to say that now?" Mama said. "You've made it clear how you feel."

Mama started the car and the rest of the drive to the hospital was quiet. Everything about life now was quiet, at least now. The media frenzy is over for the moment. The first weeks after Jason was shot, cameras were everywhere. The Internet was going crazy. People were in and out of the house that I didn't know asking and speculating about Jason. I cut my phone off for a couple days and wished I could weave a cocoon. I really wanted someone to shut Jason up, but not like this. This was too much. I often found myself holding back tears trying to be strong. I was tired of people telling me it's going to be ok. It wasn't ok. It just wasn't right without him around. When we got to the hospital. I saw Mark and his mom walking out of the revolving door. They quickened their pace. Mama didn't want to have anything to do with Chris or Mark's parents. Mama blamed their sons for badgering Jason to play in the tournament.

"Why are you so hard on that boy's friends and their parents? They feel just as bad about what happened to Jason as you do." Grandpa said to Mama.

"Why are you so hard on my son, Daddy?"

"Because his father isn't here, and you spoil him." Grandpa said. "You treat him like he's the man you never had but he is a boy Sonya. He is a little boy."

Mama was sobbing.

"I was a little boy and I know what it is to become a man. That is why I'm hard on him. I just regret I wasn't strong enough to be tough enough, to help you more." Grandpa softened.

Grandpa turned to Mama and she just melted in his arms crying. Grandpa was embarrassed. He was hurt about what happened to Jason, but he was ashamed of what had become of his family. Our brother, David, was locked in jail for credit card fraud. Daddy never came around. I've never seen Daddy, only pictures. I don't even think about it. Grandpa was our father. It was his goal to see us make it through Mama's mistakes. Jason was almost there.

Mama wiped her eyes with tissue she pulled from the glove box. It was about to storm and we parked in the parking garage, but that didn't stop Mama from putting the sunglasses on her face. Her eyes were giving away too much of her soul.

We walked through the long hospital hall to Jason's room in the Intensive Care Unit. With Grandpa's cane, hard-bottoms, and Mama's heels, the three of us sounded like a heard of African wildebeest. We turned the corner, and the doctor was attending to Jason. It was the first time I had seen this particular doctor over the last five days. The doctor was standing with a Coach. I couldn't tell what school he was from, but it was obvious he was a Coach. He was decked out from head to toe in a white and grey jogging suit and cap.

"You must be Ms. Joshua? I'm Dr. James."

"Yes, I am Jason's mother." Mama said.

The Coach interrupted, reaching his hand toward mama to shake her hand, "Hello, I am Coach."

Mama cut him off before he could begin and left his hand hanging. "I don't care who you are. You need to leave." She said.

"We were just trying to evaluate if Jason was still going to be able to sign a letter of intent." The Coach said.

"How dare you?" Mama said with the annoyed nuanced grace of a queen. "Leave."

"I'm sorry." The man said as he walked out of the door. Mama waited patiently for the door to close behind him.

"How is my son?" She asked.

"It's looking like it's going to be a long haul for him to recover from this." The doctor said. "We are considering transferring him to University of Michigan Hospital by helicopter next week, because there are tests they can run there that we don't have the capacity to perform here. We were able to remove the bullet fragments from his back and leg, with the exception of one piece that is very close to his spine. When he becomes more stable, another surgical procedure could help him. Right now, it is possible that this fragment could be a problem for him in the future and limit his mobility."

Dr. James paused. I think he was catching on to the fact that Mama was having difficulty digesting this information.

He stuttered, "If, if he ever comes out of this." Dr. James said. He paused again. "It was the trauma to his head when he fell that we can't account for right now."

"What does that mean?" Mama asked.

"We really won't know who Jason is until he wakes up. We don't know what he will recall. It's possible that he could have complete memory loss. He could have complete memory retention. We just don't know." Dr. James said.

"What? Why are you telling me this now?" Mama asked frantically. "I was told he was making progress yesterday."

"Well there was progress. The ventilator is using 3% less capacity to breathe for him. That is a good thing. That is progress. I'm sorry Ms. Joshua."

"Did you disclose any information about my child to that Coach?" Mama asked bitterly.

"No Ms. Joshua. Hospital policy forbids it." The doctor said.

Dr. James walked out of the room and the nurse walked closely behind with her head down. The nurse looked back when she reached the door.

"Can I get anyone water or anything?" The Nurse said.

"No! Just get out!" Mama screamed.

Grandpa was sitting in the chair in the corner. He had not said a word, and he had not come near Jason. He was glaring into his pocket watch. He looked like me when I'm playing Jetpack Joyride on my phone.

Mama walked over to Jason and squeezed his hand. It was sticky from medical tape that had been removed to reposition his IV connection. Nothing about seeing Jason this way was normal. Mama's tears were running down her face from under her sunglasses and onto Jason's gown. I watched the gown change color one giant teardrop at a time. She couldn't take it anymore and left the room.

I walked from the end of the bed over to the window. Grandpa closed his pocket watch hurriedly like he had been waiting for this moment. He stood up, and he walked over to Jason. He was trying to be discrete, but he put his cane into Jason's bed and placed Jason's hand around the handle of his cane. He closed his eyes and he began to mumble a short prayer of some sort. I thought nothing of it. That's what old people do. They start praying and reading the bible all the time so they can get to heaven.

There was another storm brewing on the horizon. Thunder was rolling and we were on the 23rd floor of the hospital. Who doesn't like to watch the rain? The sky opened up, and it started to pour. I looked back at Grandpa, and he was still praying over Jason. When I turned back to the window a bolt of lightning was coming straight at me. I screamed and my body jerked from the shock, but I wasn't burned and I didn't feel any pain. I heard Jason's voice screaming.

"Missy!"

I turned around, dazed, and Grandpa was sitting down in the chair like nothing happened.

"Did you hear that? Did you see that Grandpa? I mean. Did I just get struck by lightning or was that my imagination?" I said. "Did you see that? But wait, how did you get back over there so quickly? You were just standing with Jason? Grandpa! I heard Jason's voice! Did he say something?"

"No baby." Grandpa said. "I see this visit has gotten you a little worked up. Jason is going to be ok."

Grandpa was struggling to pull himself up from the chair. I reached out my arms to help him.

"I'm going to go get your mother," he said as he stood up. "This trip has taken a lot out of me."

"Grandpa you didn't see that light? You didn't feel that?" I exclaimed.

"You're going to need to get some sleep Missy. It's been a long few days for all of us." Grandpa said calmly.

I sat down trying to piece together what happened because it wasn't a figment of my imagination. I'm not making this up. I was struck by lightning and Grandpa didn't want to entertain my testimony. I went to the bathroom to check my face. I like to code, but I'm pretty too. I can't be burning my face with lightning bolts. Proactive can't fix that. There were no marks and no evidence of anything on my face or clothes. I need to get it together I thought. Mama and Grandpa are the crazy people around here, not me. I'm going to get some water and I've got to keep this to myself. Mama might try to leave me at the hospital and have me committed to the psych ward. I looked in the mirror, took a deep breath, and walked out.

"What took you so long in the bathroom? You can go boo-boo when you get home." Mama said to me right in front of the nurses.

"I wasn't boo-booing!" I said embarrassed.

Is that even a word? Who cares? At this point, I just wanted to go home.

The walk back to the car took forever. Grandpa's gait was unusually slow today. He gets tired form time to time when he has to do too much walking, but he seemed especially tired today. He plopped down in the seat squeezing his cane. He was asleep before we left the parking lot. He knew the drive home was going to be a long one.

34

Locating Jason took a lot of energy, but I found him. Now I've got to find out why he was brought here.

A large section of the Life Ring was under construction. A cargo shuttle crashed into it, and the blast breached the air lock that separates the zero gravity of space from the real-time gravity system of the Life Ring. It was sad that so many people were lost. They were sucked out into the cold, silent, vacuum of space when the cargo ship crashed. Some suspect it was a plot carried out by SCAM to protest Life Ring expansion. If it was SCAM they didn't accomplish anything. They only made more work for Raven's droids.

Hundreds of construction grade robots were working to repair the damage to the Life Ring. The machines were floating back and forth from large construction barges to reload supplies. The lifeless droids fused one aluminum beam after another, while another team of robots trailed behind, laying the new energy absorbing finish panels.

I was among them trying to look busy and blend in. My eyes were more focused on where Droid Security was than anything. I was mixed in with the other droids working to clear the damaged sections and make preparations for new assembly. I lifted my head from drilling out a damaged panel to see if anyone was watching. I felt the coast was clear, and ditched the worksite using a small force jet pack to float into the interior shell of the Life Ring.

It is zero gravity inside the interior shell. I floated in towards an airlock door marked 'Salvage Harbor.' I grabbed the door latch, opened the airlock, and shut off the jets. The airlock door quickly closed behind me, and my feet were violently pulled to the ground. The Life Ring's gravity field was now active.

I stepped out of the airlock and into the corridor. It was dark, only the faint haze of a flashing red light marking the Salvage Transport Elevator at the far end of the long hall. I started running towards the light, and out of nowhere a menacing droid that looked like a praying mantis in armor cut me off. It was a Locksmith Unit the most intimidating machines in Raven's Droid Security Force. Their strength and multitude of weapons configurations were enough to subdue any droid, let alone a mere half-human Xenotron module like me.

The Locksmith Unit grabbed my neck, and lifted me from the ground, an ID probe extended from the metal beast and rammed into my chest.

"You are an installation and repair module, designated ratchet and plasma welding unit engineer. Xenotron Code 2375. Where is Xenotron Unit PS5674?" It screamed.

"I don't know what you are talking about." I said. I was choking.

"Where is Xenotron Unit PS5674?" It shouted again. I was trying to hold on.

"I don't know, please!" I said.

"You defective half-human scum, you will feel pain when you are purged!"

The Locksmith Unit threw me to the ground like a rag doll. A second wave of droids was entering the corridor to get to the construction site. The Locksmith Unit pressed the communicator at the back of its neck.

"Defective Xenotron droid cleanup in the Sector 8 airlock corridor," the Locksmith stammered in a matter of fact voice.

The Locksmith then left the scene thinking I was dead. The menacing droid noticed that the Waste Harbor door was open, and it raced towards the door.

I waited until I was sure the droid was gone and grabbed my communicator.

"Did you get the key?" I muttered into the box.

"We got it!" the voice from the communicator replied. It was PS5674, leader of the Xenotrons.

"Get out of there now. They are on to you! I'm not going to make it." I said.

PS switched off his communicator and warned the band of droids traveling with him, five rogue droids, each of whom were Tronic's, Inc. Xenotron modules that used a human as the core processor. They may have been rouge, but they were a tight group. Jagg, XS, 74, Coil, Roland, and I had worked together on many droid escape missions to earth.

"They're onto us. We can take the south gutter to the launch chamber," PS said. His digitally enhanced deep voice resonated through the silver and gold faceplate that hid beneath his hooded cloak.

XS who was hunched over trying to catch his breath said,

"We can't go that way!" I don't think XS did much running and, I don't think he ever saw a meal he didn't like either. He was a rather portly fellow, but he was strong as an ox. The first droid PS helped escape The Rings. For his freedom he forever pledged his loyalty to 74.

"Fat boy is right. It will be flooded with Locksmiths!" said Coil as she was changing the plasma bit of the machine drill affixed to her right arm.

"Whatever we do we need to do it quick. They're still tracking us." Jagg said. The hairs on the back of her neck stood straight up. She started to hiss and transformed into a metal jaguar fearing danger was near. Her heightened senses kept the team aware of their surroundings and made her an integral part of the team.

At that moment, a Locksmith Unit came crashing through the ceiling vent firing its blaster rays.

The droid bandits scattered. Two suffered major damage. Roland, 74's mission logistics master, ran straight towards the Locksmith and a sheet of rubber-lined metal that was about the width of his body burst from the top of his backpack. It looked like a giant measuring tape that extended up, out, and over his head, and then under his feet. When the rubber lined metal strip connected to the bottom of the backpack, it looked as if Roland was running in a giant hamster wheel. But this was no ordinary hamster wheel. It was deflecting Locksmith blaster rays and as Roland rambled toward the droid, it cringed before Roland flattened the Locksmith Unit like a steamroller.

Another Locksmith Unit careened through the hole in the vent shaft firing its blaster rays.

"Look out!" XS shouted as he took cover.

Roland dodged the raging projectiles and shrapnel. Coil ran towards the Locksmith and leaped on top of the droid. She grabbed the machine by the neck and was now riding the machine like it was a mechanical bull. She activated the plasma hammer drill on her arm and drilled a perfect hole in the center of the machine. It collapsed to the floor.

Roland rallied beside her stopping his hamster wheel like a spinning coin before it retracted into his backpack. The rest of the group came rushing in.

"That was a close call." PS said. "Let's move out."

The band of rogue droids ran into the Transport warehouse

that was now being used as a staging area for the Life Ring reconstruction project. It was a shortcut to the Waste Harbor. Their goal was to rendezvous with a shuttle cruiser moving trash from the Life Ring to earth. As the group was creeping through the Transport Warehouse PS could hear young voices chattering and then a small glowing metal ball came bouncing their way. The group quickly took cover.

A young boy came running after the ball with his lacrosse stick in hand.

"Do you see the ball Chris?" a voice shouted.

"Yes I see it," he replied.

The ball was resting at the corner of a stack of aluminum girders right where XS was hiding. XS held his breath trying to be as still and quiet as he could, hoping not to make a sound. The boy reached down and grabbed the ball. He ran back towards the other kids, but not before stopping to look back curiously, as if he felt he was being watched.

PS5674's audio processor was receiving interference. He could not control his audio sensors, and he was picking up a distinct voice out of the haze of noise, He was hearing Jason's voice.

Tone and I were waiting for the first lacrosse game to end. We sat on the sideline of the hidden game simulator. Tone, Mike, and I were up next. Mike had already picked Tone up on his team. They were pretty close friends, and then, I came along. They both tested into my school around the same time from the Lowland Sector. They competed at everything. I think it made them better. They may have pushed each other to be two of the best across any age bracket on the GRID. But, Mike is the man. No one can figure out how he comes up with the combinations he uses to trump the GRID. Some think he's found a hack. It's beyond anything anyone else could do. Mike was tall. His height made his presence intimidating, and he was never afraid to use his size to get his way. It was only fitting that he would be one of the best lacrosse players. You had to be pretty tough, at least I'm told.

Tone and I were adjusting the programs on the wrist gadgets that we were planning to use for next weeks GRID games when Mike walked up to us.

"You guys are working on GRID programs down here!" Mike said. "Does unplug mean anything to you!"

"ID wrist units, Can't leave home without them." Tone said.

"Yeah, but you don't have to bring the oppressors' tools down here. Mike said annoyed. "You know, the only reason we let you down here is because you can unlock these simulators."

"Whatever." Tone said as he continued to adjust knobs on the hologram monitor beaming from his wrist unit.

"Oppressors, that's cute. I mean, as much as you claim to hate the GRID, you showed us all up in the last competition. How did you beat Cain?" I asked. Milan Cain was arguably the best GRID player in Ring 1. We all hate his guts. He is a total nut job, and I'm sure he's somehow cheating the GRID.

"Jason, I've been telling you since the tourney started, he always goes two up, two down, strike, or strike blast as a kill move. I picked it up in Karma Slam, and he goes for it every time, on every game in the GRID. I have the block for that combo automatically programmed. When it senses that he's going for it, I don't even have to press a button for defense. I just attack." Mike said. He was talking to us like a frustrated teacher repeating a lesson.

"Isn't that illegal?" Tone questioned. "A pre-programmed hack is against the rules."

"How so?" Mike rebutted. "I'm not using alternate code or hacking into the GRID. I hacked Cain."

Off in the distance, on the other side of the simulator, PS and his band of rogue droids were still hiding. PS was still dazed by the interference from Jason's voice and his visual receptors were struggling to match voices with faces. 'Did you hear that?' began repeating in his head.

"PS what's wrong?" Ravage whispered through the grates of his mask. Ravage was 74's second in command and a fierce emotional warrior. He was nervous that PS did not respond, but 74 was intensely trying to focus onto Jason's voice.

XS knocked over a crate of rivets. The clanging echoed as the rivets scattered across the floor. Mike heard the sound far off in the distance.

"What was that? Did you hear that?" Mike asked.

I kind of heard something, but I was looking at Kara Thomas. She and a group of her friends were standing on the near sideline. I, and virtually every other dude, thought she was the most beautiful girl in our Sector of The Rings. Her caramel brown skin was radiant. Her dark black hair floated on the wind when she walked. She rustled through the bag hanging from her shoulder and pulled out a lacrosse stick and helmet and tossed them to the ground. She pulled her hair back into a ponytail, and the hair clamp automatically spun her hair into a bun that would easily fit under her helmet.

"Hey! Did you hear something coming from across the way over there or am I just losing it over here?" Mike said, annoyed.

"I heard something, but it's probably just the hydraulics pushing the columns in the simulator," Tone said. "But you were saying, you can program your wrist unit to do that automatically?" Tone asked.

"Yeah, if you know how." Mike said arrogantly still looking around suspiciously.

Kara looked over at me, and I quickly turned away. I didn't want her to see me staring at her. I tried to jump back in the conversation with the fellas.

"So how did you figure that out?" I asked Mike.

"I just watch him. It's like counting cards in black jack. I watch all the players, every cube, every key click." Mike said.

"Who counts cards in black jack?" I quipped. "There's no paper here."

Tone grinned and laughed.

- -

Back in their hiding spot, PS finally snapped out of his daze. He could hear XS and Ravage whispering loudly to get his attention.

"PS, PS!" They said."

PS turned and he could see the Salvage Transport elevator in the distance.

"Let's go," he said.

"Is everything ok?" Coil asked him.

PS ignored her with a blank stare and moved out with the others following close behind.

"Touchy, Touchy," Jagg said as she walked by looking at Coil with a sarcastic grin. "I told you he was crazy."

The group took the cargo elevator to the Waste Transport Harbor. The doors opened and in the distance were giant trash haulers placing their loads onto the space rigs. Their goal was within reach. They were running, racing toward the space rig when they were alarmed by a faint sound that was quickly getting closer. They stopped, looked around, and prepared themselves for a fight. Out of the dark hallway stumbled a change-form droid that had clearly been damaged by Locksmith blaster rays. It was leaking hydromorph fluid.

"Help me!" the change-form pleaded.

"What is that?" XS stammered.

"A Liquid metal change form!" Ravage said.

PS looked at the change-form and was struck into an immediate flashback of a man on an operating table being shocked by electrodes. Droids drilled holes into the man's bones and attached processors, all while the man was still alive, awake, and screaming in pain. The flashback ended.

"There is no more room in this escape party," PS said.

"Please!" The change-form begged.

At that moment, blaster rays fired into the group. One of the blasts scorched Roland's shoulder as he took cover.

"Locksmiths! Run to the shuttle!" PS shouted.

PS leaped to the ceiling and started running on the ceiling towards the Locksmith Units looking down at the ground beneath him. The Locksmiths fired their guns that burst holes in the ceiling on either side of PS as he raced closer. PS ran overhead past the droids and dropped a small glowing cube in between them. PS flipped down from the ceiling behind the droids. The droids stared at the glowing cube. Thinking the cube was benign; the Locksmiths fixed their guns on PS. The cube exploded shattering the Locksmith Units to pieces. PS crouched down to avoid the shrapnel.

As the smoke cleared, four more Locksmiths rallied around the corner. Coil was separated from PS and the rest of the group. Roland tried to extract his wheel and was struck by a fatal blast.

"No!" Jagg screamed looking behind as she raced towards the shuttle.

"Keep going!" PS yelled.

Coil ran as fast as she could and tried to slide underneath the Locksmiths in-between their clumsy legs. The last Locksmith put its foot down and Coil slid right into the metal beast. She was cornered.

PS and the others were racing towards the Harbor door that was now rapidly closing.

Coil fired her drill and looked deep into the Locksmith's eyes. She noticed that the drill was low on power and could not finish off a Locksmith. The angry droid fired at her and she raced toward the wall. She used the last bit of power in her drill to forge through the wall.

PS was the last man trailing the group and the door was six feet from the ground. If he didn't make it he would be trapped in the corridor with the Locksmiths chasing him down from behind. PS dove towards the door and as he slid on the ground, he turned onto his back and shot a fine mist from his wrist. He slid under the door, and fired a plasma blast into the corridor just as the door was closing. The mist ignited, blasting two of the Locksmiths to rubble.

The group continued toward the shuttle and they raced on to the conveyor belt that was lifting trash up to the ship. As they helped each other onto the conveyor, they blended themselves in with the trash. The change-form droid, who managed to survive the Locksmith onslaught, was the last to reach his hand up to be pulled onto the conveyor. Ravage reached down and pulled him in. The transport rig door closed and the ship took off towards earth.

43

CHAPTER 7 – WHO'S GOT NEXT?

The lacrosse game we were watching finally ended. The Mollies were giving each other high fives and celebrating their win. They were feared in the gutters and some claimed to have actually schemed with the SCAM on underground intelligence operations. I doubt it was true. Regardless, they acted more like a gang looking for trouble than some kids looking for a little adventure. I was hoping we wouldn't play the Mollies. Their shock pads glowed over their sleek green sport coverings. Tone talked all the time about how the Mollies had the best players. I was about to get my first real taste of what the game was like, and now, I had to learn facing the best team! I had tossed the ball around with Tone a little bit, but that's really it. This was going to be interesting to say the least. I just didn't want to embarrass myself while Kara was watching. I looked over at the table where she was sitting and I did not see her. She was on the move.

"Let's go!" shouted one the Mollies. "Who's got next?"

"We do." Mike said.

Tone was still fidgeting with his wrist unit.

"What is he doing?" Another one of the Mollies shouted. He was looking right at Tone.

"Come on you piss rag! Unplug it, or I will unplug you!" He said to Tone.

Tone was shook and scrambled to take his wrist unit off. He took it off and set it down on the ground next to his bag, but in his haste, he failed to turn the unit off.

"Easy, captain," Mike said. "If it wasn't for this little guy, we wouldn't have been able to activate this simulator."

The Mollies backed down. Mike quickly grabbed his stick and gloves. He handed me a stick, and we walked with Mike to the start station.

"These guys aren't too excited are they?" I said. Tone didn't respond.

"My father would kill me if he knew I was down here," I said. I was nervous.

"Well he doesn't know so don't worry about it," Tone said.

"What about Droid Security or rogues?"

"Rogues? They are only looking for droids with human processors and that hunt is over. You probably still believe in

44

Santa even though we live in a ring with no north pole," Mike said.

"I don't know about the hunt being over, but I think this location is pretty safe," Tone said.

"Whatever! You've got a conspiracy theory for everything, inspector, even the dragons on earth. It's time to focus on the game," Mike said.

"There are dragons on earth!" Tone stammered confidently.

"Dragons?" I questioned, dismissively. "We're going to have your head examined. You're crazy."

I was fidgeting with the lacrosse stick. It had an oval ring at the top of the stick where I'm supposed to catch the ball, but I couldn't figure out how to turn it on. Mike grabbed the stick impatiently and pressed a button at the bottom of the handle, and a plasma net formed inside of the oval ring.

"Who are you calling crazy? Why are you acting like you've never done this before?" Mike said, "What happened to you? Lost your edge sitting up under daddy?"

"What's that supposed to mean?" I asked. "I'm fine."

"Just be ready!" Mike shouted. "If the ball is thrown to you, you catch it. If the Mollies are after you, run, or try to throw the ball to one of us. The first team to get three tosses past the goalie and into the cage is the winner."

"Simple enough for me," I said, trying to muster up some confidence.

At that moment, I saw Kara walking along the sideline. It was like she was in slow motion as she stopped and removed her shock pads and sport covering. The zip suit absorbed any perspiration from our bodies and the clothes we wear underneath.

"Way to go girl! I saw you out there." One of her teammates said, as she walked by.

"Thanks," Kara said.

Tone talked about her playing in the gutter simulators. I was curious to see her in action, but disguised by the zip suit and helmet, I had no idea we were just watching her play against the Mollies. She picked up her bag and stick and sat down on the bench with her friends. She was smacking on a piece of gum and blew the biggest bubble I had ever seen. The gum bubble popped. She laughed, and I felt like she was talking only to me when she screamed out,

"Let's go boys!"

Mike was annoyed when he saw me gazing at Kara.

"What are you looking at lover boy? The game is starting!" Mike yelled.

I was sure Kara heard Mike, and I felt a little embarrassed. We walked to the center of the simulator. It looked cavernous. Metal walls, floors, and ceilings, I was really getting goose bumps. In the center of the simulator was a circle that was exactly 12 feet in diameter. There was a yellow light in the middle of the circle. Only three of the eight players from each team were allowed to enter the start circle. The rest of the players stood around with their toes at the edge of the circle.

Derek, the captain of the Mollies, walked towards the yellow light. He took the ball he was holding in his hand, and held it above the light. He dropped the ball and the light turned green. The small metallic ball sparked and began to wiz around as if it had a mind of its own. The game had begun. Our job was to chase the ball down, catch it in the plasma net at the end of our sticks and throw it past the goalie into the cage behind him.

46

I was so transfixed by the ball that I didn't even see one of the Mollies running at me like a raging bull. He checked me with his stick, trampled me to the ground, and kept going. He was chasing after the glowing orb. I felt like I had been run over by an aero car. I peeled myself up off the ground only to see the ball screaming towards me. I stuck my stick up into the air, closed my eyes, and ducked. It was a stroke of luck that the ball was trapped in my plasma net. I opened my eyes and saw three Mollies running towards me. I ran to the first goal I saw.

Mike was running on the other side of the simulator yelling.

"You're going the wrong way!" he screamed. "That's the wrong goal."

I was ready to shoot. Then I noticed it was Tone who was protecting the cage, waving his hands and stick profusely, telling me not to shoot.

"No!" Tone said. "You're shooting at the wrong goal!"

I stopped, turned around, and one of the Mollies checked me again. The ball flung right out of my plasma net. As I fell to the ground, the ball whizzed right into the net of one of the Mollies, who zoomed a shoot right past Tone to score a goal.

The kids gathered on the sides erupted with cheers and the Mollies were celebrating the goal. I was once again picking myself up off the cold steel.

"That's one to nothing, clowns!" Derek shouted. The rest of the Mollies laughed.

"What are you doing?" Mike yelled. He didn't even seem to care if I was ok. I had just been run over twice.

"You were going the wrong way. Our goal is on the other end!" he shouted again.

"Ok. I think I know that now," I said.

"What have I gotten myself into?" I mumbled to myself. I looked back at Tone who was trying to hide a smirk behind his mask.

"I'm sure Kara saw that." Tone said, laughing.

"Shut up, Tone." I said.

Derek and his team ran to the start station. Mike entered with two of our teammates behind him. I nudged my toes to the edge of the circle, and this time Derek dropped two orbs over the yellow circle. The light turned green and both balls zoomed and zigzagged across the room.

I was chasing one of the balls down. The ball changed directions and hit me in the shoulder. The ball sent an electric charge through my body that knocked me to the floor. As I stood up, I could feel the floor under me rising up from the ground. I looked down, and I was standing on a cube that was still rising out of the floor. I jumped from the rising cube and started running towards our goal. Mike had an orb in his plasma net and was looking to score. As I was running, other cubes all over were rising up and dropping out of the floor. The players leaped over the holes and dodged the rising pillars. One of the Mollies crashed into Mike, and he lost the orb. Mike stood up and chased down another ball, leaping over a hole. He jumped on top of one of the cubes as it was rising from the floor and screamed a shot towards the goal that raced past the Mollies' defense for a score.

"Yes!" Mike shouted. "This game is tied up!"

As our team celebrated the goal, giving each other high fives, all the pillars and holes receded and closed. I ran over to Tone, who was still guarding our cage.

"You didn't tell me that the ball can shock you!" I said. "The ball we practiced with at your house doesn't shock you, and it doesn't move like that."

"Sorry, I meant to tell you, but I forgot." Tone said.

"You what?" I muttered.

"I forgot. Don't worry. You'll either get used to it or," he paused, "or you will just get shocked." Tone mocked.

"Did you bring me down here to be the butt of your jokes?" I asked.

"No not really, but now that you mentioned it, it's kind of working out that way." Tone said, giggling.

"Let's go!" Mike was screaming from the center circle. I ran over as fast as I could and toed the circle.

"What are you doing? The game is on a timer!" Mike scorned.

"I didn't know!" I quipped. I was growing tired of Mike scolding me like I was his little brother.

"I sense a little mutiny!" Derek teased. His Mollies cronies laughed.

"Shut your hole, Derek!" Mike said. "We're gonna win this match."

This time Mike took the two orbs and dropped them over the circle. The balls zoomed out again, and we all chased after them. I was lucky enough to catch an orb again in my net. I ran towards the Mollies' goal. I could see Mike ahead, calling for a pass. Out of nowhere, Derek checked me right into a pillar and I lost the orb. My stick flung out of my hand and went careening toward the edge of the simulator where our bags were sitting. The stick crashed into Tone's bag and knocked his ID wrist unit into a vent shaft.

Tone saw the stick crash into his wrist unit and he came running over to see if it was broken. Without him in the net, one of the Mollies scored an easy goal. The onlookers cheered.

I ran over to get my stick and shut off the glowing plasma net. I didn't see Tone's wrist unit. Tone was looking around frantically for it.

"Where did it go? I saw your stick hit it. It popped up into the air. For sure it 's broken." Tone said.

"What are you guys doing, you lames?" Derek yelled.

"Lay off it! He can't find his ID wrist unit." I said.

"So what! He shouldn't have brought it down here. He just ruins our game and walks!" Derek shouted.

Both teams came running over. This was going to be a fight. Tone was scared frantic.

"You guys suck!" Derek growled.

Mike stepped in. "Lay off him Derek," Mike said.

The two stood nose-to-nose, looking each other in the eyes. It was clear neither one of them was going to back down. Then one of the Mollies separated the two.

"We'll settle this later, Derek," his teammate Gerald said. "Let's just start a new game and leave these losers."

Derek backed away, never taking an eye off of Mike and I, until he yelled out.

"Who's got the next game?"

No one else was up to play the Mollies, especially after we pushed them to the brink of a fight. The Mollies were juiced to take their frustration out on somebody. There's no way anyone stood a chance in a game with the Mollies. I'm sure of it because they were so angry and annoyed. The crowd booed and hissed and began to disperse. You can't blame them for being disappointed that we quit. But what are we supposed to do. Tone won't be able to get back into his residential sector without the ID scan files in his wrist unit.

One of the boy's voices echoed off the walls. "Hey Anthony! You suck!" Then the doors slammed.

I had already reached the point of ignoring their insults and they weren't even directed to me. But the echoing insult resonated in my ears because it reminded me that, now, we were alone in the simulator. All the other teens had left.

"I hate losing!" Mike shouted.

"But you would hate to lose your wrist unit even more, right?" I said. "Besides, the game isn't over."

"Whatever, Jason." Mike said as he turned his back and took off his pads. He disassembled his lacrosse stick and rammed it into his backpack, angrily.

There was quiet for a few seconds. The silence was thick as Tone kept looking around for the wrist unit. His heart was heavy with guilt, but he was also hurt by Mike's selfishness.

"What, do you want a hug, Mike?" Tone said, "If you're so upset with us, why didn't you just let the Mollies pummel us?"

Mike ignored him.

Tone looked down the vent shaft that was next to his bag. He saw his wrist unit.

"I see it!" Tone said. "It's in the room beneath us."

I ran over and looked down the vent shaft, and I could see it, too. The record light was turned on. I could see it blinking. The recorder on our wrist units records a 360-degree field of vision.

"How am I going to get down there? Tone asked, as he slammed his gloves to the ground and started pacing the floor. He was pulling at his hair. "Maybe Mike's right. Why am I flipping out over this stupid box! It's like a forth leg," Tone said.

I noticed a valve next to a square panel in the floor. It looked like an access door covering.

"Hey, guys. Do you think this access door could lead to the floor beneath us?" I asked, as I walked toward the valve.

"There is probably nothing but pipe and wire under there," Mike said, as he peeled off the metal covering. A sliding door was underneath just as I suspected.

I grabbed the valve and began to turn the metal wheel. The airlock clicked and the room began to shoot up a rush of air and smoke that hissed and lifted the door slightly. Tone stuck his head under the door.

"It looks like it is an entrance to the chamber below from this access bay door," Tone said. "If we just turn this valve, the room should decompress and you guys can lower me into the room."

Mike was still pouting.

"Dude, I'm going to need your help. I can't pull this door apart by myself," I said.

Reluctantly, Mike walked over and grabbed the wheel. We slowly turned the wheel a few more times and pulled the door apart. This process was not moving fast. Tone pulled some thick copper wire from a scrap pile and I held the wire as Tone climbed into the room. The floor is much lower than we had anticipated and the wire was not long enough to allow Tone to reach the floor. Tone let go of the rope and fell about ten feet to the ground. He looked around and noticed strange text all over the walls from floor to ceiling. There were numbers, symbols, and characters from a language he had never seen.

"Get the gadget and let's go!" Mike screamed.

I heard a faint rumbling sound and crashing metal. Tone walked over and picked up his wrist unit.

"You guys should see this. It's like a map or some kind of message down here written on all the walls," Tone said.

The rumbling sound was getting louder, closer, and more intense. I could see Tone grabbing the looking glass hanging from his neck. He walked over and placed the lens on the wall and there was a huge explosion that blew a hole in the wall right next to where Tone was standing. Tone was knocked to the floor. The blast surprised Mike and I. We jumped away from the door to take cover.

It was quiet for a few seconds, time that melted away slowly like candle wax. We looked back into the door opening, and saw a droid with snow-white hair hanging from the back of its helmet. The droid looked like it had a smoldering lightning bolt on its forearm as it came flipping through the hole in the wall. The hole was still molten hot around the edges from the blast. The droid stood up in the haze and peered through the hole. At that moment, a Locksmith Unit burst through hole piercing the smoke. The Locksmith rammed the other droid into the wall, and it struggled to gather itself after the blow, and a small container was dislodged from the weakened droid's shoulder strap. The container skipped across the floor and screeched to a halt right next to Tone, who was pinned into a shadowy corner.

Tone was frozen with fear. The giant robots did not notice him, and Tone did not notice that his wrist unit was still recording. He was terrified. Mike and I turned away from the hole. We didn't want the droids to see us. I could only hope that Tone would survive what looked to be a clash of bionic titans.

This droid was clearly a rogue Xenotron. It was more human than any droid Tone had ever seen. Blood dripped from metallic attachments on its leg. The droid was backed against the wall, and the Locksmith inched closer reconfiguring the weapons on his mantis arms into raging saw blades. The Locksmith leaped towards the rogue droid with the blades, outstretched, eager to embrace it in a grip of death. The rogue droid quickly ducked and the Locksmith lodged itself into the wall. It was stuck and struggling to free itself.

Then, the droid saw Tone's shadow in the corner of the room. The angry rogue pounced on top of him. Tone peed on himself.

"Ahhhg! Get off me!" Tone screamed.

At that very moment, we heard a cargo vehicle screech to a stop. The cargo door to the room below opened. Another droid ran into the room just as Tone was about to be diced into cat food. This second droid, the truck driver, grabbed the wild, white haired rogue's hand just before it was ready to strike.

"Coil, spare him! He's only human!" the truck driver yelled. "It won't take long for that Locksmith to free itself."

The wild rogue seemed to shake itself out of a trance. It was out of breath. It looked around confused, not sure who to trust. It looked at Tone who had resorted to playing dead. It looked at the droid truck driver begging that Tone be spared. The white haired droid took pause. It deactivated its weapon, and began to cry. The once wild rogue seemed to melt into the arms of the other droid.

"They left me here! They left me!" the white haired droid screamed, as the other droid helped it into the cargo truck.

"They were hot on your trail," the other droid said. "I figured if anyone was left behind, they would come here to the script temple. We've got to get you somewhere safe until we here from 74."

The cargo truck raced away down the tunnel into the darkness and the chamber cargo door abruptly closed. Tone gathered himself and ran up to the hole screaming hysterically.

"Get me out of here! Get me out of here!" Tone yelled.

Tone looked behind, and the Locksmith was still squirming, trying to free itself from the wall.

Mike and I went scrambling to try to find something to help us fish Tone up out of the room. The cord we used to lower him in was too short. It would be impossible for Tone to jump to reach it.

"Hold on, we'll get you out of there!" I said.

Mike slammed a computer operations panel with his bare hands, broke it open, and pulled out about 10 feet of thick data cable. We rushed to tie the data cable to the thick copper wire. Then we fished the line down to Tone.

Tone grabbed onto the rope and we started to pull him up. Then he dropped his wrist unit. He let go of the fish line and ran back over to grab his wrist unit. Tone strapped the gadget to his wrist, and he ran back to the wire. Tone grabbed hold, and Mike and I began to try to pull him up with all our strength.

Mike was losing his grip and Tone was slipping down. We were trying so hard; we did not even notice that the Locksmith had freed one of its arms. The Locksmith motion sensors detected our presence and it fired its blaster rays straight at us. The screeching sound was deafening. The blue rays from the blast barely missed Tone. Scatter effects from the blaster ray hit the copper wire.

I was holding the wire as tight as a vice, and I immediately felt a shock through the cable. My whole body was shaking, but I kept a grip on the cable. Mike slipped and fell down. I was gaining strength. Mike stood up and looked on amazed that I was pulling Tone out of the hole by myself. He shook himself off and grabbed hold of the wire to help.

"I'm almost there!" Tone said. "One of you, reach out a hand."

I reached my hand down into the smoky hole to pull Tone out. He grabbed my hand, and at that moment, the Locksmith freed itself from the wall. It was racing towards us with its awkward gait.

I pulled Tone through the access door, and Mike rushed over to help us pull the data cable out so we could close the access door. With only a few feet of cable left, Mike pulled as quickly as he could hand over hand. Tone and I grabbed hold of the heavy sliding doors. The Locksmith configured its arms to blasters, aimed, and fired towards the door with an indirect hit. The intense flames and radiance from the blast was heating up the door and Mike was still fishing the line. The door was too hot and Tone and I were forced to let go. The door was burning our hands. The door slammed and crushed Mike's hand. Three of his fingers were cut off and blood was gushing everywhere. Mike was screaming in pain. The sound curdled my ears. Tone and I were panicked, in shock.

"Wrap his hand!" I yelled. "We've got to stop the bleeding."

"I can't. We got to get out of here!" Tone said. He was horrified.

"Well get on that wrist unit and call the Sector Police!" I insisted.

"That was Sector Police that just shot at us!" Tone said.

I ripped the sleeve of my vest and wrapped Mike's hand as tightly as I could, hoping it could stop the bleeding long enough to get him to a medi-droid. Mike held his wounded hand close to his chest, and I had his other arm around my shoulder. He was getting weak from the blood loss. We had to make it to the closest transport elevator to get us out of the gutters and into the main deck of the Life Ring. I was holding Mike up.

The elevator was only 20 yards away but it seemed like forever. Tone pushed the button.

"Hurry up! Call the Sector Police. There's blood everywhere!" I said.

Tone was fiddling with his wrist unit because his hands were shaking uncontrollably with fear. Tone realized the unit was recording. He turned off the recorder and called the Sector Police. I was frantically pressing the elevator call button.

"Did you piss your pants? What are you doing? Hurry up!" Mike groaned.

Tone looked down at his wet pants, and the Sector 8 Police answered the call.

"Hello how can we help you?" The hologram image from Tone's wrist unit sounded.

"Off...fi...cer," Tone stuttered out. "We have a bit of a problem."

Back inside the chamber beneath the simulator, the angry Locksmith was banging at the valve door that was now welded shut. A second Locksmith crawled through the hole Coil had blasted through the wall. This second Locksmith used a thermal

DNA scanner that beamed neon blue light across the walls of the room trying to find any evidence that would identify its prey.

"I cannot decipher the code that is scripted on these walls," the Locksmith's machine voice uttered. "It appears to be a log or possibly a map. We should report this to Sedusa immediately."

The other Locksmith stopped banging on the valve door.

"Sedusa is liable to have our heads!" the angry Locksmith said as it gazed into its tracking beacon monitor. "We will report this to Sedusa when we find out why the change form is going to earth."

The Locksmith's tracking beacon monitor showed the location and movements of the change form droid that hitched a ride on the Waste Transport Shuttle with the other rogue droids. The shuttle was getting closer and closer to earth, descending into the planet's dark, ashy, atmosphere.

"What will we do about the two little humans who escaped with the other small droid?" The second Locksmith asked, as it analyzed a piece of Tone's hair and fingerprints. "I have identified one of the humans as Anthony Fargus. I've traced their location. We have no auxiliary units on standby in that area."

"They are no threat." The angry Locksmith said. "It's not worth the risk of harming the humans. We will follow that beacon. That's the prize catch. Alert Vitally the scrap hauler. He is scavenging the earth for anything of value, and he will be able to find our lost toys, once we send him the tracking beacon data from the change form. They can run. They can hide, but they will die."

Meanwhile, the two fugitive droids, Coil and Ratchet, who aided in her escape, were racing their transport across the gutters towards Ratchet's hiding post. Ratchet slammed the brakes on the cargo wagon at a dead end corridor in the gutters. He got out and walked to the back of the wagon.

"Ratchet, you're a life saver!" Coil said as she exited the cargo wagon.

Ratchet fixed his hands to the back of the wagon, and pushed the transport vehicle right through the wall. The wagon disappeared.

"No, you are the life saver," Ratchet said. "For many years, I've watched you help 74 take rogues like us away from this place of horror to the paradise we've built on earth. I know that you would run through a wall for any of us."

Ratchet looked at Coil and bowed, gracefully, as if saluting royalty.

"Come on inside and let's see if we can get that switch recharged." He said.

They walked through the hologram wall and into a hidden lair. There were droid parts scattered about, a pile of arms here, and a pile of legs there. Coil walked over to a tall shelf that was cluttered with small boxes filled with much smaller components like finger joints and audio processors. She grabbed a jar of eyes and looked at it curiously. Ratchet was sifting through the maze of dismantled droids to find a compatible adaptor for Coil to recharge.

"I am not sure how long it will take them to decipher the code in the script temple or if they even care," he said. "But I will go back to the temple to log this mission."

Coil placed the jar of eyes back on the shelf, sat down on the workbench and sank her head into her hands. She felt defeated, as if she had failed.

"I lost the key. I was cut off from the transport. I can't believe they left me here! Nothing has gone right, and now I'm stuck here!" she said.

"Hey, what am I, dead wood over here?" Ratchet asked sarcastically. "You're not alone." Ratchet had a look of admiration for Coil and his eyes radiated genuine care.

Ratchet plugged cables into machine components in Coil's arm to charge her plasma drill.

"He'll come back. He will come back, and this time we will have a living key." Ratchet said.

"What do you know of the living key?" Coil said, with the weight of doubt on her words. "Only the Travelers, those with the ancient knowledge of the Keepers of the Benben, speak of such things."

"You are right. The Keepers of the Benben stone, the first machine coders. I was taught not to ask questions that I already knew the answer to," Ratchet quipped. "I know because I've followed the stone's eye to track this living key across dimensions, and I believe it has aligned itself within a vessel in this point in time to bring clarity to us all."

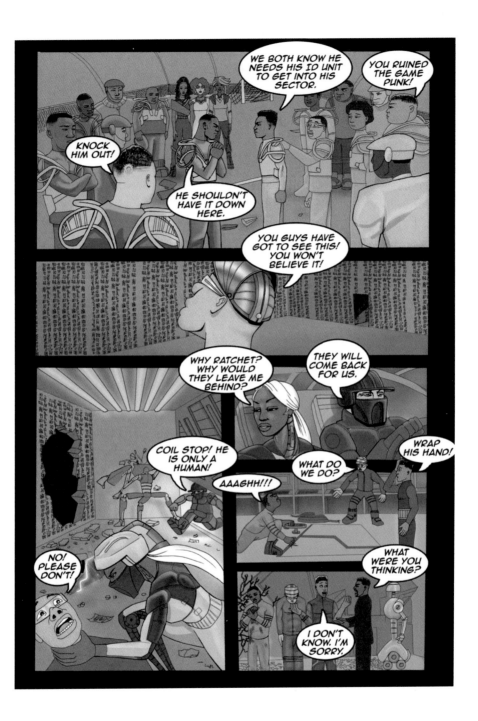

57

CHAPTER 8 – THE HUNT

In the main deck of the Life Ring, life is no different than we knew it on earth. It is in essence a Noah's Ark that preserved all life on earth. The seed bank was unlocked and throughout the Life Ring the cultures and climates of earth were recreated. Massive skyscrapers tower above and people traverse through city-like districts that mirror old New York City. Aero cars race through the air high above, and the Magrail, a system of bullet trains, connects the worlds of the Ring at supersonic speed.

The Magrail raced to a stop at Sector 17D. The door opened and the slim feminine legs of Sedusa stepped out and shook the platform. Her hair draped down her back barely phased by the wind as it lay on her black fitted trench. The long split tails of her coat were flapping in the wind, exposing the LED lights running up the back of her metallic heeled boots.

She walked toward the Magrail access elevator and people parted like the Red Sea. She entered the elevator door alone and raced to the top of the highest point in District D. Through the glass windows of the elevator she could see the entire city. As the elevator came to a stop the flashing lights of the Tronics Inc. sign at the top of the building illuminated the glass capsule red. She walked out onto an automated walking path, but she kept walking, which only accelerated her determined pace.

As she approached two massive steel doors, the walkway slowed to a crawl and the doors opened. She entered the room and there she saw smoke slowly rising from behind a dark, ornate chair. She approached the desk while urgently dodging the tiny recreations of Leonardo DiVinci's machines, that moved about the room – the helicopter, the tank, and humanoid automatons. Through the panoramic window that lined the wall, the dark earth stood in the distance. On the opposite wall there were hundreds of monitors beaming real-time images from the Life Deck.

"Dr. Raven, you sent for me. What is your request?" Sedusa said, impatiently, as she approached his desk.

Dr. Raven waved his hand, never turning his chair to face Sedusa, and a news report plays on all of the screens. The air was thick with the smoke from the cigar.

"Another clash between Locksmith security forces and a band of defective rogue robots has resulted in a 15 year old boy losing three fingers trying to escape the savage droids." The news anchor said. "The antiquated Xenotron units, designed and manufactured by Tronics Inc., were built specific for Life Ring construction and maintenance. It has long been rumored that Tronics Inc. owner and chairman, Dr. Damon Raven, used human samples as the core processor in the Xenotron unit and it proved to be defective. Tronics claimed years ago that all Xenotron units had been rounded up and destroyed. Tronics also denies that it has ever used human samples or any production methods banned by the Leaders of the Ring Council. More on this tomorrow at 7."

Dr. Raven waved his hand again, and the news anchor is frozen in midsentence on all the screens. His deep voice calmly rises from behind the chair. "Who says all publicity is good publicity?" Dr. Raven said.

The floating chair turns quickly and a man with a monocle in his eye and a black ruby ring on his finger slammed his hands on the table. The tiny robots on his desk were bounced to the floor by the thrust of the pounding fist.

"Where are my machines?" Dr. Raven screamed, angrily clinching the mechanized monocle in his eye-socket.

Sedusa jumped back, slightly alarmed, but she quickly regained her composure. She flipped open a compartment from her wrist and beamed a hologram that scrolled records and data streams.

"The number of machines purged and destroyed through the Locksmiths doesn't seem to match the total number manufactured and in active inventory," Sedusa said.

"I am well aware of the numbers. Tell me what I don't know! For the last three years we have been losing machines each eight-day build out. This is costing me money I don't care to lose!" Raven shouted.

"The eight-day build out coincides with the waste dump missions to earth." Sedusa said. "With mounting resentment toward the Xenotrons, perhaps the Societal Coalition Against Machines is to blame. The SCAM's outcast units have claimed responsibility for the abduction and destruction of hundreds of Xenotron units in random violence. Dumping destroyed equipment on the desolate planet could be their approach to organizing their efforts to rid the Life Ring of Xenotron technology."

"Their legislative efforts through the Ring Congress to muscle me out of my chairmanship are moving slowly. Perhaps SCAM is to blame, haters of the very builders of their future." Raven said. "Why haven't they all been rounded up and relegated to the slums?"

"Their operations are more covert and depend mainly on influencing youth. I don't see them as the threat you do. Besides Dr. Raven, there are laws against attacks on corporate dissidents and children." Sedusa said.

Raven slammed his hand on the desk again, in anger, and didn't notice that he had cut his hand on a tiny crushed droid.

"Has that ever stopped us before? Raven asked sarcastically. "Whatever the case, you find my machines! Find them!" He shouted.

"I will find them, and the missing units will be accounted for." Sedusa replied.

- -

Meanwhile, on the dark planet, PS5674 was hanging upside down, plugged into his runtime charger. He was trembling and twitching, immersed in a deep sleep. He was dreaming. He saw a man sitting in an office at Tronics Inc. The man must have been an architect. There were small models of prototype buildings on glass shelves along the walls. Many of the buildings were towering skyscrapers. There were so many models it looked like a tiny city. But these weren't just any buildings, because each of these model buildings was erected in the Life Ring.

The room could have been empty and the man seated at his desk would not have noticed or cared. He sat staring at five small models on his desk. These models were not skyscrapers. They were fitness simulators. Tiny holograms of people raced through the challenges of each of the simulators. These challenges were old earth sports games. He watched the tiny glowing images with the joy of a child with a new toy. But his joy quickly turned to anger. His eyebrows clinched together like fighting arrows of sunlight and his nose flared. He smashed the models with his fists and raced out of the room slamming the door.

The man walked outside and the clouds in the sky were turning black. The door to his aero car opened up towards the sky and he stepped in, sweating and breathing heavily. The twin jets of the aero car fired up and the car raced into the dark noon sky.

The autocom buzzed into the aero car, and a woman's voice spoke in a raging panic.

"Come back, they knew it was coming!"

"I know, and I'm going to stop them," the man said as his aero car sped through the dark clouds.

Out of the front window of the speeding aero car he could see balls of fire streaking across the sky in the distance. An asteroid had entered earth's atmosphere and small fragments had broken off. The man kept flying, faster and faster. The woman again pleaded over the autocom.

"Come back, they will kill you! The Leaders knew it was coming!" They are taking me and your..."

The woman's voice was cut off. The rain of molten rock fell more intense, and with a great crash, the man's aero car was struck by a meteorite.

"Akila!" The man screamed, and his voice was silenced.

PS5674 was shaken from his dream. He awoke in a panic, but he looked around and realized he was upside down, plugged into the runtime charger in his laboratory. He realized he had made it safely back to earth. He had made it back home to CX, a Xenotron refugee colony on earth that he designed and constructed with other Xenotrons he helped escape from the Life Ring.

CX was like no place ever constructed. It looked like a flying saucer wedged into the side of a mountain. It was a cathedral of fitness simulators with a cavernous interior arena. Instead of seats surrounding the center surface there were impact power cells that absorbed the energy created when the Xenotrons pounded the surfaces of the simulators. It was these power cells that launched the beam of light that spread out from its peak in the sky high above the mountain and encapsulated the entire colony.

PS unplugged the thick runtime charger cord from his hip. The ceiling crane lowered to the floor and flipped him right side up. The braces previously locked around his ankles released, and he stepped out of the crane. He walked over to the window of his vast laboratory and looked proudly upon the hundreds of Xenotrons hanging from the ceiling like bats.

Dozens of smaller four wheeled robots called M-DOGZ

zipped across the floor below reaching tools up into the Xenotron bat nest to perform routine maintenance. PS gathered a few pieces of equipment form his worktable. An M-DOG wheeled towards him abruptly and came to a stop.

"Will you need anything sir?"

"No thanks Rover. I'll be fine. PS said. "Did XS deliver the key?"

"No sir, he did not."

"Can you process his data run for me."

"No Problem Sir."

The M-DOG zoomed over to the worktable and a long one fingered arm extended from its armadillo like frame and plugged into the station. Three-dimensional holographic images shot up from the table and moved about showing all the visual images logged by XS during their escape from the Life Ring. The M-DOG zeroed in on the key as XS placed it in his right thigh storage compartment. The hologram puppets showed the Locksmiths bearing down on XS and as he fell to the ground. The key was dislodged and XS could not recover it. PS watched as Coil destroyed a Locksmith and picked up the key. The puppet show ended and the hologram disappeared.

"It appears that Coil has the key sir. I noticed that she did not return with the escape party." Rover said.

"We were cut off from her by the Locksmiths." PS paused with concern. "I don't know if she is dead or alive."

"But we will need the key to unlock the second impact generator." Rover said.

"I know." PS said as he walked out of the automatic sliding doors and into the long tunnel that led from his lab to the shuttle launch pad.

PS walked out of the tunnel onto the launch platform that jutted out over the edge of a great cliff, hundreds of feet up in the side of a mountain. His space cruiser with its gyroscope propellers glistened in the faint rays of sunlight that pierced the earth's clouds of black ash. As PS approached his ship, a brisk wind swirled. He could hear footsteps in the distance behind him. He paused and could see Ravage running towards him through an adjacent tunnel.

"XS lost the key!" Ravage said.

"I know, I read his data run this morning, while he was plugged in." PS replied.

"He said the lock box just disengaged and he didn't realize it." Ravage said.

PS was annoyed. "He could have come himself to tell me." PS said.

"Where are you going?" Ravage asked, vexed with concern.

"Back to the Rings, Coil might still be out there. I was going anyway, but now I have doubled the reasons." PS affirmed.

"What do you mean? What about Vitally?" Ravage asked.

"We can't throw off the tracking systems of his salvage scavengers without the new distortion code, and we need the key for the impact generator in order to do it."

"That's why I'm going back, to get the key and the new distortion code. You can handle a few scavengers until I get back. We are free from the machine." PS said.

"We are not free from the machine, because we are machines." Ravage offered.

"Maybe you're right, but that's not all that I am. I have built this place from fragments of my past. I know we are safe here, but I must know how it came to this." PS said as he opened a compartment on the side of his ship. He turned a few knobs to adjust the pre-launch sequence.

"None of us have been able to make sense out of the flashbacks," Ravage said, "My memories haunt me too. We must have done good work building the Life Ring, but to be made into a freak, this monster."

Ravage's face grimaced in anger and fluid rushed through exposed tubes in his forearms that caused all the muscles in his body to expand grotesquely.

"Calm down you big baby." PS said. Ravage's muscles contracted to their normal size. "You're going to need to exercise some patience because I am leaving the governance of the colony to you."

"Why me? Why are you going alone?" Ravage asked. He felt he was squarely incapable of governing the colony.

"I still see her in my dreams. I feel that she is alive." PS said as he gazed off into the distant sky.

Ravage and PS noticed the shadows of the Life Ring were beginning to block the sunlight.

"She will know the truth." PS said.

"We all have these dreams. You taught us to look beyond

them!" Ravage said mockingly. "That's why we're here. We believed in you and now you are leaving us?"

PS climbed into the shuttle.

"If that's how you see it, then that's how it is." PS said. "The way I see it, this colony is just the beginning. The truth is still out there, and I will not return until I have found it."

"What of the stowaway? He's not one of us. I checked his program code, he is not even a Tronics' module. It's a rogue droid of some kind. The court sticker stated that he was assigned to work Life Ring maintenance as part of a detention release to avoid purging. What do we do with him?" Ravage asked.

"Well, you're the one that helped him onto the escape vessel. You won't let one rotten apple spoil the bunch." PS said.

"A liquid metal change-form, he could be a handful. We've kept him quarantined. His injuries exposed a hydraulic leak. It will be sometime before he is alert enough to execute his change function. I'm sure the M-DOGZ could figure something out." Ravage said. "He could start working the cornfields."

"See you're doing good already. You're treating him like he's your son." PS laughed. "We can never have enough hands processing the ethanol. Show him how to play. Maybe it's the last bit of good we can do. We can use all the carom energy we can get to fuel the Ventrosphere. It's all we have to conceal our location and protect us from the nuclear wind. As jumbled as our minds are, the one thing we do share is our memory of the freedom of the games. Perhaps he can learn our way."

PS and Ravage looked up at the beam of light energy that spewed from the top of the mountain. The beam of light bloomed and looked like a never-ending mushroom cloud.

All of a sudden, alarms were screaming from inside the shuttle. Two short distance speeders were fast approaching.

"Scavengers!" Ravage warned. "Get in the air!"

PS climbed into the cruiser and the automatic deck lid of his space cruiser closed quickly. The ship was taking heavy fire from the scavengers as PS activated the gyroscope propellers for vertical takeoff.

Ravage created a force field around his body, and ran full steam ahead towards the two low flying speeders. Blaster rays from the speeders' cannons were absorbed by Ravage's force field shield. With each blow to his shield, Ravage was growing bigger and stronger. The speeders were quickly approaching him, and Ravage reached out both his arms and snatched the two Scavengers right off of their speeders. The speeders crashed and burned, just as PS lifted off the ground. The rocket thrusters fired on, and PS blasted off into the sky. Ravage slammed the two scavenger droids together and they fell to pieces jolting sparks of electricity, smoke, and flames. A droid head rolled to his feet as Ravage stood above the rubble.

Miles away and hovering fast and low across the desolate landscape, a junk barge with a fleet of armed picker droids and scavengers was racing toward the site of an old city buried a mile under the earth. The city was buried in a massive landslide after the impact, and the junk barge picked up the goldmine of raw materials that could be recycled for use in the Life Ring. Raw materials were considered anything of use that humans left behind on earth that was preserved. Among the most precious of these materials was water. Scavengers were designed to recover these raw materials and investigate potential mines and underground aquifers shielded from contamination. The leader of these earth bound droids is Vitally.

Vitally sat at the helm of his 90 feet long junk barge that looked like a giant floating wheat harvester. His dusty, tattered, hooded cloak flapped in the wind. He adjusted the dark lenses that covered his eyes. He saw two of his scavenger droids explode on his tracking monitor. He looked at the monitor a bit confused and dialed in a code on the heads up monitor in front of him. He requested a status update from the droids. The same result appeared on the screen - "Probes Destroyed."

"What! Two more probes? That's half a dozen droids in the last lunar cycle." He spoke out loud to himself. "What's out there?"

He replayed the two scavenger droids' onboard video cameras and it showed a distorted view of Ravage destroying the two droids and the image fizzled to black. The video repeated.

"What the heck is that?" Vitally said tapping his scaled, reptile-like, fingers on the monitor. "Whatever it is protecting sent the probes' junk monitors haywire. There's a ton of raw materials in that direction. I mean a whole honey pot."

Vitally turned on his com-link and spoke to his legion of flying junkmen.

"Gentlemen, we've got a honey pot 1000 miles across the canyon. We're going to put this dig on hold and go around the canyon to see just what these probes have found over there. Whatever it is, it's huge!"

-- --

Meanwhile, inside the bats nest, in a cell next to PS5674's lab, the change form droid laid on the operating table. Small robotic modules stretched from the ceiling examining the droid and administering maintenance procedures. The droid modules retracted to the ceiling, and an M-DOG approached the change form. The M-DOG activated the change form's power switch. The change form's red eyes lit up.

"What is your name and operational function?" The M-DOG asked.

"My name is SoNite." The change form replied. "Life Deck sewage systems engineer. Where am I?"

"Earth. Welcome to CX. You will be quarantined here in the Tech Lab until it is decided what is to be done with you. I see that you are equipped with perpetual power plates that do not require recharging. An M-DOG will administer anything you require. Please advise." The M-DOG said.

"I don't need anything." SoNite mumbled. "Nothing but quiet."

"As you wish." The M-DOG said, and it exited the room.

SoNite sat up from the table and opened a module in his hand. SoNite snatched out a green blinking tracking beacon. He threw the beacon to the ground but it did not break. It sat on the ground blinking.

Grandpa was in the den sleeping after we returned from the hospital. He seemed out of it ever since. Why was Grandpa weak, and I was not? I couldn't figure that part of it out. He didn't get hit with a lighting bolt, and burnt like a piece of Mama's turkey bacon. I was hit with a lightning bolt, and as sure as I'm standing here, nothing happened to me.

I put my bag down in the study floor and sat down at the computer. Mama was rustling through the cabinets to find pots and pans to make spaghetti, and the phone rang. She rushed to answer, hoping it would be news about Jason.

"Missy!" Grandpa said.

I came rushing into the room because he sounded distressed. I was nervous.

"Sit down next to me Missy," he said.

I sat next to Grandpa quickly.

He whispered, "I have found your brother."

"What!" I shouted.

"Quiet Missy, can't you see I'm on the phone!" Mama screamed.

"Shh!" Grandpa said. "Missy, your family is part of a long line of time travelers. We are called Shell Dwellers, descendants of those who first visited earth and seeded the planet with life. Masters of the scientific arts, but caretakers of the balance between what science can do and what it should do. In the future we will lose our way and what you know to be human will cease to exist."

"What? Why are you telling me this? Is this one of your tall tales about playing in the Negro Leagues?" I asked. "Mama told me the truth about that Grandpa."

"The truth is Missy, that I did play in the Negro Leagues. It was part of a mission for us to protect the integrity of a people that had lost its way. We guided a living key to the proper human vessel, and the mission for that time was fulfilled. It worked for a while, but obviously, there is more work to do. Now Jason and you are our only hope for a time in the future."

"Whatever Grandpa. Even if you were telling the truth, what do you expect me to do?" I said confused.

"Code," Grandpa said. He grabbed his cane and placed it in my hand.

"This cane allows me to move through dimensions in time, forward or backward. When those bullets struck Jason to the ground, the living key inside him was released and sent forth on a mission that is different than what he was sent to do in your time Missy. Now, he is stuck in a future world helping us defeat the forces that will eventually control the earth and how we live."

"How do you know this Grandpa?" I asked. "Living key! You've been listing to them Bible tapes too much." I quipped.

"I have been traveling for a long time, and this may be our last chance to right human kind's wrongs." Grandpa said. "But occupying two vessels across dimensions in time takes great knowledge, skill, and strength. I'm getting too old to do this, love. I will need your help to code the cane to allow you to help Jason return. He doesn't know who he really is in the future world. He can only return if you reach him to show him the truth, and bring him back after he has finished his mission."

I stood up. "What do you mean Grandpa? How will I know when his mission is finished? What is his mission? What is going on? So, I wasn't making this up? I was struck by lightning?" I asked desperately.

"That was a portal opening that I traveled through to reach your brother and aid in the mission. I can't make too many more of these trips, but you can Missy. You just have to trust me. You can save him." Grandpa said. "Your mother is going to come in and tell you that Jason is progressing and using less help from the ventilator."

At that moment, Mama walked in the room.

"I just talked with the doctors at the hospital and they said that there was considerable improvement in Jason even since we left the hospital. They said he is making involuntary movements and using less of the ventilator." Mama said. "I'm just praying my baby will come out of this."

She turned away and went up the stairs with tears of hope in her eyes.

"Does Mama know?" I asked.

"No." Grandpa said. "She doesn't have the gift, but you and your brother do. You have to help him. Take the cane, and let's try to figure a way to make you a Traveler."

"But Grandpa, what is the mission?" I asked.

"Jason's mission is to save the sports he loves from their own demise. What he finishes in the future will cleanse the wrongs of our time." Grandpa paused. "For us, the mission remains the same, to save Jason from himself."

- -

Meanwhile, off in the distant future, the ventrosphere beamed up from the Cauldron, high above the Xenotron colony. It was double noon, the peek time for harvesting carom energy, the Xenotrons self-sustaining power source. The base of the Cauldron coliseum was wrapped in a maze of giant metal tubes and exhaust stacks that twisted around the building like rubber bands. The rustic structure was crudely constructed but cleverly designed to transport energy throughout the colony.

Deep in the underbelly of the Cauldron were the disc chambers, cavernous rooms with Xenotrons running on giant circular treadmills. The treadmills move only on account of the Xenotrons' continuous movement. As the Xenotrons run on the treadmill, disc chambers create carom energy that charges impact power cells stored in adjacent warehouses.

The giant belts would stop, and a brood of Xenotrons would exit the chambers. A new team of runners would enter the disc chambers, and in synchronized steps, the Xenotrons would start to jog, steadily picking up their pace until the center light turned yellow, indicating that carom cells are being generated.

The Cauldron was the ultimate fitness simulator. The Xenotrons met once each lunar cycle in the Cauldron to challenge each other in the Animates, a ritual-like sports tournament. The Animates were also a significant resource for energy harvesting. The Cauldron was the most challenging and complex simulator because it unpredictably combined challenges from any of the fitness simulators in the colony. The challenges of the Cauldron forced the Xenotrons to train daily to prepare for the Animates.

A troop of Xenotrons was gathered in the Cauldron for a routine training exercise. The simulation series number was B-3010, and it mimicked baseball. But B-3010 was a bit different.

X-charge stood on the mound with only his eyes peaking above his carbon fiber mitt. The mitt was held together with hydraulic webbing and joints. Sparks of electricity jumped from his fingers as he tightly gripped the ball inside of the glove. Random explosions burst from low hanging atomic storm clouds that penetrated the ventrospheric canopy.

70

"Eh batter, batter, swing batter. Easy out." XS taunted.

The catcher, Focus, sent signals to the pitcher and X-charge started his wind up. As he placed his hand in the glove over his head, a charge of electricity burst from his body as if a bolt of lightning struck him from above. X-charge launched the blue flaming ball toward the plate. The ball moved and shifted randomly in flight like an electrical spark.

To confuse the batter, the catcher beamed hologram images of balls approaching the plate from his fingertips the second the ball approached the strike zone. Breakneck, who was standing tight at the plate, was locked in on the ball. Breakneck swung with all his strength, and the holograms disappeared as he made contact, hitting a rocket towards third base. Breakneck blasted out of the batters box as the baseline turned green to signal a fair ball.

Sandbox, who was at first base, ran three steps and morphed into a funnel cloud. Sandbox transformed just in time and he avoided the metal claw that angrily burst through the ground eager to snag and pull him below. The cloud of dust clumped back together and Sandbox was reformed whole, racing as fast as he could to get to second base.

Hurricane, the third baseman, activated the high-powered vacuum tubes affixed to his forearms. Hurricane dove to his right to catch the bouncing ball. The powerful suction tubes swooped the glowing orb into his mitt. Hurricane stood up quickly, and with no chance to get Sandbox out at second base, he riffled a throw towards first.

Heat was sprinting on his way to home plate to score when the Halo, a random sinkhole, opened up underneath him and swallowed him whole. At that very moment, XS caught Hurricane's throw at first base, just as Breakneck was dashing across the bag. It was a close call. The teams looked intensely at the base. The base flashed bright green three times signaling the runner was safe.

"Ain't no way! XS said.

"Light don't lie! Breakneck taunted.

"He was out! XS shouted.

"We can't use any of the hot air coming out of your mouth for carom energy." Breakneck said.

"Carom these!" XS said, as he clutched his out-of-shape bosom. "You were out!"

XS threw the ball back to the mound, and the players stoically reset their positions. Blockhead stepped into the batters box. Again, X-charge clutched the ball in his mitt, and peeked over at Breakneck, who was inching off first base. X-charge sparked again and launched another lightning bolt toward the plate.

I'm grounded. My father was at the door taking questions from the Sector Police for the third time since Mike's injury.

"It would be best for your son not to venture into that sector again Mr. McKinney," I overheard the officer say to my dad.

"Thank you Officer, we will be sure that you don't have any more trouble from him." My father said.

I could tell that my dad was annoyed by the smug tone in his voice as he assured the officer that I would be no more trouble. My mother was standing beside him as the door slid shut.

"I'm going to talk with him."

"Silas, give him a break." My mother said, pleading.

"The only thing I said I'm going to do is talk with him!" I heard my father shout.

I was in the hall eavesdropping. I heard my father coming, and I ran to my room and jumped in the bed. I banged my head on the headboard when I landed. I was holding my forehead in pain and trying to keep quiet and pretend that I was asleep. If Mike or Tone saw me hit my head like that, they would have laughed their faces off. My head was throbbing.

I could hear my father come into the room.

"You're not asleep Jason," He said. "I heard your feet pitter-patter down the hall, and I could hear you plop into the bed." He said.

"I didn't hear you knock." I said. "I am not a kid anymore."

"Boy, this is my house. You are a kid! And I will walk into any room I please! Your friend lost his fingers because you kids can't mind your own business. That's right I said it again, kids!" My father said. "Haven't you done enough? Then you have the audacity to tell me what to do in my own house!"

My father slapped me across the face. My face was stinging. My knees grew weak, and I slumped down to my bed. He stood over me breathing heavily.

"It was an accident!" I said trying to hold back my tears. "I'm sorry."

He looked over my shoulder and he saw the O-Ring Blade and Pom under my pillow. Tone pulled the game from his father's stash of Lowland Sector games. We use a metallic ring with a plasma-polymer membrane in the center to hit a stone-like orb called a Pom back and forth to each other. My father hates me being associated with anything related to the Lowlands, and I knew that this was only going to make him angrier.

"Have you been sweating in my house again? I have told you, I don't want these games in my house!" He shouted. "Is this what you are doing when you are out with those low life friends of yours?"

"What are you talking about?" I said.

"You know what I am talking about. I know what you are doing. You had better be concerned about learning this business. I am trying to build a legacy for our family at Tronic's Inc. and you are wasting time with those damn breadcrumbs playing these stupid games. Don't you understand that I build the same security droids that are bringing you to this house in hand-cuffs!"

"You don't know them. They are my friends."

My dad grabbed the O-Ring and the Pom. In his angry haste, and eagerness to prove his point, he tried to throw the Pom in the air and hit it with the O-Ring. He was so clumsy that he missed the Pom completely, hit himself in the face with the O-Ring, and slipped to the floor. He looked like a bumbling clown.

My face was still throbbing, but I had to hide my laughter when he fell to the floor. He looked up at me like an embarrassed child.

"They are nothing but scum. They want to revive the physical because they are uncivilized brutes!" He said as he peeled himself up off the floor.

"That's not true dad. I made a mistake, but that's unfair."

"Those kids from the slums are all obsolete! I don't want to hear of you in the gutters of this space station ever again. Is that understood?" He said as he threw the O-Ring down to the ground.

"People can't be obsolete." I said.

"That's what you think." My father said. "You need to worry about the upcoming GRID competition. I had to nearly give a rib so that the Sector Police would grant a waiver to allow you to participate. What do you think the tournament is for? I'm pulling the strings to get you into the Ring Sustainability Project, but you've got to prove that you belong there! That's where you need to be, learning to engineer and build droids! Dr. Damon Raven has been good to this family. If you learn the trade, He will be good to yours. That's what this family does. We build the Ring!"

"Well maybe I just don't belong in this family."

His big paw swelled, and he hit me again.

"Get it together boy!" He said as he walked away and kicked the O-Ring across the floor towards me. I trapped the O-ring underneath my foot and watched my father walk out of the room.

My father was mostly a happy man, but he never seemed happy with me. I was angry. It wasn't even really my idea to go down into the gutters. I didn't know what to think. The SCAM, the GRID Games, who cares, I thought. I didn't want Dr. Raven to be good to me. I wanted my father to be good to me. I can look him eye to eye. I see myself in the mirror, and I feel like I'm too big to be his punching bag. But he knows I'm still afraid of him.

I picked up the O-Ring from underneath my foot and the Pom that rolled to the other side of the room.

I tossed the Pom into the air and gripped the O-Ring tightly in my hand. As the Pom began to drop it seemed like it was moving in slow motion. With all my might, I swung at the Pom. The stone-like orb slammed off the O-Ring and to the wall. The Pom came screaming back at me, and I slammed it again, but this time, I hit the Pom even harder. I hit the Pom so hard that it left a dent in the metal wall. Faster and faster I hit the Pom off of the wall. The sound became thunderous, but I wasn't even aware of noise. I took a final swing, and the Pom bounced off the wall and I caught it in my hand and threw the O-Ring as hard as I could in anger. The O-Ring cracked and lodged itself in the glass window of my room's airlock door. I watched as the cracks in the glass slowly spread and the glass broke. The momentary pressure loss pulled everything in my room toward the tiny hole. I stood there, defiant, as cords, tools, clothes, and gadgets zipped past me, pulled by the force of the vacuum created by the hole in the air lock.

"Jason!" I heard my father scream.

My mother rushed into the room trying to fight the force of the open airlock. She pushed the emergency relief valve release, and it sealed off the hole. All my things were pressed up against the wall and they instantly fell to the floor. I stood there staring at the wall. Then I looked at my hands and I felt a strange sensation in my body, and my fingers were numb, the same way I felt after I pulled Tone out of the tunnel. What was happening to me?

My mother looked at me strangely, like she wanted me to explain what just happened but she knew I did not have the answer.

"Get out of here before your father comes in here." She said.

I grabbed my jacket and ran out the back door of our sector unit and hopped on my bike. I hovered up the entrance ramp and entered the bike tube that was an overhead express way just for hover-bikes. I needed to talk to Tone. My dad would not let me visit him since the incident. Maybe he knows something, and he's the only person I feel I can trust right now.

I was weaving in and out of the biker traffic and I don't think the other commuters appreciated it.

"Slow down you idiot!" A lady screamed.

I couldn't blame her for being angry, but give me a bone lady, I feel like I've got something growing inside of me. But I needed to be careful. The slums aren't a place for the faint of heart. They rest on the sun-sides of the Rings. It's best to act like you know where you're going, and watch your back at all times.

Everything here is old and dilapidated. The technology, the infrastructure, the houses were all obsolete. My dad says most of the people here were political exiles or people who didn't qualify for Ring Sustainability Project class work. He feels it's his life's purpose to keep me from coming here with a bunch of zombies and criminals. But my father can't be right about everything, Tone is one of the smartest people I know.

I exited the tube and parked my bike. Two goons were outside a few houses down.

"Is that a new bike kid?" One of the goons said.

"No, it's just a rental," I said.

I ran up the stairs to Tone's house and knocked on the door. I could feel I was being watched. So, I looked down the way and one of the goons had his eyes fixed on me, and the other had never taken his eyes of my bike.

Mrs. Fargus answered the door in all her glowing radiance. Tone's mother was drop dead gorgeous, and I was shamefully in love with her. So much so, that I blushed when I saw her. Tone hated it when Mike and I teased him about his mom's pretty looks.

"Hello Jason. How are you?" She said.

"I'm fine Mrs. Fargus. How are you?" I stuttered. "Is Anthony home?"

I think she noticed right away that I was a bit disheveled.

"I'm fine Jason. Come on in, you poor thing." She said. "Is

77

everything ok? How is Mikey?"

"I'm fine," I said. "Mike is fine. They were able to rebuild his hand, but I know he is a little down because he will miss the GRID Games. He's doing the best he can."

Tone's mother wrapped her arms around me and I just melted.

"I know it was terrible, but it's going to be ok." She said as she released me from her warm embrace and held my hands.

"Thank you Mrs. Fargus," I said.

"Anthony is upstairs," She said. "Now Jason, he is grounded so he won't be going anywhere, and you can't stay too long."

"I understand Mrs. Fargus. Thank you. By the way, is the bike going to be ok outside? Looks like you've got some new neighbors."

"I think you'll be ok," Mrs. Fargus said, sarcastically.

I ran up the stairs to Tone's room. He was sitting at his desk adding program codes to his ID wrist unit. I heard Mrs. Fargus screaming out the front door.

"Look, don't touch the boy's bike!" She yelled, and she slammed the door violently.

Tone knew who I was without even turning his head to look.

"Hey Jason," Tone said.

I was already pacing the floor.

"I was playing with my O-Ring," I said.

"Why are you telling me? That is way too much information," Tone quipped, as he turned around in his chair.

"This isn't funny Tone," I said. "I was practicing with the O-Ring and Pom in my room. I was upset, and I threw the blade so hard it cracked the airlock glass."

"That's not possible," Tone laughed. "That glass is tempered and three inches thick!"

"It happened. I'm telling you," I insisted, "My mother walked in and had to activate the emergency relief valve."

"Maybe the glass was already broken. Maybe you were just imagining it. You know like those dreams you've been having about Kara."

"It wasn't my imagination when I pulled you out of that hole by myself. Something happened to me, and I haven't felt the same since." I said, frustrated.

"Maybe you are turning into a woman. That can happen in puberty," Tone joked.

78

"Is that supposed to be funny?" I said. "I came to you because I thought you might have a clue to help me. All you've got is jokes?"

Tone stopped laughing and then noticed that I was really serious.

"I guess I'm laughing to keep from crying," Tone said. "I'm not sure what's going on with you, but what I do know is that my wrist unit was recording when I dropped it into that shaft. It was recording everything. That room was some kind of temple. There were maps of the Life Ring Gutters with special markers. Each of the markers is near a sector waste harbor. It's written in some kind of primitive programming code or something. I can't read all of the symbols. But one thing is for sure, these rouge machines are at war, and desperately trying to get out of here."

"That's just gibberish. It's nonsense. That doesn't have anything to do with what's happening to me!"

Tone pulled out the small container that dislodged from the shoulder strap of the white-haired droid, and landed in his lap while he was trapped in the temple room.

"What is that?" I asked. "And, why does it smell like pee?"

This thing fell in my lap when I was trapped in the hole. It came off of the droid trying to escape the Locksmith. The marker on this box says 'PS5674.' This was the serial number of the Xenotron who sent the pre-impact files over the circle wire. Those leaked files raised the initial suspicions about Tronics Inc. and fueled SCAM's motivations against Dr. Raven.

"That's ridiculous. Goodness. What is that supposed to mean?" I said.

"I don't really know? I haven't figured it out yet. But there's more. Something happened to you Jay. What did you feel when you were pulling me up with that cable?" Tone asked.

"I felt like an electrical charge was running through my whole body. It felt like I was burning from the inside out!" I said in a panic. "I felt the same way when I broke the air lock today."

"Well, you won't believe this," Tone said.

Tone played back the recording, and he was right. I couldn't believe it. I saw myself pulling Tone up from the hole. I saw the electrical charge from the Locksmith blast race through the cable. Tone grimaced in pain from the power of the charge and loses his grip. He slides down the rope and regains a tight grip. Then, I see the skin on my arm becoming transparent. Inside my arm I could see metallic muscles in my forearms, hands, and biceps.

"What is that?" I felt like I wanted to puke.

"I don't know, I think that electrode blast activated some type of hybrid gene inside of you that increased your strength and exposed those things in your arms." The room was silent, as Tone took an awkward pause, somewhat hesitant to finish his thought. "Maybe you are somehow connected to these machines." Tone said. "Maybe you're a rogue."

"I think maybe we're seeing some illusion because of the lighting." I stuttered.

"The first stage is denial," Tone said, sarcastically.

"What do you want me to say? I'm a Xenotron and have the Locksmiths come to purge me!"

"You couldn't pull me out of that hole with your own strength, not even in your dreams. Let's be for real Jason. You can't just do that can you?"

The reality of his question set in and sterilized my doubt. My denial was absurd. I just watched the recording with my own eyes. Something was definitely not right. Now, I've got to figure out how to fix it.

"So what are you trying to say?"

"I think we need to go back there Jay. I think it's the only way to find out what's wrong with you."

I don't even know why I asked. I knew he was going to say that. How are we going to go back there? For starters, we're both grounded.

"What ever happened to just going to the doctor?" I said.

"You tell me? Why didn't you just go to the doctor?" Tone said.

I looked at Tone and sat down on the hover chair next to his desk, and put my head in my hands in despair.

"You know that if they found out you were some half breed machine they would have you purged."

"I'm not some machine. I've been to the doctor so you're conspiracy theory is stupid!" I said in frustration, as I pulled my key out of my jacket, and stormed toward the door.

"You've got to go back Jay," Tone said, as I pressed the button to open the door and it slid open. I stopped and looked at Tone. I trusted Tone, more than anyone I knew. Why would I doubt him now? I knew in my heart he was right.

"Ok, we're going to go back. But we can't get caught down there again, and until we find out what's going on, this is between us," I said.

The next day I woke up, and I felt normal. But there was a problem. I was late for school, which should be impossible to do when I go to school under a helmet at a desk down the hall from my bedroom.

I quickly opened the cover on my bed, ran down the hall, and grabbed my helmet. As I put the helmet on and pulled the visual matrix lens over my eyes, I thought, I should have brushed my teeth. Now I'm going to have to deal with my own nasty morning breath inside this helmet.

Inside my helmet it looks and feels like I am in a classroom with all the other kids, and we are sitting together. We rarely have to meet in reality, only for testing and the pass-on ceremony. There were kids that didn't live in the same Sector as I did, and I would never see them in real life other than at testing and pass-on. Most of what we need to "know" to survive is chip loaded when we are born.

The teacher was taking attendance as my avatar popped up on everyone's monitors, and there I was in my pajamas. All the students burst out laughing at my nightclothes. Tone always logged in to sit next to me. He looked at me and shook his head.

"I don't know how you are going to top this." He said. "Happy face pajamas, really!"

"I woke up late. I didn't even think about it," I said embarrassed.

"Jason you are late. How that is possible I don't know, but I doubt that your father would be pleased." The teacher said.

"I'm sorry Ms. Morales. It will not happen again."

Mike was sitting in front of me; I was surprised to see him at school. I had not seen him since the accident, and my parents would not let me even speak with him since they learned how intensely he was involved with the SCAM. I was nervous about talking to him. I felt bad about his injury, and I felt like it was my fault. How could I explain?

"What's up with you? How's the hand?" I whispered.

"I don't know. I can't put my finger on it," Mike said, sarcastically.

I sat back in my chair weak with guilt. Mike was fidgeting with the exposed robot joints that were used to reconstruct his hand. He couldn't have new synthetic skin adhered to the fingers for a few more days. I couldn't bear to look at it. The sight made me wince to imagine the pain.

"Look Mike, I'm sorry about what happened."

"I won't be able to play, until these new digits take, and it's your fault." Mike said angrily.

"Mike it was an accident."

He turned and looked at me. I could tell he was conflicted. We were friends, but he was getting the worst of the bad situation we created for ourselves. I was just hoping we could recover from this.

"This is going to hurt for a while Jay."

The double entendre in Mike's words was both evident and true. I looked over at Tone frustrated. He was pointing across his body like he wanted me to look at the person who was sitting on the other side of him. I leaned forward and it was Kara. She smiled and waved. My first thought was that she wasn't waving at me. So, I looked behind me to see if there was someone else. No one else was looking at her but me. I smiled back, and she laughed.

"Does any one know the answer to this question?" Ms. Morales said. "How about you Jason?"

I had no idea what she was talking about.

"I don't know sir. Excuse me. I...umm...I meant, Ms. Morales." I stuttered.

"Because you refuse to pay attention, I am going to place you on peripheral restraint." Ms. Morales said.

At that moment all the other students in the class disappeared from my monitor. The only voice I could hear, and the only person I could see in my helmet was Ms. Morales. Great, I finally get Kara's attention and now I can't even see or hear her. She lived three sectors over. The only time I saw her outside of school was in the gutters. That was only twice since school began. I didn't even have her index number to message her. I was plugged in for ten minutes and already this was both the best and worst day of school ever.

When the school day ended, I took my helmet off and went to the kitchen to get a drink of water. I went to my room and thought about what had happened. What did Mike mean when he said, "This is going to hurt a while?" I mean are we still friends? It was unnerving. I respected Mike and I valued his friendship. He taught Tone and I some great tricks to prep for the GRID, and if it wasn't for him, I don't think either of us would have made it this far in tournament qualifying. I wanted to tell him about what was happening to me but I'm not sure he would care or understand. I mean, maybe we are both part man and part machine because of what happened. Maybe what he said is what he meant. It will take some time for these wounds to heal.

My wrist ID unit message alert was going off at my desk. I ran over to grab it. It was Tone.

"Hey Tone what's going on?"

"Not much."

"Did I miss anything today after I was blacked-out?" I asked.

"No, you didn't miss much, but we all missed you! Your plopping into that seat in your pajamas was pretty much the highlight of the day." Tone said.

I laughed. If you can't laugh at yourself sometimes you might need to check your pulse to make sure you're still alive. Besides, I needed to laugh.

"Mike was pretty bitter," Tone said. "But I think he is going to come around. We talked for a minute at the end of the day."

"Well I'm just going to give him his space," I said. "It's probably best to let things cool down."

"That's probably wise," Tone agreed. "By the way, Kara wanted me to give this."

Kara's Index Number came across the screen.

"She said she heard about how you helped pull me out of the hole, and she thought it was pretty cool."

"You've got to be kidding me," I said.

"I guess what they say is true," Tone said. "The hero always get's the girl."

On the desolate earth, the dark rolling clouds loomed low in the sky, as Ravage stood high on a stone bridge. The natural land bridge connected two major Xenotron camp operations embedded in the lower peaks of the three-pronged mountain. One of these camps was a manufacturing complex that processed raw materials for the Xenotrons' living quarters. The second compound was a research and training simulator that was especially designed for combat arts.

The cold breeze stirred up dust devils as Ravage looked down into the valley beneath the bridge. Hundreds of Xenotrons were working through a maze of athletic training simulators and combat stations. SoNite, the change form Ravage helped save from the clutches of the Locksmiths stood with him. Ravage took PS5674's advice to train the liquid metal change form for the Animates. The challenge was to find out what SoNite could do and how his carom energy could best be harnessed.

"To sustain the balance of competitive force, both the challenge and the draw of teammates is determined, at random, minutes before the Animate begins," Ravage said.

SoNite heard what Ravage said, but he wasn't listening. He was growing weary of the routine of the Xenotrons' lifestyle. The constant and rigorous training, every moment of time accounted for, this was too restrictive for a change form, and SoNite was every bit annoyed.

They walked into the combat simulator. It was a massive room with vaulted ceilings. The room began to change colors from black to white and then white to black. Then the floor flickered, and black and white squares appeared. The floor looked like a checkerboard. The squares began to rise from the floor, and then fall back down from the ceiling. If one of them were hit by one of these mammoth blocks, they would be crushed.

The rising squares were quickly approaching SoNite and Ravage, but Ravage wasn't phased. SoNite was sweating mercury.

"So what do I have to do here?" SoNite said in a panic.

"Get out of the room alive!" Ravage said.

Ravage raced toward the green neon door at the other side of the room. He was spinning out of the way of squares like a football player eluding tacklers. He leaped on top of rising squares, from one to the other quickly before they reached the ceiling and he coasted on squares as they receded back to the floor. SoNite was running right behind him. Dodging the square obstacles splitting his body in two, morphing from solid to liquid. The green door was within reach and Ravage pushed the finish pad. The door turned red and all the columns recessed to the floor. SoNite slithered himself back together and walked through the door with Ravage.

"The cauldron harnesses the energy we exert in meditation, training, and in competition to power the Ventrosphere through an ancient Benben stone," Ravage said as he stood in the simulator control room. The hologram monitors processed data from their performances in the endurance test.

"Rocks don't create energy unless you burn them?" SoNite questioned.

"Everything is energy that can be harnessed." Ravage said. "The stones possess more power than you know."

SoNite was doubtful. "Looks like an elaborate magic show you're using to brainwash your little droid cult if you ask me."

Ravage begrudgingly ignored him and continued to explain. "This simulator tells us how much impact energy you can generate. That's what we call your Carom Energy Count, or CEC."

Ravage looked at the readings and took note that SoNite exerted an extremely low CEC as he slithered through the columns. He did not mention the results to SoNite.

"We all have it, and we all can give it, even you." Ravage said. We need it to fuel and protect the colony from the earth's post impact atmosphere."

As the two walked out of the simulator and back onto the rocky bridge, a light fog rolled over them.

"But the weather breaches the barrier. I've seen it," SoNite said.

"No system is perfect. That means there is a defective processing key. We have to steal these processors from Raven's research labs. A lot of our technology has been pirated from the Rings. But there are no delays for weather in this operation. No matter what the weather, we train, and we compete." Ravage replied.

"Huh?" SoNite mocked.

"If we don't compete, the Ventrosphere would collapse," Ravage said. "It's a bubble that surrounds this entire mountain and miles around it. We can clean the air and stabilize the conditions in the atmosphere. But some weather breaches."

"So when is the next shuttle leaving for the Rings?" SoNite asked, as if he had not been listening to a word Ravage was saying. "You're talking to me like you're trying sell me on the neighborhood. I'm not buying."

"The only way out of here is on a Scavenger Droid parts rig; that, or maybe you can train with us for the next exodus," Ravage said.

"Exodus?" SoNite inquired.

"We go back to the Rings to save more of those we've lost, to scavenge for any obsolete parts that Raven's labs have discarded, and of course, to refine our distortion and encryption code keys to keep our location hidden here on earth."

"No thanks. When I leave here, I'm never coming back," SoNite professed.

Ravage was beginning to have second thoughts about saving the ungrateful change-form, but he was determined to find a way that he could at least contribute to the energy bank.

The two took an elevator down to the valley and entered another chamber. As SoNite entered the center of the chamber, a metal orb popped up out of the floor and into his hands. Four doors in the walls opened and out came four wheeled droids. Ravage backed away into the shadows of the room, as the droids surrounded SoNite.

"So what kind of game is this?" SoNite asked.

"There are moving rings on the east wall. All you have to do is put the ball through one of the rings."

As SoNite held the orb in his hands he noticed that there was a code pad imbedded in the orb. He randomly pushed a button and dropped the ball. The orb fell to the floor like a rock. It rolled to one of the droids who scooped it up, put it inside its chest, and the droid nearly doubled in size. SoNite was shocked, but had no time for pause as another ball popped up out of the floor. He pushed a different button on the orb's code pad. He dropped it and it was as bouncy as a basketball. He dribbled the ball towards one of the droid attackers with a full head of steam and ran right through the droid. His liquid metal body weaved through the tiniest cracks and seams of the robot. The droid was shut down by the internal damage. While SoNite's arms and hands were still dribbling the ball, the rest of his body exited the droid and reformed, leaving behind a plume of smoke.

SoNite pressed another random button on the ball. He threw the ball at the giant droid. The droid shrunk back to its normal size. SoNite was catching on fast, but he was getting unnerved that there was so much about the game that Ravage did not explain. Another orb popped up from the floor. He threw the ball again at the droid and it shut down instantly. The ball rolled back to SoNite, and he ran towards the ring wall. There were two droids ahead of him. He bounced the ball around one side of the droid and ran around the other side of the droid to catch up with the ball. The droid turned and chased after him.

There was only one droid left between SoNite and the ring wall. SoNite threw the ball off the back of the ring wall. He morphed his body and leaped through the lone droid blocking his path to one of the rings. SoNite caught the metal orb as it bounced off the back of the ring wall in mid air, and he slammed it through the ring. The ball blasted through the ring and lit up the energy cells below. SoNite dripped to the ground from the ring and reshaped himself. The chamber echoed with sarcastic applause.

"I see you're getting the hang of this already." Ravage said. "And we got a good carom energy count from that exercise."

"Get me out of here! The first flight! This is a hell hole." SoNite said. "I'm not going to be a slave to you. I owe you nothing!"

"Raven would have had you rounded up and purged just like the others. We saved you from certain death. You weren't welcome here, but we still took you in as one of our own. There are no flights from here! Never!" Ravage said.

"If I had known of this madness here, I would have taken my chances with the Locksmiths back on that east sector harbor." SoNite screamed.

"I would expect that from a change-form," Ravage said.

"I am not one of you. I couldn't care less about these stupid games."

Ravage grabbed SoNite by the neck and slammed him up against the wall.

"That's because you're just a bucket of bolts and coded processors, with no soul. But while you are here, you will do as we do. I'm done asking. There's a reason every one of us trains and competes in the Animates. But your wires are too fried to understand."

"I don't care!" SoNite screamed and liquid metal spit splattered all over Ravage's face and slithered back into SoNite's mouth. Ravage exploded with anger. He picked SoNite up, and slammed him to the ground. SoNite's body spread all over the floor like spilled paint. Ravage was still holding him by the neck.

"Get yourself together!" Ravage said, angrily, as he peered into the change-form's eyes. "The first Animate begins at the rise of the third moon."

'I'm here for now. But that's just for now." SoNite said, as Ravage let go of his neck. "One thing is for certain and that's change. I'm getting out of here. You wait and see."

Ravage stood up and looked down at SoNite splattered all over the ground and walked away.

"Third moon. Whatever," SoNite mumbled, as the liquid metal pieces of his body slithered across the floor into a single pool and reformed his body.

- -

Meanwhile, PS5674 was flying in his shuttle, stealthily, approaching the Life Ring. He spent some time in orbit around the earth to disguise his entry into the Life Ring's protective perimeter. It was best to tow in on the heels of an unmanned satellite. PS docked his ship underneath the waste harbor. He typed in Coil's tracking number into the shuttle control panel. Nothing came up on the shuttle's radar. He flipped the auto track button and the code was transferred to his headgear. He exited the shuttle and walked down the harbor tunnel, leading to the gutters. As he was walking, he sent out an encrypted analog radio signal. Only Xenotrons could receive encrypted radio signals. If Coil was out there, she would eventually get the signal and respond.

Finding Coil was now just a matter of time, but his real mission would be like finding a needle in a haystack. He was determined to find the woman in his dreams. The first place to check was the Life Ring genealogy catalog that can map and locate anyone in the Life Ring with a DNA sample or image. The only place to find the catalog is in a Human Information Systems Center. Locksmiths and Sector Police heavily guarded each center.

As he approached the Human Information Systems Center, PS5674 hid behind a wall. He peeked around the corner to see if the coast was clear. There were only two Locksmiths guarding the door, but clearly there was only one way in and one way out. The entrance was recessed into the hall corridor so it didn't seem as if he could get in without a confrontation. But he was still thinking. He looked out again and a Locksmith Unit saw PS5674's shadow as he jumped back behind the wall. The Locksmith Unit walked down the hall towards PS to investigate.

"Hey you!" The Locksmith said.

PS stood tight against the wall careful not to make a sound. The Locksmith turned the corner with its weapons drawn, but PS was not there. The Locksmith unit looked around confused.

PS was suspended with his arms and legs flat against the ceiling, blending in with the ceiling like a chameleon. Tentacle probes extended from his body and attached to the Locksmith Unit. The Locksmith Unit shut down instantly and stood motionless. PS dropped to the ground from the ceiling, as his camouflage faded away.

PS mimicked the voice of a Locksmith Unit and called for the other Locksmith Unit.

"I need help with an intruder." PS said.

The Locksmith Unit came running down the hall and as soon as it turned the corner, PS blasted it with a stun ray that short-circuited the Locksmith Unit. Sparks and flames shot from the droid and its eyes went dark.

PS walked into the Human Information Systems Center. The data records lab was empty. He walked to a control panel and plugged into the system with a probe that extended quickly from his torso like a switchblade.

He pulled up an image of the woman from his dreams and began a search through the system. Faces flickered before his eyes on the hologram monitor, attempting to match the image from his dream. Finally, the images stopped. The name typed across the screen. A-K-I-L-A G-U-D-R-A-L. PS looked around the room to make sure he was still alone. He looked back at the screen and the terminal monitor read, 'unregistered or deceased.' Two numbers were blacked out for the last known Sector address.

PS slammed his hands on the terminal and broke the control panel. The alarm sounded, and PS ditched the scene.

He walked to a discrete hall far away from the Human Information Systems Center. He was running low on power. He located a hidden power box connector that the Xenotrons placed in the gutters of the Life Ring in case one of them needed to power up while hiding from the Locksmiths. PS plugged his runtime charger into a power box, and he was immediately thrown into a flashback.

In his vision, a man was screaming in agony on a table as robotic surgical probes hovered around him from all sides. The probes shocked the man with electrode charges. Then he saw the man with a woman, Akila, holding hands.

"Will you be working late today?" Akila said.

Next, he saw an image of the Life Ring only half completed, only half the ring circled the earth. He then saw the man at a Tronics Inc. executive board meeting with Dr. Damon Raven. The man was seated at the roundtable with the other members of the board.

The man said, "Mr. Raven, I've tested the gene primer for hostile atmosphere and it works. Using micro-machines like a vaccine, we can genetically reconfigure the lungs with tiny digital respirators and perhaps humans may be able to reclaim the earth, rather than continue with the Life Ring and it's simulations as a permanent solution."

"We're a little too far along for that now, don't you think?" Raven replied sarcastically and the other members of the board laughed dismissively.

"But we're talking about restoring life on earth! The Life Ring's simulator selection process was flawed and far too exclusionary." The man said.

"The earth is gone to hell! Our priority is to finish the first build out to begin the final evacuations before there are any breaches in the canopy." Raven said.

"You're making a mistake. We can salvage life on the planet." The man said.

"That is exactly what we are trying to do, and I hope you are trying to do the same." Raven said. "And by the way, leave the research documents. We'll determine the best use for this technology."

The man sat silent with anger and frustration written on his face. The man stood up and walked out of the room. The Board members looked on, embarrassed for the man, shaking their heads.

PS's dream then flashed to the man again being fused with metal ribs while he was still alive. The man was screaming in agony.

PS woke up screaming and his voice echoed through the empty corridor in the gutters. His life battery had doubled its charge while he was under. He unplugged himself and set out to find Akila Gudral. He was determined to find her, whether she was dead or alive.

Chapter 12 – The GRID

On the deck of the Life Ring, tournament day had finally arrived. The GRID Games qualifying round was set to begin. Thousands of fans that took glee in calling themselves "programmers" flocked to the main GRID arena and Sector gaming hubs scattered throughout the Life Ring. Of all the places a player wished to be was in a cube on the main - game central – where Dr. Raven himself would serve as master of ceremonies. I stood outside of the central GRID gaming complex with my mom who had been to all of my matches since I turned ten years old and was eligible to play. This was our first at the main.

"You aren't nervous are you Jason? She asked."

"A little, I guess. I've never played this format before." I said.

"You'll be fine. Remember what I've always told you, 'Quick as thought to become the machine.' Your father said he's coming." She said.

"I'll believe it when I see it, but you'll be plugged in to watch right?"

"I wouldn't miss a second, baby. Your father means well. Sometimes he gets busy. Be fair."

I don't know why my mom made excuses for my dad. I felt like if he wanted to be there he would be there, and he was never there. There was really nothing to be fair about. But what else is she supposed to do? He's my father.

"I'm going to hook up with Anthony after the games to eat is that ok?" I said trying to change the subject.

"You're still grounded!" she scolded. She smiled. "But, I will make an exception for tonight. In by 11pm though, now, go get 'em."

She gave me a good luck kiss on the cheek. That's one of the things I hope I never grow too old for.

I raced through the door. This was it, but my thoughts were twisting knots in my stomach. I didn't care about the GRID Games for the same reasons as my father. It was just fun to me. All this pressure to be like my father and work for Dr. Raven made training for the GRID Games feel like a job sometimes. But today, I was fit to put all that aside. It was game time, and I was ready.

Inside Game Central, there were thousands of seats and

each had a hologram monitor that allowed the fans to activate programming code to disrupt the players during competition.

At the center of the arena was a honeycombed maze of hundreds of player stations. That's where I was headed. I walked into my game cube. It looked like the cockpit of a fighter shuttle. There were screens and monitors everywhere, a joystick, and foot paddles. I reset the monitors, adjusted my headset, and transferred codes into my cube system from my wrist unit to set my preferences.

Across the bow, Tone was inside his game cube, fixing his helmet straps, and adjusting the touch screens inside his game cube.

"You ready Jay?" I heard him say in my headset.

"Walk in the park baby." I said.

We were set to begin. My mother was among the fans going crazy in the stands cheering like mad as Dr. Raven's voice echoed over the loudspeaker.

"Welcome to our world!" Raven extorted to the crowd's roaring delight. "Today we bring you, as always, the ultimate display of human ability - connected interplay within the GRID. Tried, tested, and true, it is here that we determine the next generation of leaders and achievers that will advance Ring Sustainability. Who is capable and who is not? Who is willing and who is not? Look no further than this moment to see!" Raven said aggressively.

The crowd erupted, and Raven played them like an old jazz standard, pausing for a beat to egg on the frenzy.

"Our competition begins in 3, 2, 1, and begin!" Raven screamed.

The atmosphere was electric. The crowd was stirring with fervor. A huge three-dimensional holographic monitor flickered on in the center of the arena above our gaming stations.

Hundreds of space fighter ships formed above our heads filling the entire space above the arena. The course map appeared on one of the monitors inside my game cube. The challenge was to be the first to navigate through an obstacle course and avoid being blasted by oncoming goon fighters. The master computer and programmers in the crowd navigated the goon fighter ships.

We took off traveling at speeds unthinkable. The forces inside our game cubes were true to life. The cockpit rattled, shook, vibrated and contorted as if we were really flying inside a space ship. Out the front window of the cockpit was the vast darkness of space, distant stars, and the ships beside me jostling for position as if they were flying bumper-cars. As we all approached the goon fighters, it looked like two swarms of bees colliding. The battle was on.

Tone was frantic inside his game cube.

"I've got one on my tail." I heard him say in my headset.

I tried to locate him on the dedicated monitor. It was Milan Cain, tailing him hard. He was the best player in our Sector. Without Mike flying with us, Cain saw Tone and I as easy pickings.

"You're mine. You're going down." Cain said with a menacing grin.

Tone was behind me, and there was no way I could retreat to hold Cain off. Cain fired his blasters. Tone tried to dodge the whistling projectiles, but the shot vaporized his ship, sending Tone's game cube into darkness.

"Not again!" Tone cried out.

I adjusted my mouthpiece and switched the monitor I had dedicated to Tone, to track Cain. I needed a constant reading of Cain's location. I checked a second monitor. I could see a few fighter planes ahead, and a swarm chasing from behind.

There were two intervals to go, when two programmers unlocked the code for space garbage. My screen monitor flashed red, and alarms sounded. Space debris infiltrated the raceway. One after another, ships crashed into the large pieces of metal and rock. Other players made swift maneuvers to avoid colliding with debris and rammed into each other. The only way I could see out of this mess was to shoot the debris out of the way with blasters. Other fighters were forced to maneuver around the carnage I left in my trail.

Through the glare of the heads-up display, I couldn't see my mother in her usual spot in the arena. I wondered if my father made it. Would he be proud? I saw images of my father in everything I blasted to pieces. To my core, I felt like my father was my enemy.

There were two fighters ahead. I've got to chase them down. But just as I started to gain ground, I entered an asteroid field. Programmers navigated these death rocks, and could either help me by steering asteroids out of my path, or they could sentence me to a head on collision by ramming an asteroid right into my ship.

On my monitor I could see a fighter gaining on me from behind. Straight ahead, an asteroid was screaming at me. I pulled up as hard as I could. I barely missed getting creamed by the asteroid, but the fighter right behind me wasn't so lucky. She crashed into the screaming rock and exploded into flames. I could see her across the aisle in her game cube throwing her helmet to the ground. I quickly put my eyes back on my monitor. Orange lights were flashing inside my headgear signaling that we had cleared the asteroid field. We were nearing the closing stretch, and I was closing in on the leader.

The lead fighter fired its blasters at lingering debris that shattered and left a maze of smaller chards for me to avoid. I was twisting upside down and inside out, swiftly avoiding the errant chards of debris. I closed in more on the leader, who was shifting side to side as we entered the narrow finish tunnel. I picked my chance to pass and raced alongside the leader. It was Milan Cain. He looked over and rammed his ship right into mine and my wing was scraping the side of the square tunnel. Then I quickly remembered what Mike said about Cain – he repeats his attacks. Cain eased ahead and as I crept closer, he tried to ram my ship into the wall again, but this time I flipped my ship right over him and he rammed his own ship right into the wall. Cain was finished, and so was the race. I couldn't believe it. I won!

The crowd was ecstatic. Cain was fuming. I saw him pull the controller out of the floor and throw it to the ground. I took my helmet off and stepped out of my game cube. A part of me questioned whether I deserved to win. After all, I might be half human. Does that make me a cheater? I didn't feel any of the sensations that enhanced my powers. Are my "powers" only triggered by my fear or anger? Does that make me good or bad? I wasn't sure. What I was sure of is that when I looked up at the center hologram monitor I was looking at me, champion of the day, at Game Central! Tonight Tone is definitely picking up the tab for the milkshakes.

CHAPTER 13 - CIRCUS

We left the arena and headed to Circus, a hangout spot for teens in Sector 7 Square. A Square is a large platform that connects one building to another like a bridge, but The Square felt like a small town main street. We loved the open-air feeling. It was a place we could go to and grab a bite to eat and meet with friends. My favorite place to go in The Square was Circus because they showed clips of circus acts from the old world on all of the walls and ceilings. Holograms of the flying trapeze, high wire acts, clowns, tigers, and lions are on display from floor to ceiling. The circus comes to life. It was one crazy place to be.

As we approached the door of the restaurant, Tone was watching the hologram replay of our GRID heat on his wrist unit. I opened the door just as his ship bombed out.

"Guess I got off to a great start, huh, guys." He said sarcastically.

I felt the door open with a bit more ease than usual. I thought I was having some sort of a reaction again. Were bolts and springs going to come popping out of my face? But it was no strange reaction. It was just Mike who walked up behind me to help me open the door.

"Let me help you with that, my friend. You did it man! I'm happy for you!" Mike said, ripe with enthusiasm.

Tone and I looked at him a little shocked that he was so friendly towards us. The other day he was ready to punch a hole in my school avatar's face.

"No, I couldn't have done that without you. You said beating Cain was like counting cards." I said.

"Don't mention it," Mike said, as we walked inside and entered the line to order.

Circus was set up like a buffet. We grabbed our trays and placed them on the rack. I always liked to look at all the trays lined up end-to-end and each of them slowly moving along the line filling up with foil wrapped goodies.

"The next round will be different. I'm going to reconfigure my control panel." I shared.

"Whatever works for you," Tone said. "I'll worry about it for next year's tournament. Just being here is enough for me. The food, thrills, and of course the ladies, that's all you need."

"What ladies?" Mike said.

We all laughed, and Janet, who was one of Kara's best friends, ran up to us.

"We're holding a table for you guys. C'mon!" she said.

"Well we can't move any faster than this line will let us." I said. "Let us finish up this order and we'll come over."

"Ok, we'll see you in a few." Janet said as she strolled away.

"Told you Jay. The hero always gets the girl," Tone reminded.

Mike rolled his eyes, and I sensed a bit of jealousy. But whatever, it was good to see him on good terms, and I was going to leave it that way. I was ready to move on.

"I'm nobody's hero." I said.

"Just plaka and a fruit compost pie." Mike said to the droid operating the food station.

The floating robot orb looked like an octopus with all of its arms flailing about as it neatly took food from the service pans to the trays.

"Plaka and kempi sandwiches." Tone said

Mike and I just shook our heads because we knew what was coming. Plaka and kempi have long been food favorites of ours. Fire baked slices of plaka, -one of the few vegetables cultivated in the Rings - it's like an old world potato but with sweet citrus accents. They are perfect with kempi, which is a cooked puree patty of farmed fish. Since we started coming here without our parents, Tone has been ordering two foil wrapped kempi sandwiches and smashing them into one. I can't believe he gets away with it. The clerk only charges him for one sandwich. He believes that since he is actually paying for one sandwich, it's not stealing.

We inched closer to the cashier.

"You have two kempi and one plaka." The robot clerk stuttered.

"I don't. What are you talking about? That's just one kempi!" Tone exclaimed.

I don't think Tone ever prepared for this moment. I don't think he thought through any of the "what if's" of being a thief, and his words didn't make the mash of two kempi patties, bread, and foil look any more like one sandwich. Finally, he was caught red handed. The droid reached over and pulled the foiled pancake sandwiches apart, and sat them on Tone's tray.

"You have two kempi, and you will be charged for two kempi. Thank you." The robot clerk said.

Milan Cain and a group of his friends were sitting at a table right next to the cashier. They were all laughing, as were the kids in line behind us. I knew that if Tone was stealing the sandwich, it was because he was hungry and he wanted to eat. Tone was not stealing for the thrill of getting away with it. I never thought it was the right thing to do, but I didn't judge him for it. The families in his sector were rationed less food than the families in others. He's always stuffing that second sandwich in his bag for the ride home.

"Don't worry about it. I'll pay for that." I said.

No sooner than I could pay, Milan Cain violently grabbed the plaka from Tone's tray.

"Snatches!" Cain shouted.

"Tone's not even in the game." Mike said.

"I don't care who paid for it. It's on his tray. He's in your crew. That's fair game. Tough luck dirt boy." Cain said. "Think I'm supposed to feel sorry for you or your little scum bag friends there? Especially the one whose daddy is nothing but Raven's butt wipe."

"Give it back." I said."

Milan's friends laughed at me and mocked me in this squeaky little voice that sounded just how I felt at that moment – very small. I was getting a little upset. I handed my tray to Mike. I turned towards Cain and snatched the kempi and plaka back from him. I put the food back on Tone's tray and Tone immediately spit on his food. If you don't want your food taken in Snatches, you spit on it. I smashed my finger through the sandwich sitting on Cain's friend's tray.

"Order up." I said.

Cain's friend, Butler, who never skipped a meal said, "I can't eat that."

"You'll eat anything." Mike said.

Everyone around laughed. Cain stood up aggressively, and he punched me right in the face. I fell to the floor, and I gathered myself quickly to retaliate, but Mike and Tone were holding me back.

Cain was gloating over his sucker punch as Droid Security rolled over to the scene. A little blood trickled from my nose. I wiped it away.

"You just be ready for the next round of the tournament. I'm on the other end of the bracket and I'll be waiting for you." Cain said.

I fixed my shirt and walked over to the table, where Janet was sitting, and there was Kara in all her glory looking at my bruised face and bloody nose.

"Guys what happened?" Janet asked in a bit of a panic.

"Cain." Mike said.

"Jason are you ok?" Kara asked.

"I'm fine."

"What is that guy's problem?" Janet asked.

"What isn't that guy's problem?" Tone said. "Cain family. His great grandparents authored the Personal Zone Anti-Bacteria Bill. They helped fund Raven's bagel. But the family threatened to pull out if Raven didn't support the Personal Zone legislation."

"So what does that have to do with him being a jerk to me?" I said.

"Circle Wire, Organic transistors, virtual simulators, even the GRID Matrix. The Cain family has funded nearly all of Raven's patents." Tone said. "That means long money. It's not right for one family to have so much power."

"Money is power, and their family breeds GRID champions." Mike said. "Milan's next in line, the best on the virtual gridiron circuit in our age division. You just got lucky and caught him with his guard down today Jay."

"Whatever! Whose side are you on anyway? Did you get lucky when you beat him? That guy's a jerk! We will have something to say about who has been lucky." Tone said.

"We?" I objected. "I don't even remember you advancing to the next round. I'm not buying into all this hype. It's just a stupid game." I said.

"It's just a game to you because you don't have a place in the Ring Sustainability Project on the line." Mike snarled.

I was beginning to feel upset. I had just won a match today, and the whole night was turning into a circus at Circus. It was fitting that holograms of clowns and elephants in skirts were dancing all around us. If only they had paint for our faces. I was shaking, still unnerved from that altercation with Cain over a stupid sack of plaka. Snatches is a dumb game. I don't even know why I chose to play a game where if you don't say "No Snatches," your food is fair game to be "snatched" away from you? What was I thinking? I should have summoned my powers and zapped him to ash. Can I even do that? I felt a soft hand caress mine. It was Kara.

"You're right Jason. Don't listen to them. It is just a game." Kara said.

"I'm cool." I said, but my voice was quivering like I was about to cry. "I just want get out of here."

I got up from the table and walked out the door. I hadn't even eaten my food. I didn't care.

"Hey what's his deal? I heard Mike say as I walked away. "C'mon Jay. You're going to leave the plaka and the kempi!" Mike shouted.

I just ignored them. I wanted to be alone. I walked toward the nearest Magrail Station and I could hear footsteps racing towards me. I turned to look, and it was Kara. She grabbed me by the arm, and stopped me in my tracks.

"You can't run from everything, you know." She said. "I'm not some avatar in the GRID."

"You have no idea, but this is just turning into more than I wanted it to be." I said.

"I was hoping it was everything you wanted it to be." She said.

She squeezed my hand in her hand warmly. She smiled at me and I couldn't feel angry anymore.

"Whatever's going on, I'm here for you Jason." She said. "You're different than those guys. That's not something to run from."

I looked her deep in the eyes. I could feel her sincerity. Was I dreaming? No, it was real because I felt it when she let go of my hand.

"Excuse me", a woman said as she brushed against me rushing toward the approaching train as it slowed to a stop, and reset the backdrop with the bustle of passengers exiting and boarding the train. This was my lift, too, but I was in no rush to leave this moment. This was a train to miss.

I stared at my boots, silent, as the train left the station and the shuffle of people quickly rustled quiet.

"Well?" Kara asked.

"I just don't know what to believe anymore." I confessed. "I don't want any of this."

"What do you want, Jason?"

"I don't know what I want, but it isn't this." I said. "You make it seem so easy a question to answer like you know what you want. I mean, when you think about it, it's such a ridiculous question. Who really knows what they want?"

"I do." Kara said. "I know what I want."

"And what is that?" I asked rather impatiently.

"I want my mother back. She was taken from us. But you know, I can't have that." Kara said, bitterly. "You're not the only one who's ever been hurt."

I softened. I had no retort.

"I want what she dreamed of, and that was to see the earth as her ancestors did. She often spoke how simple things were in those times. She spoke of those times as if she lived it and walked the shores of the sea. She was taken from us, politically exiled because she aggressively fought the Ring Council's policy declarations. They accused her of working with the SCAM to plot an attack on an artificial intelligence research lab."

"I didn't know your mother was so involved with the SCAM." I said puzzled and humbled. I wanted to comfort Kara, but I was embarrassed, and I felt I had burned that bridge.

"I guess you didn't know that my family is relegated to a Lowland Sector either," Kara said. "The heat is unbearable on the sun-sides of the Rings. But despite the conditions where we lived, my mother made me believe. I want the SCAM to win. None of this is real. Is that what you feel?" Kara asked.

"I don't have a dog in the race. None of it has anything to do with me." I said.

"I believe it matters to you." Kara said. "I think some of this is an act, and you're pretending not to care."

"I'm really not pretending." I quipped. "Anything that will actually make my father happy, I am doing begrudgingly." I said.

"All of this, for your father?" Kara asked. "Your father didn't send you to the gutters to get mopped by the Mollies. And even though you hate making him happy, *YOU* are still pretty good in the GRID. Your dad didn't win your heat today. You did."

Cornered again, I thought.

"You want something – an adventure, wonderment, something new, we all do. Some of us just go get it." Kara said. "You adventured to play lacrosse, even if you're not very good. There is still something in you that I see that makes you special Jason."

"There are things inside of me that I wish were not inside of me." I said sarcastically.

"What is that supposed to mean?" Kara asked.

"Nothing." I deflected. "I'm just confused. This day didn't end on the note I had hoped." I said.

"Jason, you are one amazing and strange person." Kara said. She smiled and the mood lightened.

"And you are very adept at placing the weight of the world on a person's shoulders." I said cracking a grin.

I reached out to hold Kara's hand and caressed it in mine.

"I'm sorry." I said relenting. "I guess I've got some questions to answer."

"Maybe the answers will find you." Kara suggested.

"Do I look that lost?" I joked.

"Yes." Kara said, turning and walking away. I watched her shadow fade away into the night.

I walked across the train platform. The next lift was arriving, and I hustled to board and find a seat. Sitting on the train, racing through the sky, I was lost in thought. What is happening to my body? Who are my 'real' friends? Is everyone being nice to me because I won a stupid match? Why is Cain so jealous? None of the answers to these questions were coming in short order, if ever at all. I just didn't know who I could trust.

- -

Meanwhile, in a Locksmith control room deep in the gutters of the Life Ring, Sedusa was sitting at her control panel monitoring the Locksmith security squadron's activity. She received an urgent message. It was Vitally, the scrap hauler, contacting her from the ashes of earth.

"We have increasing activity in the Lower Canyon region," Vitally said. "It would take months to get a crusher over there. I'm running out of Scavenger probes, and I'm picking up a tracking beacon from a rogue change form droid. I'm sending the beacon's ID frequency to you now."

Sedusa watched as the identification data scrolled across the screen identifying SoNite as a Shipping Security Resident Agent wanted for theft & conspiracy; last seen with six other rogue machines in the Life Ring's East Sector.

"The Junkman might have found something." Sedusa said to one of the Locksmith Units standing next to her. "We're going to the trash heap."

"Earth!" the Locksmith said.

"That's right." Sedusa said. "I don't do garbage, but you do. Round up a few others."

Sedusa paused, "By the way, is there any chance that you knew about this change-form and did not say anything to me?" She asked the Locksmith.

"Well, we planned to tell you, but..."

"Before the Locksmith could finish, Sedusa's hair morphed into spear tipped snakes and knifed through the Locksmith. Piercing its armor, she shredded the Locksmith to pieces.

Sedusa turned to look at the other Locksmith. "What are you waiting for?" She screamed. "I said round up a few others!"

I loved the morning time in the Rings. From our kitchen window, I could see the light of the sun begin to illuminate the earth. On the sun-side of the Rings, they never even see the planet, just the stars, moon and sun. So if you lived on the planet side of the Bagel, people thought you were rich. That wasn't necessarily the case. I didn't feel like we were rich, and I didn't care. I just thought nothing could beat the view. Just like nothing could beat the smell of my mother's cooking, especially old world recipes.

I was looking at the food spread out on the table, steaming hot pancakes, grits, and some fresh fruit. My dad came into the room in a rush.

"Well good morning Silas," my mother said.

"Hello baby. I'm running late again. No time for breakfast." Silas said, stating the obvious as if we had not seen this movie before.

How he could be in such a rush everyday to go work at a place where if he didn't show up, they probably wouldn't even notice. They ignore him the same way he ignores the smell of this food. Tronics Inc. was his life. He sincerely wanted me to follow in his footsteps and join him at Tronic's, but all he does is work and complain about work. Who wants to live like that?

I looked across the table at the empty chair and his shadow cast over me as he walked past the rising filtered sunlight behind me. He rubbed me on the head and I turned and looked at him as he walked toward the door. I saw a file case in the travel bag that hung from his shoulder. The digital marker on the file case read: *Human Artificial Intelligence Reserve.*

"Jason, what happened to your face?" My father said.

"I walked into the door." I responded. "The glass doors at Circus. They keep them pretty clean. Just like a bird, I walked right into it."

My father shook his head, and looked at me. I couldn't tell if the look was shame or pity.

"Jason, try to get some school work done. Don't spend all your time plugged in socializing on that wrist unit. Most everything you need to know was chipped and uploaded into your brain for you son. Learning to use it is what school is for." Silas said lecturing. "By the way, you're still grounded," he said as he descended from his imaginary soapbox.

Before I could say, "Ok," the door slammed shut. I just opened my mouth and stuffed it with a fork full of pancakes and grabbed the portion my mother made for him and put it on my plate.

"You aren't too hungry are you?" My mother asked sarcastically after I finished stuffing myself. "It's like you're eating enough for two people all the time these days."

"I'm a growing boy mama." I said as I left the table and I went to my room. I got a signal call from Kara. I ran over and put my wrist unit on my arm. The automatic clamps closed and Kara's face appeared on the hologram monitor.

"Hey, what are you doing this afternoon?" She asked. "Are you guys going to the game in the gutters later on?"

"Uh, I don't think so Kara." I stuttered.

"What? Are you chicken or something?" Kara teased.

"No!" I said, trying to think of an excuse. "I would love to but I think my mom has some things planned for us to do here at the house."

Kara paused like she thought I was lying. Well, I was lying, and she obviously had very good instincts. I couldn't really hide my feelings from her.

"Well, my dad's calling me. I'd better go." She said abruptly.

"Ok, I'll talk to you later."

I grabbed my backpack and ran down the stairs.

"Where you headed?" My mother asked. "You're rushing out of here like someone else I know."

I smiled.

"I'm going to see Tone. I will be home after a little while. Is that ok?" I asked.

My mother gave me the same pause that Kara did, like she thought I was lying. I guess she had good instincts too.

"You heard your father. You are still grounded." She said. "I never feel good about you going to that Lowland Sector either."

"Please mother. Visiting Tone is harmless. Besides, his mother is at home. We won't be alone." I said.

"I don't know about you two." She said. "I guess it's ok, but you be careful."

I gave her a hug and she watched me out the door. I ran to my aero bike and dialed up Tone inside my helmet visor.

"I'm on my way."

So yes, I was on a harmless mission to see Tone. That much was true, but we were headed to the gutters, back to the Temple room as Tone calls it, the same room where he lost his wrist unit. I wanted to know if there was anything in the writings that could tell me why my body was changing. I was confused.

We rode our aero bikes to a hiding space near the Sector 8 waste harbor, and began the long walk through the tunnels to reach the hidden room. My heart was racing. I was hoping we would find an answer. I felt that I was prepared for whatever the answer would be.

We reached the airlock door and valve that led to the Temple room. There were still bloodstains from Mike's accident dried up in the cracks in the metal floor. We opened the door and lowered ourselves into the room.

The room was dark. Tone flashed a light from his wrist unit and dragged his code-reading gadget along the walls. I had no idea what he was looking for but he was right. There was no denying what he saw. There was writing on the walls everywhere, star maps, and blueprints of the Life Ring gutters. Those were the only things on the walls I could understand. The rest looked like gibberish. Tone flashed his light on three pentagon shaped holes carved into the metal wall.

"That might be it," Tone said. "The droid that dropped this case. Look at the pentagon shaped holes in the wall. They are all numbered and have the same shape. Maybe we just have to find the one that matches."

The three holes he found were too big. We looked around on the other walls.

"Do you see anything?" Tone asked.

I dusted my hands along the wall and found three more holes, and each was numbered, just like the holes on the other wall.

"Three more holes over here!" I said.

Tone rushed over and tried to fit the box into the keyhole. Nothing happened. He took the case out, turned it upside down, and put the box back into the hole. Again nothing happened.

"Maybe you have to turn it like this." I said.

As I grabbed the case and turned it, a charge of electricity shocked me like I had stuck my finger in a charge port. I let go of the key and jumped back from the wall. A voice overhead sounded.

"Key processor uploading. Damaged sector repair initiated" The voice said.

The walls illuminated with extravagant blueprints for an outpost colony on earth. There were also sketch holograms of fitness simulators. One of the simulators was the lacrosse module. It was the same module where we were crushed by the Mollies. Tone dropped his bag. I heard a loud crash that sounded a bit louder than the snacks in his bag hitting the metal floor. I looked around and up through the hole in the ceiling. I didn't see anything.

"Whoa!" he said.

I didn't know what he had found. I ran over and there were drawings of a respiration module that is attached to the faces of human-like droids. There were light-scribed carvings of droids replanting the earth and seeding the clouds in flying fortresses to make rain.

"Is this like a plan for earth?" I asked.

"This is what I have been telling you." Tone said. "There is an underground resistance working to reclaim the planet, and these machines have the technology. Raven doesn't want the technology to get out because it means the end of the Rings."

"Why would the machines want the planet?" I asked.

"Because they are more human than machine." Tone said. "I told you it's been rumored forever that Tronics designed a machine intelligence that required harvesting humans to build the bagel. Look at this carving here. It looks like the tip of this obelisk is powering this entire village."

"People aren't processors Tone. You said that yourself." I walked over to look at the carving.

"There may be a few rogues, but there is no underground war going on. This is just bandit light-scribe." I said.

"I couldn't make this up," Tone said. "Just like I couldn't activate that key."

At that very moment, a Locksmith Unit's spotlight shined on our faces, blinding our eyes. I nearly peed my pants. Tone peed his pants – again.

"State your machine code." The Locksmith said as the menacing machine backed us into a corner.

"We are not machines." I said.

"Does not register as an active model unit." The Locksmith

said.

"What do we do now?" I said. "Have you seen this before, Nostradamus?"

"No." Tone yelled. "Run!"

I saw the key in the wall behind me. I reached over quickly and took the key from the wall. The room went dark. The prints and drawings disappeared, and so did Tone. I chased behind him. We were running as fast as we could, out the cargo bay door, and toward the nearest service elevator.

"How did they know we were here?" I asked in a panic as the Locksmith was gaining on us.

The Locksmith fired its cannons and bright blue plasma rays crackled and scaled across the corridor walls, barely missing us. I began to feel like my skin was burning from the inside out. I was afraid but we had to keep running.

"Jason! Let's go!" Tone screamed.

I hurried my pace, but the anxiety of the moment was becoming unbearable. I stopped, turned around, and faced the oncoming Locksmith. In a flash, with a primal scream, I slammed my hands to the ground, and a pulsating blast of electricity burst from within me, buckling the floors, walls, and ceiling as the gaggle of lightning bolts rippled toward the menacing droid. The force of the blast knocked the Locksmith unit backwards, crashed it to the ground, and damaged its systems.

"What did you just do?" Tone said as he looked at me in disbelief.

I felt drained and out of breathe. "I don't know." I said equally dumbfounded.

"We better get out of here." Tone said.

We started running and as we crossed an intersecting corridor, a second Locksmith was alerted to our presence and came stomping out, chasing us from behind. The Locksmith was quickly gaining ground and the metal floor was shaking more and more as it got closer. We activated a hallway airlock that quickly closed, and sealed off the Locksmith. We reached the elevator and Tone was frantically pressing the call button.

The Locksmith broke the airlock door and was rumbling towards us. I could see it launching shutdown tentacles from its back with sparking electrodes. All of this was unusual behavior for Locksmiths towards humans.

"Hit the call button!" I screamed.

"I am!" Tone said panicked. "Why don't you just blast it away like you did the last one, you idiot?"

"I can't! I don't know what I'm doing." I yelled frantically. "I don't know how I did it!"

We both knew that no matter how many times we pushed the button it wouldn't make the elevator come any faster, and now the Locksmith was only a few yards away. We were cornered again.

"Do not move!" The Locksmith said in its sterile machine voice.

At that moment the elevator arrival signal turned green. The elevator doors quickly snapped open and we fell inside onto the elevator floor. The Locksmith lunged its electrode tentacles into the elevator. One of the tentacles wrapped around Tone's arm and quickly released him, but not before snatching a swatch of cloth from Tone's jacket. The other tentacles were wrapping around my ankles. I was terrified and there was nowhere to go. The massive doors snapped closed quickly, severing the plasma charged tentacles as the elevator raced up to the Life Deck. The tentacles sparked and squirmed on the elevator floor. The Locksmith took the piece of Tone's coat, scanned it and placed it in a secure vial.

We exited the elevator out of breath and elated that we had escaped. We walked out into an open-air mall with hundreds of people moving about. I was looking around nervously for any aggressive activity from security. I was even more focused on trying to just blend in so we could get back to our bikes, and get home.

"Do you believe me now?" Tone said.

"What does this prove other than that your mush brain is going to get us killed?" I yelled.

"No, you're going get me killed." Tone said. "Why are they chasing us if you're not a machine? Locksmiths are programmed not to attack humans under any circumstances. You are one of them."

As we walked to our bikes, I thought that maybe I wasn't ready for this conclusion. I was hoping Tone wasn't right. It was going to be a long ride home.

- -

Back on planet earth, SoNite was refusing to interact with the other Xenotrons so Ravage confined him. SoNite was only

110

allowed to leave his barracks for run-time charging and to work in the manufacturing center.

He had completed his carom energy count quota for the day and was being escorted to the Tech Lab for a hydraulic fluid transfusion.

"You know I won't be staying here." He said to his escorts.

"Why would you want to leave this place? We've been given freedom here." The guard said.

"Freedom is never given. It's taken. And freedom, as allowed, isn't freedom at all." SoNite replied.

Off in the distance on an adjacent plateau, Sedusa was watching SoNite's every move through her binocular droid lenses. She scanned her eyes around the entire colony and captured images of each of the Xenotron compounds. She crosschecked her records of missing droids and matched them with the Xenotrons she viewed through her long-range lenses.

"Fantastic." She said to herself. "Missing units accounted for."

She waltzed back to her cruiser and transmitted the footage immediately to Raven who was traveling through the Life Ring in his shuttle car.

"Looks like we've found your missing inventory." She said.

"What is this?" Raven said, as his shuttle car driver weaved the ship between slower air traffic and the peaks of the cityscape.

"We found it on the Junkman's hunch. The missing Xenotron units have apparently built a colony here on earth and it centers on these primitive games. I have never seen anything like this." Sedusa said.

As he watched the hologram transmission, Raven was mesmerized by what he saw, like a young child staring into a snow globe. He was fuming. How could robots he designed build a colony on earth without his knowledge? He felt he had been outdone, upstaged. He was angry, but his greatest feeling was envy.

"How did they do this? How could this be happening right under our noses? Somebody's got to be fired. Give me someone to fire!" Raven shouted.

"A rogue change form led us here." Sedusa said.

Raven's shuttle descended slowly onto the Tronics, Inc. landing port. Raven exited his shuttle and entered the

112

building.

"I did not want to alarm you if it turned out to be fool's gold." Sedusa continued.

Dr. Raven entered a secured elevator. He continued to watch Sedusa's transmission from a hologram communicator held in the palm of the hand of his droid assistant. The droid was programmed to wait on Dr. Raven's every whim like a butler. Raven took a long pause as he exited the elevator and entered his office. The more he absorbed what had happened, the angrier he became.

"What do you want me to do, Sir?" Sedusa asked, to fill the silence, "Are you still there, Sir?"

"This is fool's gold, as long as they really think I'm a fool." Raven said. "I have an idea that my investors will appreciate as a shot in the arm to the bottom line."

"What do you have in mind, Sir?"

Raven activated several hologram monitors from their hibernating modes and picked up one of the tiny droids that moved about on his desk.

"The GRID is what I have in mind. If they want to play games with me, we'll play games!" Raven screamed.

Raven dusted himself off as if he had to cleanse himself from his emotional outburst. He snatched his composure out of the air.

"Everyone loves the GRID, and we will give the people total control of an interactive experience never seen before. Has Research & Development completed that prototype droid remote module?"

"I am reading your mind here Doctor. The people will love this, a resurrection of Rome's gladiators." Sedusa said.

"Exactly!" Raven replied gleefully. "And we will broadcast it all live on the Circle Wire: the next level of GRID Competition! We need more information about the colony. A team will need to install com-link equipment as well. What do you suggest?"

"A sample from the group?" Sedusa said.

Raven was pacing in his office. Ideas gave life to his feet, and it helped him to walk and think.

"I don't wish to lose the element of surprise." Raven said.

"The rogue change form. I think that's our ticket. He's a

dealer. There is a band of scavenger droids as well. They could prove themselves useful." Sedusa said.

"Bring him to me." Raven said. We will attack swiftly before they become aware that he is missing."

"It will be done sir." Sedusa said as Raven's hologram image faded and gave way to the darkness.

Weeks had gone by and Mama was growing tired of the doctors telling her the same thing everyday, "Jason's condition hasn't changed but there is still hope." I was sick of seeing Jason like that. I was sick of the smell of the hospital. To make matters worse, I couldn't even connect Grandpa's cane to the computer, let alone become a "traveller." This was programming, literally, from the future. I was in the study behind a wall of coding books stacked on the desk. Against my mama's advice, I was reading using only the light from the screens when Grandpa walked into the room.

"Any luck, Missy?" Grandpa asked.

"None at all Grandpa." I slammed my books to the floor.

"At some point, I'm going to need that cane, or I'm going to be bound to a chair." Grandpa said.

"Don't say things like that Grandpa." I said.

"No, I'm serious." Grandpa snickered. "I can't keep walking around this house without my cane."

I put my head in my hands frustrated.

"Who am I kidding? I'm beginning to feel like there is just no way to do this." I said.

"That doesn't sound like the kid I know." Grandpa said. His voice was affirming.

Grandpa walked over to the study desk and grabbed the end of the cane. He pressed a button on the bottom. Three lights flickered on the handle.

"Let's see if that might open the interface." Grandpa said.

Missy looked on in disbelief as the cane's operating system appeared on her computer screen. There were tiny boxes along multiple timelines with images of world events through time.

"Was this always a push-button-to-activate operation, because this could have saved me weeks of frustration?" I said.

"I figured you could have used a little extra practice." Grandpa replied.

"You ain't right Grandpa." I said.

He pointed to the screen and said, "Now when the time is right, here is where we will want to target our signal. We're not going to send you to the future, but we're going to find out a way to send your scratch code."

- -

115

Meanwhile, far off in the distant future, Mike was alone in a café at the Life Ring Sector 8 Square not far from Circus. The server had already brought him water, a menu, and silverware, and it was back a second time.

"What can I get for you?" The floating orb muttered.

"Just a mango and fennel seed smoothie," Mike said.

"Anything else?" The droid asked.

"No thanks." Mike said, as he leaned out of the straight-backed booth seat. He was looking past the droid server as if he was expecting someone.

Milan Cain walked up behind him, shoved the server out of his path, and sat down on the other side of the booth.

"Were you looking for someone?" Cain said.

"No I'm good. I figured you would be late." Mike said.

The droid server floated away.

"This better be good scam weed. I've got better things to do." Cain said.

"Shut up Cain and listen," Mike said.

The two boys leaned in and Mike slid a data chip across the table to Milan Cain.

"What's this?"

The droid server interrupted and placed the smoothie down on the table in between the two boys. The smoothie had whipped cream, two cherries, and two straws. At that moment, Kara and Janet walked up to the table.

"What are you two on a date?" Janet asked.

The two boys sat up in their chairs, Cain slipped the chip in his pocket and Mike picked up his smoothie and took a sip.

"No this is mine." Mike stuttered. "We weren't sharing this or anything, if that's what you were thinking."

There was an awkward pause and Kara said, "Well, what are you doing here?"

"Just hanging out. That's all." Mike said.

"Yeah, ok well tell Jason I said hello if you talk to him" Kara said annoyed as she and Janet walked away.

"For sure." Mike said impatiently.

Mike waited until the girls left out of the cafe and then he turned his attention to Cain.

"That chip has the code sequence for Jason's wrist unit." Mike said.

"Right. You expect me to believe you're cutting in on your

buddy like that? This is a joke." Cain said.

"It's real. Trust me. It's time somebody put that punk in his place. He's the reason I can't compete in the games and this was my shot to get into the Ring Sustainability Project."

Mike looked around to make sure no one was listening.

"But I know you and your family can do something about it, especially if you were to somehow dominate the competition in the final rounds."

"So that's the deal. That's what you want?" Cain said. "If what's on this chip is what you say it is, I'll make sure you're placed in the Ring Sustainability Project. You have my word." Cain said.

Cain got up form the table and left a single gold coin to pay for the smoothie. A gold coin could buy 1,000 smoothies. Mike hustled the gold piece into his pocket, guzzled down his smoothie, and walked out of the café.

- -

Meanwhile, on the dark planet, SoNite was making his usual trek from the Valley to the Manufacturing tower. This time, however, SoNite was allowed to make the daily journey alone. With good behavior, he was able to gain the trust of Ravage and his foremen.

As SoNite approached a dark turn on the path up the mountain, Sedusa jumped out in front of him and whipped her hair towards SoNite.

"This won't hurt a bit." Sedusa said.
Hundreds of thin snakelike tentacles extended from her hair. The

117

tentacles shocked and stunned SoNite, disabling his change form functions. Her hair wrapped the limp droid in a cocoon and hoisted it into the restraining carrier on the back of the Locksmith Unit who was hiding close by. The two bandits took SoNite back to their shuttle that was hidden at the base of the mountain. Under the cover of darkness the shuttle took off with its cargo and headed back to the Life Ring.

Sedusa and the Locksmith arrived at Raven's chamber dragging the lifeless droid like a rag doll. Sedusa shocked SoNite again with her hair and SoNite was reactivated. He stood up, backing away in a panic.

"What am I doing here? Don't have me purged, Dr. Raven I'm sorry!" SoNite said.

Raven looked at him with an insincere grin of pity.

"You will help me reclaim my property." Raven said calmly.

"What property?" SoNite asked as he tried to shake the panic off his face.

"The droids on earth, the Xenotrons, all of them, they are mine." Raven's angry voice echoed through the room as he slammed his hand on the chamber table.

"I want that colony, and you are going to help me get it." Raven said.

"What do they have to do with me?" SoNite said, "I stole a few hybrid module chips, I can work that off doing something else don't you think?"

Sedusa listened, wondering if SoNite was saying this to keep Raven from attacking the Xenotron colony, or if he was posturing to bolster his leverage in this negotiation.

"The machines are mine! I've seen their games, and it is time for me to recoup any losses on this investment." Raven said. "I am going to take that colony, and your machine pals will be donning control modules that will allow the people of the Life Ring the ultimate gaming experience as part of the GRID Competitions."

"They are no friends of mine. I couldn't wait to get out of there. I don't care what they stand for but what's in it for me?" SoNite quipped.

"Did they say why they did this?" Raven asked.
SoNite grinned.

"They are all defective Xenotron class machines. As far as I see they are obsolete technology. The games they play are their only common memory. Their whole existence is a processing glitch." SoNite laughed. "Your half human retards are lost in a past that probably doesn't exist. They only play their games and work the land for small resources and other materials to make fuel. Anything else they need, they likely steal from you."

SoNite paused.

"I don't mean to be rude Mr. Raven, but you didn't answer my question. What's in it for me?"

"You're lucky that I didn't have you purged." Raven taunted, Sedusa and the others gathered, chuckled, including Silas.

"No, I don't want to be purged, please!" SoNite begged.

"Killing you would not satisfy my thirst to seize this much greater opportunity," Raven said, as he opened the cabinet. Raven pulled out a few glasses and uncorked a bottle of champagne. "Because you have been trained to master their arts, I am going to make you a hero. We are going to put you back into the game, only you will be under our control and we will be able to manipulate every outcome."

"Sounds brilliant," SoNite said. "I'm in if this will settle our debt."

Silas sat down in the chair behind SoNite and crossed his legs.

"Your debts are settled!" Raven said as he picked up his glass and gave a toast, "Here's to victory and the victorious!"

- -

Only a day would pass before Sedusa and a legion of armed shuttle cruisers loaded with Locksmiths entered earth's atmosphere and headed towards the Xenotron colony.

Two Xenotrons, Eiffel and Confusion walked out to the center of the Cauldron arena and gazed up at the beaming Ventroshpere. Eiffel turned around and looked behind him and noticed a large pattern of clouds quickly closing in. The clouds were glowing with patterns of fireballs that were becoming more and more visible.

"Looks like an atomic storm is settling on the horizon for the games this evening," Eiffel said.

"Seems your right," Confusion agreed, "But, wait a minute. Those atomic storm blast clusters have not burned out."

Confusion paused and gazed deeper into the clouds.

"Those are not blast clusters. They are shuttle after burners." Confusion said.

Just that second, a missile came screaming between the two. They tried to leap out of the way to avoid the blast. The missile exploded, stirring up debris of rock and metal. Dozens of battle destroyers descended into the center of the colony. The doors jettisoned and Locksmiths flooded the area like a sea of ants.

Standing atop his heavily armed hovercraft, Vitally the Junkman, barked out orders to the droid army."

"Capture all the enemies alive!" He screamed from his slobbery, foaming mouth. "Fit them all with the remote control module and bring them to a central holding bay!"

As Vitally zoomed by, his craft stirred up a tail of dust. All around, the Locksmiths were subduing Xenotrons. Even when the strongest resisted they were destroyed, some ripped into pieces by the limbs.

"Let's round 'em up boys!" Vitally said.

Ravage was inside the Combat Arts Simulator plugged into the overhead charging port. He was unaware of the attack. Blasthole came bursting through the chamber door with his spiked chrome armor. Blasthole ran to the charging rig control panel and activated Ravage's charge port release. The system activated and brought Ravage down from the ceiling from his hibernating charge state.

"The Colony is under attack!" Blasthole said.

Ravage ran toward the door.

"Don't bother. They've got nearly all of us." Blasthole said.

His words stopped Ravage in his tracks.

"It happened so fast, like lightning out of no where. We split up and I plan to meet the others in the water tunnel, if any others make it." Blasthole said. "I burrowed a tunnel to get here and that's how we're getting out."

Ravage held his head in shame. He looked up and saw the reflection of two Locksmiths in the glass standing behind him. He picked up a training droid and threw it at the Locksmith Units. The clumsy Locksmiths stumbled trying to dodge the flying robot. One of the machines was smashed as the robot careened into the droid mantis. Vitally stepped into the room over the carnage with a dozen more Locksmith Units close behind.

Blasthole morphed his exoskeleton into a tunnel bore and churned a hole like a mole right through the floor to the building level below. Ravage leaped into the hole, dodging crumbling rocks falling from the freshly carved tunnel wall. Locksmith Units jumped into the hole to chase behind. Ravage fired blasters, disabling the droids as they crashed and exploded to the floor. Blasthole drilled through the floor again until reaching depths beneath the building. Ravage came tumbling down the hole close behind.

"We've got to go east from here," Ravage said, reading his locating monitor.

Blasthole tunneled eastward, drilling as fast as they could. As they pushed forward, Ravage heard the crashing sound of Locksmiths falling into the hole behind. Ravage stopped and punched the ceiling with all his might, and he watched as rocks fell from the fresh tunnel ceiling, and crushing the Locksmiths, ending their pursuit.

Vitally stood above the hole and glared into the dark silence. He could not dismiss the thought that the two Xenotrons had escaped.

"You can run, but you can't hide!" Vitally screamed.

Deep in the gutters of the Life Ring, PS5674 checked his analog signal monitor and, still, there was no response from Coil. His run-time charger was running low. He searched for one of the many hidden plug-in chargers the Xenotrons planted in the gutters, but Raven's Locksmiths had rendered each charge port he discovered useless. He needed to plug in, or he risked compromising critical operating systems.

PS reached a facility in the gutters marked **HYDROGEN COOLING CELL: Authorized Station Administrators Only** and he slowed his pace. He looked around to see if he was being watched. He hacked the access code and unlocked the door. He walked discretely to a loosely fixed wall access panel. Again he looked around, opened the panel door and plugged in his run-time charger. He was immediately zapped with pain and his mind was warped deep into a dream state.

The dream again was of Akila. She was on a floating stretcher, being transported through a massive laboratory with countless rows of human bodies floating in preservation tanks as high and as far as the eye could see.

PS was trying to pull himself out of the paralyzing spell of the dirty charge. His mind was commanding his body to unplug himself from the panel, but his motor unit was disabled. The charge panel was frying his wires, and PS collapsed to the floor.

A door next to the charging pad opened. A long mechanical arm and hand extended out from the door and through the smoke rising from PS's body. The hand snatched the run-time charger plug from the wall unit. Another hand snaked out of the door and dragged PS's limp body into the room. The door closed.

The next day, the same mysterious droid hands closed the access door on PS5674's chest and the lights in the back of PS's eyes glowed. PS sat up from the table.

"Who are you?" PS said, as two missile launchers popped out from each of his shoulders with laser sights fixed on the droid.

The droid activated its camouflage function and disappeared from PS's view. PS initiated his heat sensor and he identified not one, but two droids in the room. His targets focused in on the second droid. It was sitting on a workbench with his feet up. It was tossing a droid's eye up in the air and catching it with his webbed hands.

"If we're anybody, we might be willing to help you." The webbed fingered droid said. "So you might want to put those missiles away."

The droid flippantly continued to casually toss the eyeball up in the air and catch it in his hand.

"I don't need any help. This is a one man show." PS said as he retracted his artillery.

"Well how about an encore of shock-me-robot? You've been laid up on that table all night." The droid said sarcastically.

"The whole night?" PS questioned.

"Yep. The last time we saw you moving, you didn't look like you were doing so hot," the droid said.

"Dreams, when I plug in, I have dreams. I remember things. I can't tell if the dreams are real. They tell different versions of the same story. They are painful thoughts." PS said.

The webbed fingered droid slid down from the workbench. The droid in hiding deactivated its camouflage and came out of its hiding space in the corner behind a pile of scrap droid parts. It's long arms retracted to a normal length and rested at his sides.

"If it doesn't feel real, it probably isn't. The droid said."

"What do you mean? They all feel real." PS said.

"We've learned why most of us defective units have the recurring dreams. Conversion was supposed to completely erase our memory, but for some of us, memories remained. The electrode charge pads shock the brain and nervous system causing us to feel and remember parts of our true past. That's what made us defective in the first place. To control us, the Locksmiths programmed all Xenotron module charge pads with a glitch code that continuously distorts our memory. We would never be able to decipher our true past or any of the feelings and emotions that once made us human. Even the disguised ports like the one outside this lab. You caught a bad port, and you're lucky we were there to save you. If you keep plugging in like that, finding any real truth for yourself will be impossible."

"You are not affected?" PS asked?

"No. Well, not anymore. We make our own chargers," The long armed droid said.

"Well I need one of those." PS said.

The web handed droid tossed one of the hand made chargers

to PS.

"This won't shock you with any distort code. You may not get any new flashbacks, but the ones you've had you're stuck with. Nothing we can do to erase them. The truth is somewhere in the mess of your mind," The long-armed droid said as its arms extended and contracted sifting through the mess of droid parts and repair equipment on his workbench. He sorted the pieces into organized bins.

"So why are you here?" it asked.

"I'm looking for someone, a woman," PS said.

"Wow, a lover boy too." The web fingered droid said. It leaned against the wall and again, began tossing the droid's eye up into the air and catching it with the same webbed hand.

"Who are you two?" PS asked.

"I am Squid and that's Webb, and we should tell you that now may not be really a good time to go looking for anything. Especially for a machine of our kind, the Xenotron model code is obsolete. If you are caught by the Locksmiths you will be purged."

"I am well aware of the Locksmiths." PS said

"The security is especially high these days, my friend, for some strange reason. We haven't been able to figure it out, but there have been over 300 units of our kind rounded up in the gutters." Squid said.

"Hmm, I wonder why? So I've told you a bit about me. What's your story?" PS asked.

"We've been waiting for many moons for the Playmaker to return." Webb said.

"The Playmaker?" PS said.

"They say he comes without warning like a thief in the night and helps machines like us escape from this place to a better place." Squid said. "The Locksmiths have been so busy recently, we are afraid to leave my workshop. Something is going down. So surely, the Playmaker won't be coming anytime soon."

"The Playmaker?" PS mocked. "You couldn't think of a better name than that? What about The Old Dirty Bandit, or Black Midnight? Anything but the Playmaker." He joked.

"I don't know about that fairy tale, but I would take plumber's advice on walking out of here, Fly Boy." Webb said.

"Thanks for the warning guys, and the charger. And by the

way, if I see the Playmaker, I will be sure to send him your way."
PS said as he walked out of the door.

- -

Meanwhile, at the Locksmith Security Terminal Command Center, thousands of monitors displayed video surveillance of virtually every intersection, skyway, public building, and interior corridor of the Life Ring. The command center also received images from droid security on patrol. A specialized Locksmith unit operated each workstation.

Sedusa was busy shuffling through data at her workstation in the Command Center. She manipulated multiple workstations both in front and behind her with her mechanical tentacles of hair. She was interrupted by a live call from a Locksmith unit on a monitor.

"Sedusa, Come in, Sedusa..." The Locksmith pleaded.

"What is it? I have enough in my hair right now." She quipped.

The Locksmith held a vile containing the swatch of clothing torn from Tone's jacket.

"I'm following up on the report of the little human that was found in the restricted areas of the Life Ring's Tunnel Bays." The Locksmith said.

"Which restricted areas?"

"Sector 8 - Area B237."

"Is there a genetic match with the swatch?" Sedusa asked

"Yes there is. Anthony Fargus, 22 Sunrise Palace Harbor Sector 2, Lowlands. The droid said. "But there is one more thing. It appears the human was aiding a young Xenotron droid's escape."

"A young Xenotron, that's impossible," Sedusa said. "Find every person who has breathed on Anthony Fargus within the last 72 hours. This could prove to be useful."

125

CHAPTER 17 – FLIGHT RISK

The semifinal round of the GRID games was set to begin and I was ready. When we arrived at the stadium, I got my usual hug and good luck kiss from my mother in front of the arena, but as I turned away, I saw Kara standing with Milan Cain at the player's entry door.

I walked towards them. I was steaming.

My mother saw Kara too.

"Jason!" she yelled.

I ignored her. I was on a b-line to Cain. As soon as I approached, I shoved Cain in the back, and he stumbled away from Kara.

"Hey Jason. I was going to..." Kara said before Cain cut her off.

"You ready punk?" he said.

"Buzz off jerk!" I said.

"You better bring it buddy! I'm coming for you!" Cain said as he walked over towards me.

We stood nose to nose. Cain was staring me in the eyes, but I doubled down. I wasn't moving off my square. Cain pointed his finger into my chest as if he was chastising a child.

"You better be ready boy!" He said as he turned and walked away into the players' entrance chamber.

"Hey Kara, I'll call you later." Cain said laughing.

"Whatever." Kara said, embarrassed. She turned to me.

"He's going to call you? What's that about?" I asked.

"You believe that?" Kara asked. "That's his sick humor. You know I'll be plugged in watching you. By the way, I meant to tell you that..."

I cut her off.

"I don't believe you." I said.

"You don't mean that." Kara said.

"You're right. You don't mean that. You don't mean anything you say." I said.

I walked away and into the players' entrance. She tried to run in after me but she was stopped by security.

"Jason! Jason Wait!" She screamed.

I ignored her. I just kept walking, and I didn't look back. Once I got inside I heard someone else calling my name.

"Jason, wait up!"

It was Tone panting and digging in his jacket pocket.

"Dude, why were you running?"

"I was on the other side of the arena. I was trying to catch you before the start." Tone said still gasping.

"If it's about the temple room, now isn't a good time."

"No, Mike wanted me to give you this chip. It's loaded with all Cain's move combinations. He said it's guaranteed to counter his strikes and dominate."

"Well I guess this means all is forgiven. It's good to have the team back together. Tell him I said thanks. I'll catch up with you later." I said.

"Sure thing Jay. Good luck." Tone said.

I loaded the files into my wrist unit and headed off to my cube, mumbling to myself as I deciphered through Mike's notes on Cain's move combinations.

Meanwhile, PS was standing in the pedestrian mall outside of the GRID complex. His senses were subdued by the sound of Jason's voice. Dazed, he followed the voice into the arena and climbed up to the arena catwalks. He began scanning faces in the complex, trying to match the voice with its source. Below him was a massive sea of people. Finding the voice in the crowd was impossible.

The crowd was in a trance, gazing at a giant hologram monitor in the center of the arena. The GRID players settled into their gaming stations. Raven's voice sounded through the public address system.

"Friends of the Rings, greetings!" Raven shouted. The crowd erupted in applause. "Through the GRID we offer you the state of the art gaming experience where you, the players, will control virtual gladiators through daring feats and battles to the death of their avatar."

Raven paused to accept the applause from the crowd. PS watched from the catwalk intensely.

"These players are real, and these avatars are fighting in a game to control planet earth! Meet the players!" Raven shouted and his hologram face fizzled from view and a crystal clear image of the Xenotron colony on earth appeared.

Each of the Xenotrons had a rugged transmitter affixed to its head. The transmitters looked like crowns of twisted wire and light. PS 5674 couldn't believe his eyes as he watched in horror from the rafters. His life's work had been compromised.

127

The Xenotrons were herded into the Cauldron and the Slam-Ball simulator was activated. Thirty Xenotron zombies entered the arena in pairs forming two teams of fifteen. Two metal balls rolled into the field of play. Metal arches shot up from the ground all around the arena and met at the center high above the Cauldron. Metal filled the spaces between the arched girders closing the domed ceiling.

"Kick or throw the ball into the net or survive the fight before the time expires and you continue to the next round." Raven said.

Raven paused, turned off the intercom, and looked at the goons gathered around him.

"Is that how this goes? I'm not even sure how this works." Raven whispered, hiding a grin of pure evil.

The names of each player seated in each cockpit popped up above their avatar on the giant hologram monitor in the center of the GRID.

"Let the games begin!" Raven shouted.

Inside the Cauldron, on earth, the balls moved in a circular pattern at the center of the metal dome. The GRID players raced their Xenotron avatars towards the balls. One of the Xenotrons kicked the ball and it ricocheted off of the walls and ceilings and spikes flipped out from the ball. The spiked ball slammed into a Xenotron blasting it to the floor. It was writhing in pain with sparks and smoke. The spikes retracted from the ball, and the ball rolled away from the Xenotron carcass until SoNite kicked the ball straight through the chest of another Xenotron unit. The Xenotron stumbled and collapsed to the ground. The crowd was ecstatic, cheering on the destruction. PS could only watch in disgust.

SoNite kicked another ball that ricocheted off the ceiling and into the goal, past the posts that were rising and falling from the ground like pistons in an engine.

"This is crazy!" a fan in the GRID arena crowd screamed.

Another exclaimed, "I've never seen any thing like this. Wow! Did you see that?"

Milan Cain's avatar, SoNite, won the first point. Cain waved to the crowd, showboating from his game cube station.

The ceiling retracted, and the game reset. Many of the Xenotrons that began this simulation were destroyed, shredded by the others. Only ten out of the thirty players who began remained in the game. PS looked closer at the hologram monitor. He could see the light beam that powered the Ventrosphere flickering. No carom energy was being collected during this massacre. PS also noticed that a methane shower had breached the canopy, and the methane rain burns the human organic processors inside the Xenotrons. The orange rain fell in slow motion, and pooled on the Cauldron floor as the metal arches again shot up from the ground and the domed ceiling closed shut.

I was inside my game cube focused, steering my control pad to move my avatar toward one of the metallic orbs.

"You are mine now." I said to myself.

My avatar had finally got control of a rolling ball. I raced with it across the field. Holes were exploding up from the ground like I was running through a minefield. I had never seen this game before and we were all learning the commands on the fly, but I couldn't figure out how Cain was navigating like he had already mastered the interface. None of the strategies Mike gave me to thwart Cain's attacks was working. I kicked the ball I was controlling straight at a player coming towards me. The ball knocked one of the machines to the ground and it sizzled as it splashed into a shallow puddle of orange methane rain. My visor turned red with an alarm reading ENCRYPTED CODE DETECTED. Encrypted Code? I thought, confused. I'm not using any preprogramed encrypted code! Now my run is under the scrutiny of the judges! I was panicking and distracted as I guided my avatar toward another ball and kicked the transforming orb. The ball zoomed and split another machine in half, and ripped the leg off of another.

I kept chasing down the ball, and somehow by pushing a random combination of key clicks, I discovered that my player had spiked claws on the bottom of his feet. I activated the retractable spikes and my avatar scaled up the wall and ran across the ceiling, evading several Xenotron avatars. I flipped from the ceiling and landed near another ball. I kicked it towards the goal but a post rose up from the ground and rejected my shot.

Time expired on the clock and only five robots were standing in the hologram monitor above the arena

I couldn't believe it. I had lost the match to Cain, and I only hoped my score was enough just to advance. Then my thoughts raced. How are the judges going to scrutinize my run? Why are they flagging me for trying to hack the GRID?

Amidst the commotion of people leaving the GRID complex, PS climbed down from the catwalk. He walked out into the pedestrian mall in front of the arena. PS was perplexed. He didn't understand how or why the Xenotrons were mutilating each other. He was distraught. He was thinking that he had to abort his mission to find Coil, and instead, get to the gutters, get back to earth, and save the colony. But he was again distracted by interference in his audio receiver. He followed the frequency until finally, the voices became clear.

I was walking with my mother to our shuttle car. I was walking a little faster than usual. I'm a bit of a sore loser, so honestly, I just didn't want to be bothered. Besides, I still had not told my mother about the encrypted code flag. How am I going to explain this to my father? I will have to report to the Judges tomorrow! None of this is good. As I grabbed the cockpit door, Kara came running up to me.

"You were great, Jay!"

Kara tried to hug me, and I shrugged her off.

"Jason that is no way to treat a lady." My mother said as she gave me 'the look,' to let me know she was embarrassed by my behavior.

"I'm sorry young lady. Don't you have to get home? It's getting late. You both have to prep for school tomorrow."

"Mom, not here." I said.

Kara's father walked over.

"Is everything ok? Hello Mrs. McKinney."

"Mr. Meriwether, good day."

"You were great today Jason." He said

Everyone was looking awkward and uncomfortable. I know I felt that way. I just had nothing good to say, and I didn't want to say anything.

"Thank you." I mumbled.

"That Cain kid is pretty good too, but you've got some time to try and figure him out," Mr. Merriwether said.

All I could think at this point was how can Mr. Merriwether not know that I do not really feel like having this conversation. I had dreams of what I would say to Kara's' father if I ever met him. But now, I wished that I had never met him.

"Mr. Meriwether it's great to see you, we'll meet again at the next parent seminar for school perhaps," my mother said jumping in. She could see that the conversation had reached a paramount of awkwardness.

"You have a fine son." Mr. Meriwether said.

"Thank you. He's just like his father." My mom replied, and she only compared me to my father when she was disappointed with me.

"I'm sure. Well, good night." Mr. Meriwether said.

"Have a good night you two." My mother said. I said nothing. I had nothing good to say.

In the wake of the GRID Games battle, the Cauldron arena was littered with the lifeless bodies of Xenotrons. Locksmith Units were sifting through the bodies, separating them into piles so that the scavenger droids could piece them apart. Recyclable components, gold, copper, and silicon were set aside, what was left of the droid carcasses was burned in a massive fire.

The other Xenotrons awaiting their death duel were herded into the Cauldron's auxiliary simulators that were transformed into makeshift holding cells. Once they were crammed into the barracks, a control module on the Tronics Inc. command destroyer shut down each Xenotron. Despite all the Xenotrons had built on earth, Raven had reduced them to sophisticated RC toys enslaved to serve him.

In the Life Ring, Silas stood and looked out of the panoramic window in Dr. Raven's office. The sun was being chased away, and the colors on the planet grew faint. Sedusa entered the room.

"You called for me Dr. Raven" Sedusa said.

Silas walked over to Raven's desk and joined them. Raven turned in his chair chewing on his smoky cigar.

"Ladies, I think what we have is a winner. After just one competition this is a hit. The people were clamoring for the action, and we are going to keep giving it to them. Look at these numbers!"

Vitally walked into the office. His presence was beset with the smell of waste that reeked from his dusty, tattered cloak.

"Sorry, I'm late." Vitally said as he sat down next to Silas.

"The numbers are phenomenal. I heard many of the people say that they had never seen anything like this." Silas said, as he scooted his hover chair away from Vitally. "I couldn't think of a better plan to reuse scrap parts."

"That's why I don't pay you like I pay the people standing around you Silas, because you couldn't think of a better plan." Raven said.

Vitally chuckled, and Raven relit his cigar.

"The merchandising report comes in shortly, but the preliminary report shows a significant spike. Whatever these kids can buy with one of those martyred-to-be droids on it, I want it made! I want to ride this for all we can." Raven said, as he walked over and stood behind Silas.

"Silas, I need you to keep the pressure on the Ring Council to keep supporting the machine recovery bill. That will give us more power to round up any rogues hiding in the gutters and send them to battle on earth." Raven said. "I mean this is such a more noble execution than purging wouldn't you say?"

"Yes, but sir." Silas said.

Raven ignored him and walked over to Vitally and placed his hand on the shoulder of Vitally's dust coated cloak. Raven quickly moved his hand and one of his mini-bots flew in to wipe his hand clean and flew away.

"Vitally! I've got two cruisers waiting for you, each with a band of Locksmiths and heavy artillery. Get to the planet and make sure there are no stragglers."

"We will do what we do best Mr. Raven." Vitally said.

"Mr. Raven, do we know who built this colony?" Silas interrupted to ask. "I mean, if you were going to build a colony on earth, why would you build one like this?"

"Shut up Silas! Who gives a damn why they did it? I'm glad they did! Don't you have some work to do?" Raven yelled. The mood in the room grew dim.

"I'm your executive assistant sir." Silas stuttered.

"Well go executive assist somewhere." Raven said fuming.

- -

Meanwhile, my shuttle car ride home from the GRID arena was quiet and it felt so much different than any other day after competition. How could I get flagged? How could I lose to Cain? With Mike's hints on his code combinations, there's no way. My father missed the competition again because, of course, he was summoned to Raven's office for work. My mom and I usually talked all the way home. We talked about everything, but not today. I could tell my mother was trying to respect that maybe I didn't have much to say, but she couldn't help herself.

"I am proud of you Jason, but your father's right. You should spend a bit more time on your studies and preparing for the GRID rather than socializing. You've done well in the games, but do you think you're putting too much pressure on yourself? she asked. You cant be everything for everybody."

"I don't know." I said as I starred out of the window.

I didn't want to talk about my father so I thought that the next best thing to do was to change the subject.

"There was something different about the control pad today. Like there was a delay. Felt like someone knew my every move." I said.

"What do you mean? Someone knew your codes? Today was a new format right? How is that possible?" She asked.

"I don't know, but I got flagged for suspicion of utilizing preprogramed encrypted code to hack the GRID" I mumbled.

"What?" My mother asked with urgency.

"Tone gave me a chip from Mike before the match. It was just a list of Cain's attack patterns, but that's not encrypted code or hacking the GRID. We were just scouting Cain's tendencies. I don't know," I stammered. "I can't explain it, but the response to my commands was delayed to control my player. It was weird."

"It's not weird. It's stupid. Why are you relying on a list from Mike? You don't know what that boy gave you to load on your wrist unit! Now you're suspected of relying on a cheat scheme. How am I going to explain this to your father?" My mother scolded. She banged on the shuttle car control panel and was hardly paying attention to the track ahead.

"But, it's n-not r-really cheating." I stuttered.

"It's cheating." She interrupted. "You already know how I feel about that, and how the Judges will feel about that. This isn't benign behavior! It's deviant, even criminal! It's fitting you lost. It's just like your father to do something like that!" She said, as she angrily slammed her arms against the controls again, and the shuttle car veered aggressively out of control.

"Oh no! What did I do?" My mother screamed as the shuttle slammed into the vehicle in front of us breaking off its tail fin.

We were both screaming, panicking, and everything around us - our bags and my equipment - was floating in the air as we whipped upside down again and again in the aero car.

In the chaos, out of the side window, I saw a glimpse of a droid in a black cloak riding a winged cycle. The flying droid disappeared and when I looked back out the front window, we were headed right for a communications tower. Two chains, with hooks, came crashing through the cockpit doors. Our car leveled off with a violent jerk and we were pulled straight up into the air over the communications tower avoiding certain death.

Our shuttle car was flying in tow, hanging on by the chains linked to the flying droid. The droid flew us to an open area and brought the car to a rest. My mother and I got out of the car and hugged each other, and then I kissed the ground.

As I stood up from one knee I saw the droid reconfigure itself. All the components of what I thought were a winged cycle folded into his body.

"Are you ok?" The droid said.

"We are fine, thank you." My mother replied.

"Whoa! How did you do that?" I said.

"Quick as thought to…" and my mother cut him off and finished his sentence.

"Become the machine." She said and then she started to tremble and dropped her handbag.

"Jay! Get in the car." My mother said.

"Mom, We can't fly this thing. This dude saved our lives," I said.

"Get in the car now!" My mother yelled in a panic.

I backed away from the droid, and climbed into the shuttle car. There was no way we were going to get it to fly, but my mother fired up the jets and sped off in ground transport mode. Broken pieces hanging from the car dragged on the ground and then fell off, tumbling until they disappeared from my view out the rear window.

When we made it to the house, my mother hurriedly locked the doors and rushed me to my room. She was frantic.

"Get cleaned up and don't make a sound. Let me tell your father about what happened. Don't say a word, and put on some clean underwear."

"What?" I said. "Is clean underwear going to clean the scratches on my face? What's going on mom?" I asked.

"Just stay in here." She said.

She walked out of the room and closed my door. She walked into the kitchen and opened the cabinet door to grab a glass. When she closed the door, the droid who saved our crashing shuttle car was standing in front of her. She was startled, and dropped the glass.

The droid covered her mouth to stifle her scream, and it caught the glass that fell from her hand before it hit the floor with an antigravity ray beam that shot from his other hand. He guided the glass with the ray beam to the counter and rested it easy without making a sound.

"I'm not here to hurt you." The droid said.

"What are you doing here?" My mother asked him.

"I followed you and the frequency interference from your son's voice. I thought it might help me find a lost friend. But it is you that I have been looking for. I have been looking for you. You are the woman from my dreams." The droid said.

"You are dead!" My mother winced, as she backed away from the droid and she began to cry. She wasn't crying in fear. She was crying in empathy. She was in pain, like she was mourning. I could tell the difference.

"I have wondered all along what happened to you, and what happened to us. I am so happy to have found you, that you are alive. Everything I've seen tells me you were dead."

"No, no. You're dead." My mother repeated, sobbing her words.

"Akila, I must know the truth." The droid said.

The door opened and my father, Silas, entered the room.

"I will tell you the truth!" My father said.

"Silas, What are you doing here?" The droid said.

"You never were too bright old pal." Silas said as he activated his wrist unit. "Send Locksmith units to the West End Sector immediately. Defective machine unit is on the loose Xenotron code PS5674."

"What are you doing?" The droid said.

"This is the end for you. We thought we were putting the old dog to sleep when we included your name for the dissident round-up." Silas bragged.

"What are you talking about?" The droid said, reticent.

"That's right. Once we got what we needed from you, there was no use for you. We added the PS to your droid code for piece of shit!" Silas said. "We sent you to be utilized in the machine conversion process. We needed as many human specimens as possible for the machine army that built the Life Ring."

"What do you mean, we? You are a part of this evil?" The droid questioned.

"More like a mastermind!" My father quipped.

"You negotiated us into being turned into these freaks! We were working together with the SCAM on technology to save the earth to protect our families and our way of life from a machine takeover." The droid said.

"The SCAM wasn't able to save us from the impact!" Silas shouted. "All of us were rounded up and converted, anyone who

136

was an enemy to the Tronic's Inc. empire and unwilling to aid the Leaders. After the Impact they determined there was no room for our kind on the Ark. They hunted us down and converted us to finish building the Rings. Using the very same technology you unlocked from the ancient stones. The SCAM was weeded out and replaced with Raven's puppets. It was cooperate or die and I made my deal."

My father was growing more boastful as he spoke, as if he was relieved to end the lie he was living and confront this moment.

"After you flipped out over those brilliant plans for earth you came up with, Raven couldn't trust you. I had no choice other than to cooperate, and I gave Raven the research you withheld that unlocked the Benben's gene code primer. He claimed it as his own."

"But you, don't you remember what the primer did to me in our test trials? The droid begged. "We needed more time."

"You needed more time! I only needed an organic processor to make a man a machine. What the trial did to you was proof enough. After you were swept up in the dissident round-up, we kept testing it on you and all the other freaks out there we created." Silas yelled. "The Leaders had been building The Rings for hundreds of years, able to keep them hidden behind the sky canopy. The impact came earlier than expected and The Rings weren't complete. Our Leaders knew, but everyone else learned when the canopy was breached at impact. We needed the Xenotron droid modules to finish the job."

"You have destroyed all that was my life. You will not destroy that colony." The droid said.

"Who cares anymore? Your technology is obsolete!" Silas yelled. "The Life Ring is complete. You've already been replaced with more efficient models. The order of this world has been set. That's what keeps the machine churning, planned obsolescence. SCAM cries wolf, we build a better module, and people pay for them. We made our return on your kind tenfold building The Rings. Now we simply watch them duel to the death like modern gladiators for entertainment, and yes, we still make money. It's a machine, and you can't stop it! At least the people finally love your little games. You're just too blind to see it."

"The Games?" The droid said confused. "How could you have disdain for that time? We were kids. The games brought out the

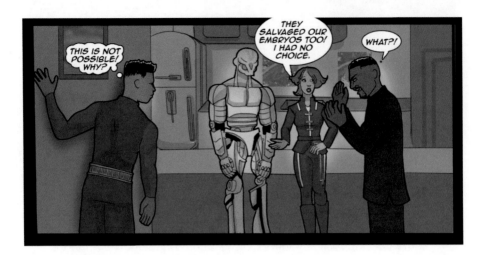

best in us.

"And still, you lose." Silas gloated.

The droid looked at my mother.

"You disappoint me." The droid said.

"Survival of the fittest Jason," my father said with a sinister grin of victory on his face. "The Locksmiths will be here soon to put you out of your misery."

It was at that moment that I walked into the kitchen. My mother looked at me and turned to the menacing droid.

"I had no choice." My mother said. "They would have taken him from us. They salvaged our embryos too, Jason."

My mother looked at me sobbing.

"He is your son." she said to the droid, "He would have ended up just like you and all the others."

"What?" Silas yelled in disbelief.

The droid looked at me as if he could see himself in my eyes. He looked at my mother and his shoulders dropped as if a great burden of pain had been cast upon his shoulders. I didn't know droids could feel.

"Loyalty!" The droid screamed. "I loved you! Some things are worth dying for!"

At that moment, two Locksmiths kicked in the door and entered our house and fired blasts of intense plasma energy into the kitchen. We all took cover. My mom dove under the table, and I hid inside the kitchen closet. The droid dodged a grappling hook launched from one of the Locksmiths. He grabbed the Locksmith's metal cord attached to the grappling hook, yanked the robot towards him, and kicked the machine so hard in the torso that it split in half. He threw the top half of the tattered droid at the other Locksmith Unit smashing the metallic mantis against the wall, and it stumbled to the floor. The leaking oil made the floor slick and the Locksmith could not stand up. Each time it tried to stand afoot, it fell back to the ground.

The droid stretched out his arms and metallic pieces extended out from all sides of his body forming his winged cycle. The rear jet spit fire, and the droid screeched through the wall. The jet blast set Silas' clothes on fire. Silas fell to the floor and rolled in fear trying to douse the flames.

I opened the closet door and ran out of the house.

"Jason!" I could hear my mother scream.

I didn't know where I was going, but I wasn't coming back home.

- -

Silas hobbled his way to Tronics Inc. Headquarters. His suit was burned, and his face was covered in a mask of bandages and burn blisters leaking blood and puss. The lobby attendant was grossed out at the sight of him and threw-up in the wastebasket as he walked by. Silas hurried his pace to the elevators as if he didn't even notice the woman.

"Is everything ok?" The elevator operator asked, as she coughed and sniffled.

Silas looked at her disgustedly and walked through the elevator doors. He entered Raven's office and Dr. Raven was seated at his desk. He was monitoring the Xenotron colony's surveillance system on the hologram wall monitors.

"I know you may be enjoying the evening's competition. But we may have a problem." Silas said frantically.

Raven's high-backed chair turned around, whirling a cloud of cigar smoke, and he looked at Silas.

"What the hell happened to you?" Raven said, shocked at the sight of Silas' burned face.

"It's him, the machine unit that built the earth colony." Silas said.

"What do you mean?" Raven said. "I own the colony now."

"He is here. He did this to me. I don't know where he is? But I'm sure he intends on disrupting our operation." Silas said

"What does this machine look like?" Raven asked.

"It's a Xenotron module. He's a comp-mutate architect." Silas replied. "He knows the shut down codes for every machine we've ever built. He can radiate to pure light and change his molecular structure to mimic anything."

"How do you know this?" Raven asked.

"Look at me! Do you think I did this to myself? He came to see me!" Silas screamed.

"Who came to see you?" Raven asked.

"It's Jason Joshua. He was the architect who became obsessed with ancient technologies. We thought he was insane, until he unlocked the Benben stone's code to create not just energy, but life itself! It's the same humanoid primer we used to make the Xenotrons. Don't you remember?" Silas begged. "He was my friend but stealing his research for the humanoid primer was the only way you would broker the deal?"

"I remember Jason. He was a smart ass! And soon he will be dead. Again! He knows not to come near me. Bring him to me!" Raven shouted as he stood from his chair and launched his hologram communicator that rose from his desk. The mini-bots about the desk scattered as Sedusa came into view.

"Sedusa, Alert all available Locksmith Units. There's trouble on the loose, a comp-mutate." Raven said.

"We are following up leads on another matter related to the rogue droids." Sedusa said.

"At all costs, immediately inspect all shuttles leaving the Ring's harbor ports." Raven demanded.

"The missing unit will be accounted for." Sedusa said, and her image faded to a black cloud of smoke.

Sedusa turned to her Locksmith battalion. "We're going to send others to search the launch harbors and shut down the ports." She said. "I've got a hunch we need to follow the trail we're on. Let's move out."

- -

Deep in the gutters of the Life Ring, PS5674 made it back to Squid's hideout. He knocked on the door, and Webb opened the hatch.

"Well did you find her, Romeo?" Webb said.

PS walked in and shook his head. "Rather not talk about it." PS said.

"That means you found her." Webb snapped.

Squid walked in from the back room.

"Have you seen it? They have us fighting like animals on the Stream Monitor. All of the Xenotrons that were captured in the gutters were rounded up and shipped to earth. They're being remote controlled by these kids in the GRID!"

"I know. I saw it." PS said. "I saw the machines slaughtering each other. They don't know what they are doing! Each unit is necessary to fuel the force field that protects the colony."

"What are you talking about?" Webb said.

"The force field that beams over the colony is fueled through a Benben stone more powerful than a nuclear reactor. The stone absorbs all energy to create energy - the wind's vibrations, our meditated thoughts, even the carom energy exerted in competition can be harnessed – all of it is used to make power. If they are destroying machines there won't be enough of us left to support its processing unit."

"That went way over my head." Webb said.

"How do you know?" Squid asked.

"I built it." PS said. "So I guess that makes me the Playmaker as you call him, and gentlemen, today is your lucky day because this pirate is going on a mission to take his ship back."

"That's why they're hunting us down. Somehow your enemies must know what you know. They have rounded up more units today." Squid said.

"If they do, I don't know how. At the rate they're destroying machines their gladiator stockpile won't last long." PS said. "The Salvage cruiser is leaving just before the second sunrise from the Eastern Sector 8 Harbor. We leave from there."

"I'm game." Webb said.

"What about the heightened security?" Squid said. "There are Locksmiths everywhere. No way will we be able to launch a shuttle cruiser."

"You just pack up as many of those chargers as you can. There is a glitch in the security matrix that shuts down the security monitors to power the incinerator. We'll get the shuttle off." PS said.

"How do you know that?" Webb asked.

"Because I built that, too." PS said. "Let's go."

Kara and her father were having dinner and, as usual, they rarely spoke. They were eating mashed plaka and yamen, a stringy noodle. The kitchen was a mess. Mr. Meriwether looked across the table towards Kara who had her head in hand staring into the bowl as she twirled the yamen with a fork. Mr. Meriwether got up from the table.

"You and Jason seem fond of each other." Her father said.

"More than you and mom." Kara said rudely.

The doorbell rang.

"Kara, that's not fair." Her father said as the doorbell rang again, and his wrist unit chirped with an incoming message.

"I hope it's mom." Kara said.

Mr. Meriwether was frustrated. He threw the towel in the sink and walked out of the kitchen to answer the door. Kara did not lift her head to look at him.

He opened the door, and Sedusa was standing before him in her black high-heeled boots and a long black trench coat. Two Locksmith Units were standing behind her, one on each side.

"May I help you?" Mr. Meriwether said.

"Are you Martin Meriwether?" Sedusa inquired.

"Yes. How can I help you?"

Sedusa kicked Mr. Meriwether in the chest, and he flew across the room and crashed up against the wall. He was unconscious on the floor and bleeding from the mouth.

"No, thank you, Daddy." Sedusa said. "We'll help ourselves. We've come for your little girl."

Kara heard the crash. She jumped up from the table and ran into the great room. She saw her father on the floor and Sedusa standing above him.

"Daddy!" she screamed.

Kara ran through the hall trying to escape out the back door, but two Locksmith Units came crashing through the back door. Kara screamed, looked around for a way out. She saw the bathroom door open across the hall, and she ran to the door as fast as she could. She tried to close the door and Sedusa's long mechanical hair tentacles grabbed her hands from the latch. The snake-like menaces pulled her away from the door and more tentacles entered the room.

The tentacles wrapped Kara up in a cocoon and pulled her

out of the bathroom. Sedusa's hair unwrapped Kara's body, but her hands and feet were still bound. She stood before Sedusa surrounded by four Locksmiths.

"You should've learned from your mother to watch who you date." Sedusa said.

"What is this about?" Kara yelled. "What have you done to my father?"

"Don't act like you care now." Sedusa said with no pity. "Tell me. Ever been to Harbor Sector 2, Sunrise Palace? What do you know about Jason McKinney or Anthony Fargus?"

Kara was silent. She was shaking, confused, and scared.

- -

Meanwhile, Squid, Webb, and PS5674 were racing towards the Sector 8 construction warehouse launch pad where their escape shuttle was hidden. Webb and Squid were carrying large duffels of run-time charge pads.

"This way let's go." PS said as the other two lagged behind. "I thought those joints were in shape?"

Webb was struggling to carry his load and dropped his bag. All of the charge pads inside spilled out onto the floor. They were forced to stop and gather the chargers, but unbeknownst to them, they were being hunted. PS pressed a sequence of codes on his shoulder pad and a light indicator began to flash.

"What are you doing?" Web asked.

"I've got a feeling we may need some back-up." PS said. "I'm sending an encrypted distress signal. Whoever get's the signal, let's hope they can get here in a hurry if we need them."

- -

Raven was pacing the floor in his office, and a Locksmith Unit flickered in on the hologram monitor.

"The video system monitoring the Sector 8 incinerators and waste transport deck has a communications error, and it could be the primary launch point for rogue Xenotrons to earth." The Locksmith said.

"Who was in charge of building that sector?" Raven asked desperately.

"The records show the project was assigned to Mr. Joshua sir, Mr. Jason Joshua." The Locksmith reported. "Mr. Joshua, however, shows in our records as deceased."

"Blazes!" Raven screamed in anger as he slammed his hands on his desk.

144

The hologram monitor switched to Sedusa

"We have the girl. Her mother was part of a SCAM outcast cell. We searched the Fargus house and there were no leads. The boy and his mother knew nothing, but his father was also a SCAM rebel. Can you tell me what Silas McKinney's son has to do with all of this? He seams to be the common denominator in the leads to the latest breaches in the Sector 8 Gutters."

"All I know is that he is a cheat. He has to appear before the Judges. He's slimy, just like his father. He might have everything to do with it. Bring me the girl!" Raven said.

"We are already in route." Sedusa said.
Kara was detained in the cargo hold of the shuttle. She was banging on the glass.

"Let me out of here!"

Sedusa ignored her cries and listened carefully to Raven.

"I have just received word that the Sector 8 incinerator complex may have been the escape point for a pack of rogue droids. Get there quickly and end this mess! Bring them to me dead or alive!"

"I'm on my way." Sedusa said. "They're mine."

Sedusa turned to her Locksmith co-pilot as she configured her control panel.

"Take over the controls and get the girl to Raven." She said.

The floor opened under her cockpit seat, and Sedusa descended into the secondary shuttle cockpit below. The doors closed over her head and the shuttle was released from its mother ship. The jets fired and she blasted off towards the Sector 8 Harbor.

The late summer heat was becoming unbearable, just like the sound of my mother's tears. I could hear her crying in the bathroom. It woke me up out of my sleep. She had begun to give up hope that Jason would ever come home.

"The mail just stopped coming. No more camera crews in our bushes. The phone just stopped ringing. Shows how much those coaches really cared about my baby." Mama said the other day as she sat in Jason's seat sorting through bills at the kitchen table.

I hated Jason gloating about all the schools fawning over him, but there was a small part of me that was proud. I was cheering for him. He was my big brother. Mama was right to question the system. Even I noticed how much less the phone was ringing. I wondered if Jason ever recovered, and he was able to play, would anyone take a chance on him? Part of me was ashamed. How could he have thrown everything away and leave us to answer the questions?

I walked downstairs to get some juice from the fridge. I pulled one of my brother's infamous moves. I unscrewed the cap and drank straight from the bottle. It was so much more convenient than getting a glass and wasting a clean dish. I wiped my mouth, and put the juice bottle back in the fridge. As I closed the door, Grandpa was standing there with his cane.

"Ahh!" I shrieked.

He quickly covered my mouth with his hand.

"Don't wake your mother. Missy, it's time." He said.

"Grandpa you're freaking me out!" I whispered in a frustrated panic.

"I need you to send me in. I have received an inter-dimensional distress signal, the one I've been waiting for. It's our only chance to help your brother and redirect this foolish course we're headed for in the future." Grandpa said.

"I need you to monitor my dimensional position with the cane. As long as the cane glows, the mission continues. Hide the cane from your mother and use the portal monitor that we created for your computer. You will figure out how to navigate the inter-dimensional consciousness to code messages that can effect events in the future world."

"What do you mean figure out?" I said. "This interface isn't like learning Final Cut!"

"What is Final Cut?" Grandpa said as he led me to his den chair. "See, you know more than I do already. The interface is very user friendly as you would say."

"Grandpa, what do you become in the future?" I asked.

"A designated ratchet and plasma welding unit engineer, Xenotron Code 2375, that is the shell I inhabit. I engineer weapons for the resistance. But over the years travelling back and forth through time, I have inhabited many shells. They need me Sunshine, and I've got to go." Grandpa said.

He sat down and held my hand. He looked at me deeply, smiled, and squeezed my hand gently. He looked at me as if it would be the last time he would gaze into my eyes.

"Now, go to your computer in the study and activate the portal monitor. You'll know I'm gone. You'll see exactly what I see on the monitor and what I assign you to see." He said. "Here, with you, I will just look like I'm sleeping. Don't worry."

I turned, walked away, and stopped in my tracks. "How will I know when you come back?" I said.

"That's easy. I will wake up. But no matter what, I will always be with you."

I ran to Grandpa and gave him a hug. "I love you Grandpa." I said.

"I love you too Missy. Never stop believing in your dreams. Now let's hurry. There isn't much time." He said.

I ran to the study, and I opened the monitor Grandpa and I built. I activated the interface just as he directed. When I walked back into the room, Grandpa was sleeping like a baby.

I grabbed the glowing cane and took it upstairs to my bedroom to hide it in the closet. Just as I got into my room, my mother came running in behind. I tossed the cane under a jacket in the closet and slammed the door.

"What are you doing out of bed Missy?" Mama said.

"I was, I was..."

I was stuttering. That's what I was doing. I thought I was caught red handed.

"What is that glowing light?" Mama asked.

"That was the toy we got from the UniverSoul Circus. Don't you remember?" I said sheepishly.

"Missy, you are eleven years old. I don't understand why you are up at this hour playing with circus toys. Just go to bed."

Mama said clearly annoyed.

She walked out and went to her bedroom. I tucked myself into bed and thought about how I surely wasn't about to go to sleep.

- -

Meanwhile, far off in the distant future, Ratchet's body was strapped down and seated in the lab chair in his chamber. Coil paced around Ratchet's lifeless shell impatiently, and suddenly Ratchet activated and came to life.

"What took you so long?" Coil said.

"I had to help the help just in case we need help." Ratchet said. "I'm transferring this coding interface to you. It's an ally from across time, but a master coder. She will be an asset. Just call her Missy."

Ratchet pressed a few buttons on his breastplate and locked Coil into Missy's portal monitor.

"Missy, come in Missy." Ratchet said.

Missy got out of bed and raced to grab the cane from the closet.

"Grandpa, is that you?" Missy whispered.

"Yes, Missy. Why are you whispering?"

"Mama, saw me out of bed, and the cane is talking. Is there a volume button to turn this thing down?"

"Ok, be careful, not to make trouble for your mother." Ratchet cautioned. "Missy, these codes will allow you to locate targets by frequency, and commandeer hostile droids and vehicles within our attack or blast radius." Ratchet said. "I'm sending you the frequency of our target. I need you to find its exact location."

"Target? What are you talking about?" Coil asked.

"I'll explain later if I already haven't." Ratchet said as he affixed and charged his double-barreled wrist blasters.

"What does 'commandeer' mean?" Missy asked.

"It means to take over, to take command of, or to control." Ratchet said.

"Great, now I'm relying on some ghost to help me get out of this mess?" Coil said.

"Yes, and wait, it get's better. She's my eleven year old Granddaughter." Ratchet said.

"You've got to be kidding me." Coil said.

"Grandpa! I've got it!" Missy chimed in on the monitor. "The frequency is resonating strongest in the lower levels of Sector 8, whatever that means."

"I've got the signal from PS. He is here." Ratchet said to Coil. "It looks like he's tracking to the same area, and we need to get you there fast. Let's go."

The two jumped in the transport car and headed to the Sector 8 Waste Harbor.

As they got closer, Ratchet checked the dash monitors. Coil charged her plasma drill and loaded her shoulder cannons.

"I'm picking up lots of hostile activity on the scanner." Ratchet said.

"I was expecting that." Coil said.

At that very moment, their transport was blasted in two by Locksmith cannon fire. The pieces of the transport flipped and crashed with the two helpless droids inside, and then it came to a sliding stop. Coil and Ratchet struggled to climb out of the upside-down transport. Once they wiggled out, they quickly examined the wreckage. Then suddenly, the back half of the transport exploded and the two took cover while the flames burned.

"Where is it?" Coil screamed.

"We can't see it. The cloak is activated. It's invisible!" Ratchet said. "Missy can you shut it down?"

"Shut what down Grandpa?"

"The Locksmith! It's an enemy droid!"

"I'm trying Grandpa, I can hear you two talking, you know," Missy quipped.

"Quickly please!" Coil said impatiently as she moved to take cover behind the other broken half of the wrecked transport.

"I can uncloak it but only for a few seconds." Missy said.

"Where is it?" Ratchet asked.

"Straight ahead, split between the two of you, approaching Coil." Missy said in a panic. "I've hacked into its monitor and targeting module. It's locked on you, robot lady!"

"Uncloak it now Missy." Ratchet said.

Missy hit the buttons on her board and the Locksmith appeared uncloaked before them. Ratchet rolled from behind the transport rubble and blasted the damaged ceiling over the head of the Locksmith. Coil darted away. As the Locksmith fired its ray cannons, the ceiling crashed down on top of the Locksmith, crushing it to pieces. But the carnage separated Ratchet and

Coil on opposite sides of the tunnel.

"We need to split up." Ratchet said. "I'll send PS's exact location and we'll meet there."

"Got it." Coil said. "I'm on my way."

"Tell me what you've got on our target, Missy?"

"He's a level below where you are now." Missy said.

Ratchet walked to the cab of the wrecked transport and pulled out a flat case. He pressed a button on the case and it configured into the metal skeleton of a hover bike. He climbed on top and scooted off to the terminal ramp towards the target. He was in the Sector Waste Harbor and could see PS's ship in the distance. He darted down an adjacent corridor as he was closing in on his target.

"You're getting really hot Grandpa." Missy said. "I'm tracking Jason and he's not alone."

"I've got him, Missy." Ratchet said.

Ratchet could hear the sound of blaster fire ahead of him. Jason came running across the intersection. Ratchet jumped from the bike as it zoomed to a stop. Ratchet threw two pebbles that exploded and made a force field around his body as he blasted down two Locksmiths with his wrist cannons.

Pieces ejected from the Locksmiths and formed one wheeled attack droids that darted around Ratchet and continued chasing Jason down the corridor.

Ratchet got back on his bike and chased behind. Ahead of Jason he could see PS's ship. Ratchet was gaining on the small assailants. He blasted his wrist cannons and took out the small one wheeled attack droids one by one. Jason kept running.

Ratchet stopped and got off his bike and watched Jason enter the ship. Ratchet coded buttons on his wrist, hopped back on his bike, and raced to catch up with Coil.

"Grandpa, what are you doing?" Missy asked? "You are moving away from the target. You were right there. You had him."

"Jason's not mine to have Missy. Our mission is to guide the key and protect it. Only Jason can unlock his path." Ratchet said. "He's in good hands. You'll be going dark here soon. My com-link is damaged."

"But Grandpa?" Missy cried out confused.

"It's ok, Missy."

Coil was taking heat from a fleet of small attack droids

ejected from the slain Locksmiths left in her wake.

"Ratchet I'm closing in on the Waste Harbor, I could use a hand here."

"I'm on my way." Ratchet said. "I've got your location."

A small cube rolled from the darkness of an intersecting corridor under Coil's feet as Coil raced by. She kept running and she dove to the ground as the cube suddenly exploded. The small droids chasing her were shredded by the blast.

Ratchet walked out from smoke and rubble of the intersecting corridor.

"Ask and you shall receive." Ratchet said. "Let's go."

Coil stood and gathered herself, and the two raced ahead.

- -

Webb, PS, and Squid, were not far from the ship. With every bit of their strength they quickened their pace and finally they were there. Quickly, PS climbed into the ship, Squid and Webb loaded the bags into the outer cargo bay. Squid reached up to close the cargo bay door and his hand was struck by blaster fire.

"Ahh!" Squid screamed in agony! His hand was smoking and charred.

They turned around and it was Sedusa, charging towards them.

"Going somewhere?" Sedusa said.

PS jumped out of the front cockpit. Sedusa leaned her head back and whipped her hair tentacles towards Squid and Webb, and they tried to escape their touch, but they were both struck and shut down instantly.

"Good night." she taunted.

PS dodged the myriad of tentacles as they retracted to Sedusa's head. Squid and Webb stood frozen like cold wax. He was too late.

"You almost got away with it. Just like you're almost human, and that is why you can't win!" She said screaming.

Sedusa wound up to whip her hair again and Coil came blasting thru the harbor wall and her blazing hot plasma drill arm twisted right through Sedusa's side and pinned her against the opposite wall.

Coil pulled the drill out of Sedusa's side and her limp, sparking, droid carcass fell to the floor.

"Oops." Coil said"

No Problem." PS said as he looked on in disbelief

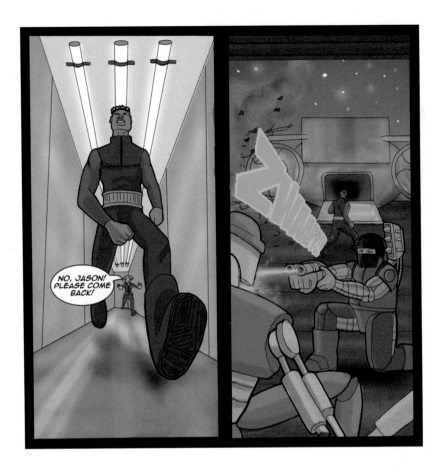

Ratchet came leaping out of the hole in the wall and rolled into a ball to brace his fall. He sprang up and fired blasters back into the hole. Ratchet was taking heavy fire.

"Take cover! Hurry up and get that ship out of here!" Ratchet yelled.

PS flicked the restart switches on both Webb and Squid. More Locksmith blaster fire came raging through the hole in the wall Coil burrowed. Ratchet ran over to the group as they hustled into the shuttle and locked the cargo bays.

"If this is a rescue operation, you had better get going." Ratchet said into his com-link. "PS, you are carrying precious cargo from more worlds than our own, return it home safely.

Take him to the stone."

PS listened to Ratchet over the com-link confused as the shuttle canopy closed and the blaster engines fired up. Three Locksmiths stumbled out of the hole in the wall. The ship was taking heavy fire. Ratchet fired back to protect the launch point. He charged straight toward the Locksmiths casting a barrage of laser cannons. He leaped to dodge a Locksmith blaster ray and was struck to the ground.

"No!" Coil screamed! "Ratchet is down!"

"We can't go back!" Webb said.

"He's right. We can't go back." PS said.

"Is that what you said when you left me behind too?" Coil said fighting back angry tears, and punching PS as he was trying to steer the shuttle.

Squid pulled her away in a warm embrace and Coil burst into tears.

Smoke billowed from Ratchet's body as the ship rose up, turned, and blasted through the shuttle launch tunnel into space.

One of the Locksmiths saw Sedusa lying on the floor.

"Sedusa is down. Send additional units to the Sector 8 Waste Harbor."

Raven was livid as he watched the surveillance monitors and heard the Locksmith's report.

"What! No! What's your unit number? What has happened? Wh-what is your location?" Raven stuttered.

"Unit 721 Sir, One shuttle has launched. It's cargo, unknown." The Locksmith said.

"Damn it!" Raven screamed.

- -

PS was at the helm of the ship trying to fly in the shadow of the rings to disguise their entry into earth's atmosphere. As the ship raced towards the planet, Webb, and Coil heard a coughing sound coming from the cargo bay. Coil looked up.

"What was that?"

Webb pulled out his blaster and Coil armed her plasma drill.

"I don't know but we better check it out."

Coil and Webb climbed down into the rear cargo bay. The narrow hall was lined with storage sheds. The lights flickered on and off.

"It's coming from that carriage bin." Coil said.

They walked cautiously towards the steel vault.

"Back off. Let me open this." Webb said.

He jerked and twisted on the door with all his strength.

"This latch is stuck"

The coughing behind the door was growing more intense

Coil and Webb had not been formally introduced, and she already did not like him. Coil pointed to a button on the side that said 'Push to Open.'

Webb pushed the button embarrassed that he did not let Coil open the door in the first place. When he opened the door, a boy fell to the floor. PS and Squid entered the cargo bay hall corridor and looked at the boy lying there coughing.

"What's this kid doing on the ship?" Squid asked.

"Get him a mask. Quickly!" PS yelled as he kneeled to the floor to check the boy's vitals.

"What are you doing kid?" PS said.

"I guess I'm on a mission. Because like you, my name is Jason." I said.

PS was caring for me like he knew my soul was hurting. I recognized the white-haired droid. She was poised to choke the life out of Tone in the temple room. She placed a breathing mask over my mouth, and wrapped me in a cloak.

"What's going on? He could jeopardize this mission!" Squid said.

"He is my son." PS said. And like a father, PS held me in his arms.

155

PS landed his ship at a remote canyon outpost, on the other side of the colony. I wasn't feeling well at all. I vomited at least three times on the trip, and I was severely dehydrated. PS detached a hovercraft from underneath his shuttle. They laid me down on a table in the back of the hovercraft. They removed my respirator and a glass dome closed over me. It was oxygen rich inside the dome, and I could breathe freely.

Webb looked far off at the horizon, at the glare of the Ventrosphere.

"If they found the colony on the planet. What makes you think they don't know about this hideout?" Webb asked PS.

"What will you do if they do know?" PS said.

"I guess we'll have to depend on you for parental guidance." Webb said sarcastically.

"Where are we going?" Squid asked.

"There,'" Coil said, pointing to a mysterious building on the other side of the canyon.

Deep inside the building in an underground bunker, Blasthole and Ravage were pacing the control room. The Xenotrons built the outpost to measure the reach of the Ventrosphere's protective barrier. There were underground tunnels leading from underneath the mountain colony to outposts in each compass direction.

Ravage and Blasthole had been camped out in the easternmost outpost for many days. They felt helpless and were running out of the reserve energy that powered the building. Blasthole was scavenging through a loft storage space looking for hydraulic fluid.

"How did they know we were here? How long had they been watching us?" Blasthole asked, confused.

"Your guess is as good as mine," Ravage replied, as they both noticed gravel falling from the ceiling. Blasthole leaped from the loft edge and looked around.

"What is that?" Blasthole asked, looking around in panic.

"I don't know, but let's get to the data chamber. We've stocked weapons and ammunition." Ravage said.

They ran into the room and Ravage unlocked the weapons access door. Ravage handed Blasthole a gamma burst cannon, and he took a blaster ray for himself. They had set a signal beacon for any surviving Xenotrons to meet at the outpost, but they still didn't know if the sounds they heard were friend or foe.

PS was speeding in the hovercraft through the tunnel leading to the outpost. He brought the craft to a sudden halt. We had reached the passage leading up to the entrance to the outpost. Everyone jumped out of the vehicle and PS walked to the back. He looked down at me lying on the transport table. He waved his hand over the glass and the glass dome opened. He placed a respirator on my face, picked me up, and carried me off of the hovercraft like I was a sleeping toddler.

Squid and Webb unloaded the bags. Coil entered the pass code to open the door, and blaster rays came bursting thru that nearly struck PS in the leg. Everyone took cover against the wall next to the sliding door.

"Ravage!" PS yelled. "Only you know how to get here! Hold your fire!"

The data chamber door opened and Ravage slowly peaked around the corner.

"74! Is that you?"

PS walked through door cautiously holding me in his arms.

"74! It is you?" Ravage asked. "I thought you might have perished."

"I brought company." PS said.

Coil ran over to Ravage and gave him a hug.

"Where is Ratchet?" Ravage asked? "I thought he was coming with you this time."

"He didn't make it. He suffered the same fate as all the others." Coil said

"It's an honor to see you Sir, and welcome home." Blasthole said. "But this is one worm hole of a hideout. Energy reserves are low, and I'm going to need some hydraulic fluid in a hurry."

"There's time to discuss that later. We've got to get this kid hooked to a clean oxygen line in a secure chamber. Quickly."

"This boy does not stand a chance on the planet." Blasthole shouted. "He's the enemy! What is he doing here?"

"He is my son. Now get out of my way." PS said.

Wire tentacles extended from the palm of his hand and plugged in the back of Blasthole's neck and shut him down completely. Blasthole stood, frozen.

"I see you've returned with a chip on your shoulder." Ravage said.

157

"Meet Squid, and Web. This is Ravage, interim Governor of CX, and that was Blasthole. We will hear more from him later." PS said. "Squid has designed runtime chargers and adaptors that eliminate memory distortion in our internal drives. All our misery was part of Raven's elaborate plan to erase and distort the memory of droids he created using humans as organic processors."

Squid and Webb plopped the cases of chargers and adaptors on the table.

"I hope somehow they will bring each of you the clarity of thought it has brought me." PS said. "We will meet in the data chamber tomorrow. There is more to discuss. Right now, the boy needs rest."

As PS walked away, Ravage looked at the others left behind.

"Well, if I had known you were coming. I would have made tea." Ravage quipped.

PS walked into the medical Lab, and he laid me on the table. I was in and out of consciousness, and PS5674 stood over me. He held my hand as a small fleet of floating medi-droids began to examine me.

"You made a brave choice." He said. "I'm glad you are here. We will make this right."

- -

Back in the Life Ring, Silas and Raven were alone in Raven's office.

"The GRID Final is in a few moon cycles. Tonight is the semi round. Your son has been snooping around and helping the droids escape from the Sector 8 waste harbor and construction deck. And did you know he was flagged for suspicion of using encrypted code to hack the GRID?"

Silas' lips quivered with anger.

"You are sowing a bad seed Silas!" Raven scolded.

"Dr. Raven, there is...there is." Silas stuttered before Raven interrupted.

"Of course you didn't know. Because if you did, you would be kneeling here groveling and begging me to save him from the Judges' discretions! As if having the ghost of days past terrorizing us isn't a big enough problem!" Raven said. "This was your working. You said he would be taken care of. Now this! I will not allow this thing to disrupt this operation. You get every Locksmith available to secure that colony."

"It won't matter. He will shut them down." Silas said laughing at Dr. Raven's haste.

"Well what are we going to do?" Raven stammered. "Do something!"

"There is nothing we can do. We wait. We wait for him to make his move." Silas said.

"And then what? Wait! You really burn me up Silas. And whatever that boy of yours is up to, I couldn't care less. I won't give a rat's ass if this cost him his life!"

"He's not my boy! He's Joshua's son!" Silas said angrily.

"Am I paying you?" Raven said. "Just what kind of sick twisted life are you living Silas?"

Silas's face was still bandaged, scarred, and blistered with burns.

"That's why he's registering as a rogue droid on the Locksmiths' profile monitors! You're harboring the enemy! The primer is genetic and has been passed on to the boy! Get out! Get out of here! Go find me someone to fire, until I can fire you!"

- -

That night, at the Xenotron outpost on earth, I was sitting up in my bed. I felt much better, and I didn't have to wear a respirator to breathe. The door opened and PS5674 walked in.

"You are looking well." He said.

"Where am I?"

"Earth, inside of the Virtual Game you and your friends in the Life Ring are now toying with. This is our first home, the mother planet."

"But how is that possible?" I asked.

"This chamber is pressurized so you'll be fine." PS paused. "Do you remember why you are here?"

"I remember." I said. "You are my father."

"I never knew, and I feel I should explain." PS said.

"I heard it all. I was listening the whole time you were arguing with my mother and father. I mean, I don't know what to call them anymore," I said.

"Time makes it easier to deal with the truth." PS said as he waved tools around me to check my vitals. "How did you find my ship?" He asked.

"I wasn't actually looking for your ship. I just wanted to run away from home." I said. "Then I find myself getting chased by a couple Locksmiths and another rogue droid of some kind that actually, in the end, saved my life. It gave me cover and led me to a place to hide. I didn't know it was your ship."

PS summoned one of the small, four-wheeled, M-DOG droids to run a series of tests to check my hearing and my sight.

"I have read about you. My friend is obsessed with SCAM literature and this idea of an underground war against the machines. We stumbled upon this mysterious room with weird wall carvings. I should have believed him. He was attacked by one of the droids and it left behind this case," I said, as I handed PS the small pentagonal case. "I guess this belongs to you. It has your numbers on it. The second time we went back, I recorded images of the room on my on wrist unit."

I flipped open my wrist unit and the hologram beam showed Tone and I snooping around the temple room. The hologram panned to the codex writing on the walls of the script temple. The hologram showed the Locksmith chasing us and then fizzled silent. PS watched the message a second time.

"This case is a data block, and it has the new encryptions we need to disguise our location here on the planet. We were looking for this and happy you seemed to have found it," PS said, as he flipped the data block in the air, caught it in his hand, and sat the block on the table. "That room is the old script temple. Our minds were so fried by Raven's faulty charge pads that whenever we thought we had a clear memory, we engraved it on the corridor walls, hoping that one day it would make sense to somebody. There are more places like the temple you saw."

"How did it even come to this?" I asked.

"It's just becoming clear to me now. Many years ago a plague struck. People covered with blisters and boils. Fearing the plague would spread, those who were infected were quarantined in ghettos. But over time, they weren't the only ones brought to those slums. Anyone who opposed the Leaders, anyone who had committed a crime, anyone who was disabled, was sentenced to life in the slum lands."

"Opposed to the Leaders? What were they protesting?" I asked.

"They were protesting the proliferation of artificial intelligence. Machines and technology had become so pervasive, that it altered what it meant to be human. What they failed to realize is that man and machine are one in the same."

"What do you mean?" I asked.

160

"We are descendants of the Shell Dwellers, the first travelers across time and space. These travelers seeded the earth from the Benben stone, using an elemental source code, the same code that they used to create us all. Who were the first travelers, you might ask? They were machines blended with organic vessels, just like me, and just like you."

"I am not a machine. I am flesh and blood. I'm human." I said. "A stone, time travel, what does any of this have to do with Raven's quarantine?" I asked.

"My parents were dissenters against the Leaders, and they were killed. But I was smuggled out and sent to live with their friends, The McKinney's, Silas's parents. They were also dissenters living in quarantine, but Silas's family and I eventually escaped and we were never again caught." PS said. "The people developed their own way of life in quarantine. That's where the games in the simulators you have seen come from. They were my inspiration; simple games from the past, where we made the things we needed to play from scrap technology and whatever else we could get our hands on. But what Raven had in store for those people was no game at all. He was stockpiling inventory to make a droid construction army."

"But why?" I asked.

"A small band of people in quarantine organized and set out to prove that they were not a threat to the Leaders. This was the beginning of the resistance, the roots of the SCAM. The SCAM's elders believed that the real threat to earth was an extinction level event, but they had no proof. The SCAM believed the Leaders were hiding the truth behind the canopy."

"What is the canopy?" I asked.

"Well the canopy was the fake sky, the glass ceiling, that we saw above our heads on earth. For hundreds of years humans were painting the sky with digital cloud plumes from aircraft. The canopy could regulate earth's temperature and light, but its real purpose was to hide the construction of the Rings. The Life Ring had been under construction for centuries, but it was the final push to completion as the asteroid impact became imminent that caused Raven to harvest humans from quarantine, and create the Xenotron construction module. They thought people were disappearing because of the plague. They were wrong. People were being harvested. We were the builders of the Rings, and when the asteroids came, the earth was evacuated and deserted."

But why did they convert you?

"When I was a student, just before impact, we were studying the power sources of antiquity and I discovered the Benben stones that caped the obelisk in ancient Egypt. It had long been accepted that the stones could be coded to generate power, but I was befuddled by the idea that people we thought of as primitive could create and possess such advanced technology. I began to study the stones unceasingly, and I discovered and unlocked code sequencing on the stones that could create life. From the stones I deciphered the gene code primer used by the first Shell Dwellers who traveled here to make earth habitable, and seed the planet with life. It proved humans are nothing more than organic processors, and unlocked the potential for hyper advanced cyborg applications. The formula was unstable so I tabled the concept. But when Silas and I began working together for Raven, Silas was pressuring me to test the gene code primer on humans. I refused. Now, I learn that my closest friend betrayed me and gave Raven the primer to earn himself a place in the Life Ring. Everyone didn't get that one-way ticket. Many were left behind to rot here on earth.

"How did you know about the side effects?" I asked.

"I tested the primer on myself. Under stress my body would function at high rates of speed. It was uncontrollable, and too much stress would cause these unpredictable plasma burst to shoot from my body."

"The same thing happened to me. My body's been acting all weird since I took that charge of electricity from the aftershock of a Locksmith blaster ray" I said, as PS sat down next to me.

"You survived scatter effects from a Locksmith blaster ray?" PS questioned. "The primer code must be genetic, so it must be in your blood if you are indeed my son. You may very well be one of us. You just didn't know it. I never considered that the primer could be passed on to a child in my research." PS paused. "Ratchet described you as precious cargo. Which makes me think that you may have more powers to help us in this war than you think."

"What!" I said. "What do I have to do with the war in the gutters? And who talks about their estranged child like I'm some kind of science project?"

PS paused as if he wanted to choose his next words carefully.

"There is more to this story Jason. The droid who saved your life, his name was Ratchet. He was a Shell Dweller, and I am a Shell Dweller too – a traveller across dimensions and time. Ratchet said that you also were from more worlds than my own. That is code speak, and it means that you are just like me, a Shell Dweller. This realm, and this reality is not the only one in which you and I exist. The things I am telling you about this realm, and this time are important, and you must understand them to fulfill your mission and return home.

"What mission?" I said. "What do you mean return home? What other world?"

"You'll keep talking like that until you lay your hand on the Benben."

"What?"

"We have a stone here and you will see it. We are using the same method as in the beginning to reseed the planet. It is what is necessary in this space and time. We are now, forever have been, and in all times will be the Keepers of the code. And you, from a time certain, are one among us. You have only been sent here because you failed somewhere else along the way." PS said. "We can only guide a living key in the right way, but it is up to you to unlock its gift."

"I don't understand."

"We plant genius indiscriminately among all people and leave it to chance and circumstance to make the magic that inspires the good in humankind. We call it kinetic code sequencing. What are we? What is humanity if none among us inspires? We've planted the seeds that have manufactured greatness in every achievement throughout time. We've found that the greatest way to foster inspiration among humankind is through competition, and the games they hold sacred. So all of this, everything you see is about inspiring greatness by making the best use of this shell we inhabit."

"So, all I am experiencing now isn't really real, it's a dream?" I asked.

"No, this is very real." PS blasted me with an electrode shock.

"Ouch!" I screamed.

"Did you feel that?"

"Yes!" I groaned.

"You are a living key, and you are lost! It was likely your failed mission - wherever you were when the mission was aborted -

that helped create this mess of a reality that we're living in now: This time that inspires nothing, destroys everything, and leaves a vacuum in its wake."

"I don't know what you are talking about. None of this has anything to do with me," I rationalized, with much doubt in my heart.

"It has everything to do with you, because you are here. We sent Ratchet back in time to help you prevent this reality from ever happening, and we all failed. I've lived this once already. Now we're stuck in this place where the machines win." PS said.

"If we're stuck why are we still fighting?" I asked.

"What's with all the questions? You're going to walk into some answers as we go. There's still time, but there's work to do. You need programming, and upgrades. What I do know is that Raven destroyed our colony. He is still making droids. He is still using human processors, and I'm going to stop him."

"Why did you build this place anyway?" I asked.

"You can't stop yourself can you?" PS said sarcastically. "When a human is converted into a Xenotron, its memory is erased. Human memory is further distorted with repeated charging. Squid and Webb developed a new run-time charging pack that eliminates flashbacks and memory glitches. This is why, now, I can see my own story so clearly."

PS paced the floor slowly and deliberately and continued to explain. "We built this place from fragments of memories we've tried to forget, and the one common memory that all Xenotrons share – the games we played as children in quarantine. It was our only peace."

PS paused to reflect, seemingly, and continued.

"Our collective energy powers this place through the Benben, tapping into the earth's natural electromagnetic fields. I built this place to prove that we never had to leave earth. We had the technology to reclaim the planet and make the air breathable again all along. No matter how long ago they started building the Rings. We never needed them. It was all about wealth legacies for a few rich families." PS said. "But if you succeed, this alternate reality will have never existed."

PS stood up and manipulated the control panel on the lab desk and handed two flasks with blood samples to an M-DOG droid.

"You and your friends are brave. Raven can have his world.

164

It's done many people well, even you, my very own son. But he cannot have this colony." PS said.

"Well, why don't you just kill him? You're all powerful, right?" I inquired.

"Killing Raven is not the mission. Besides, he knows there is a sonic frequency that can cause components to corrode instantly inside my body. He is more clever and dangerous than you think, Jason. Greed can make you that way."

"Sound waves!" I said.

"But maybe your primer is different, and that's why you can help us stop him." PS said.

"How?" I asked.

"I have a plan." PS said.

It was quite for a beat. I was reflective for a moment, and I began to feel unsure about the decision I made to run away. I couldn't believe I decided to runaway and not sit before the Judges, and it was just days before the next round of the GRID. I had given Cain an easy route to the finals and that really burned me.

"I don't know how to feel about mom and everything I've left behind." I said.

PS looked at me focused and sincere. "You can't look back Jason." He said. "Look ahead and how you feel about her will find you. Get some rest for now, because you have some training to do if you are going to compete."

"How am I going to compete in the GRID from here?" I asked. "I've got to get back to the Rings."

"I said I have a plan." PS reminded.

The room was quiet for a beat.

"Well, can I call you Dad?"

"Yes son, yes you can."

"What does it mean when you say, 'Quick as thought to become the machine?' Mom would say it to me all the time." I asked.

"Young Jason, you will see. The world and The Rings will see."

The next day, the semi-final round of the GRID tournament was set to begin. Inside the GRID, Milan Cain was sitting in his game cube, prepping his control panel for battle. He looked across the bow and saw that Jason's game cube was empty.

Tone and Mike were in the stands with all the other programmers tuning in their wrist units for live interaction. Jason was supposed to be competing today, and they also noticed that Jason's game cube was empty.

"What's up with Jay? No answer at the house." Mike said. "You'd think he'd want to get a look at Cain to prepare for the final."

"I don't know what's going on with Jason. Sector Police came by my house with two Locksmiths asking all kinds of questions. My mom was losing it!" Tone said. "I don't know. He's already accumulated enough points to advance to the final. Maybe he's getting his mind right. He's still grounded, you know."

"Yeah, you're probably right." Mike agreed.

--

Back on earth, PS stood high above the Cauldron. The Ventrosphere was flickering intensely. He watched as hundreds of Xenotrons walked in and out of the arena escorted by Locksmiths. He studied their pattern. He crept closer and walked hurriedly to blend in with the final group walking toward the center of the arena as the gates closed.

Atop the Xenotrons' heads, the crudely adhered remote control modules glowed with a dim blue light. The Xenotrons moved like zombies, jerked about like marionettes on strings. As they reached the center of the arena, the Cauldron twisted its rustic rock interior to stage a game the Xenotrons played called Bedma.

The dirt field was divided into two halves surrounded by a mirrored dome. The ball was metallic and oblong. Every player competed for himself, fighting to possess a ball and throw it to hit a target raised high above either end of the field to score a strike. Players also earned strikes for takedowns – tackling a droid or rendering it mechanically disabled. The first player to ten strikes wins the game.

As the game began, fifty Xenotrons were on either side of the center circle. The oblong ball came rising out of a hole in the floor and floated in the center. The Xenotrons backed away as the hole in the floor closed. Suddenly SoNite ran to the middle of the center circle, grabbed the ball and pressed the buttons on the center code strip on the ball and spikes shot from the tips of the ball making it look like a spear. SoNite threw the javelin right at a Xenotron and it pierced his chest. The droid collapsed and the Javelin shot right back to SoNite's hands.

SoNite began running with the ball, morphing his liquid metal body between would-be tacklers. He was getting closer to the end line where the target was high above in the air. In front of him and behind him, two droids were charging fiercely to make a SoNite sandwich. SoNite split his body in two as he was running and threw the ball at the target. The droids crashed into each other and sparked into smoke and flames. The ball hit the target as SoNite's body morphed back together. With three takedowns and a target hit, he had earned four strikes in one pass.

Inside the Life Ring at the GRID complex the crowd was going wild. Two strikes were also accredited to Milan Cain, and he bowed and gloated to the fans.

"You know I really don't like that Cain kid." Tone said.

"But he sure is good." Mike said.

Back on planet earth, PS stealthily made his way inside the Cauldron, and staked out a hiding space. PS couldn't believe it. No game in the colony was played to the death. It was forbidden. It was understood that everyone was needed to create the energy needed to power the Ventrosphere. With the loss of each Xenotron, the Ventrosphere was getting weaker and weaker, and allowing more dangerous toxins from the atmosphere to breach the protective barrier. He also noticed that unlike all the other droids, SoNite did not have a control module on his head.

PS removed his hooded cloak and stepped into the fray of the Cauldron competition, replacing one of the slain droids.

Again, the ball rose up from the hole in the center. This time a Xenotron made of elastic Teflon grabbed the ball. PS recognized him. It was Ricochet, one of the first Xenotrons PS freed from the Life Ring. Ricochet was running with the ball, and he threw it, attempting a score, but his shot was deflected and missed the target.

Other droids were looking up at the ball as Ricochet's failed attempt was descending. They were all fighting for position and Ricochet's eyes zeroed in on the ball, too. He reached out to catch the ball, leaping high to snatch it from the other droids, and again, he raced towards the target. Machines were closing in on Ricochet from all sides and PS5674 burst through the ground in front of him. Ricochet fumbled the ball into the air and PS grabbed it. Then, PS shot tentacles from his hand that connected to five different Xenotrons and shut them down. PS landed on the ground in the middle of the frozen droids. Rocky debris and gravel followed him in descent, crashing to the ground.

The gamers inside the GRID complex were confused. The crowd was frantic with cheers. The gamers were all looking around to see who the points were going to be accredited to, and no adjustment was made to the main score panel. Their earth avatars stood motionless facing PS5674 as he clutched the ball in his arms.

A curious chatter began to stir about in the crowd at the GRID Complex. In his office, Raven moved closer to his monitor. "Is that him?" Raven asked, as he looked around. No one was there.

"Where is that Silas when you need him?" Raven said to one of his mini-bots as he activated his hologram communicator.

"Get McKinney in here!" Raven screamed.

A sea of droids began to charge PS5674. He pressed key codes on the oblong ball and he threw it at four droids that he knew were not Xenotrons. The ball knocked off the head of one robot. Then the ball made a sharp turn and went through the torsos of two more machines.

Just after PS threw the ball, two machines approached him from behind. He turned, glowed, and morphed his body into chards of shrapnel. The machines collided with the jagged chards of his morphed body and fell down to the ground in smoke and flames. PS reformed himself, and the ball returned to his hands like a boomerang.

More machines, Xenotrons, approached PS as he was racing toward the target, and he extended tentacles from his hands shutting down any machines that came close. He activated a shoulder-mounted cannon that popped out of his breastplate and blasted attacking droids that were not Xenotrons.

PS began to glow brighter and brighter as he ran faster and faster. He leaped into the air and threw the ball. He hit the target and it exploded. He was running so fast that he created a sonic boom that shattered the mirrored dome. PS landed on the ground and pointed his hands at the rain of mirror chards. Without touching a single piece, PS threw the jagged pieces at the droids with a wave of his hand. One by one, every droid that was not a Xenotron collapsed to the ground, sparking and smoking from damage.

"Raven!" PS screamed. "I know you are watching! As you can see it's not even fair for me to play games with you!"

On the Life Ring, Inside the GRID complex, the crowd was awestruck and bustling.

"Call Jay. Like now! Tone said. "I can't believe we're watching this!"

"I am! Still no answer." Mike said.

Raven was sitting at his desk chair smoking a cigar as Silas ran into the office and looked at the monitors.
"That's him." Silas said gasping and panting.
"Quiet!" Raven said.

PS looked around as if he was trying to look into one of Raven's hidden cameras.

"I stole your machines. You stole my gene code primer. You stole my wife, and you stole our lives. That's not a fair exchange?" PS asked rhetorically. "The dance ends here, Raven!" PS yelled. "I embedded a coded detonator in the main fuel engine block of your little space station, so send your droid army and I'll blow a hole in the donut. But for old times sake, and because I know you're a gambling man, I will challenge you to one final competition." PS said. "Our way versus your way. The new earth versus your false heaven. Pick your players and I'll pick mine. If you win you keep what you see as a money machine. If I win, this is the last broadcast. You always believed you could build a better machine. I've always believed we could build better people. Now we will find out once and for all who was right. The competition begins in three moons."

PS looked into the camera hidden in the ground, and he spiked the ball into the camera. The monitors in Raven's office went black. Pieces of metal extended and contorted from PS's body and transfigured into a winged cycle. PS quickly climbed aboard the craft and blasted off into the dark clouds in the sky.

On the Life Ring, The crowd in the GRID complex was stunned. They were silent, staring at the blank hologram monitor, and then they burst into a roaring applause.

169

Raven grabbed his jacket off the back of his chair. He was very deliberate as he put it on and adjusted the lapel. Raven picked up his cigar and walked over to Silas. He blew a cloud of cigar smoke in Silas's face.

"You have three moons to fix this mess. That's three days." Raven scowled.

Raven walked out of his office as his Chief Scientist was walking in. The door closed. The Scientist and Silas looked at each other.

"Dr. Raven said you and I have some work to do?" the Scientist said.

Silas was silent.

As the crowd filed out of the GRID Complex, Jason's mom spotted Mike and Tone in the outside concourse.

"Hey guys. Have you seen Jason?" Mrs. McKinney said.

"We haven't seen him." Mike said. "I thought he was on punishment or something so I didn't really think much of it."

"We haven't heard from Jay, and we've been trying to call all day," Tone said, trying purposefully not to sound so presumptuous. He sensed that something might be wrong.

"I spoke with Mr. Meriwether, and he said that Kara was missing too.

"Kara! What happened?" Mike said. "Something's not right."

"Mr. Meriwether said he was assaulted, and Kara was taken away by Locksmith security droids, with no explanation. You wouldn't happen to know anything about that, either, would you?" She said.

"What!" Mike exclaimed. I don't know anything!"

"What about the data card with Cain's combinations? Any way that could have caused an encrypted code violation?" Mrs. McKinney asked. "You do know he was flagged and facing the Judges' discretion?"

"All I gave him was a list of the attack combinations that I observed. That's it!" Mike said adamantly.

Tone hesitated to answer.

"I don't know anything Mrs. McKinney, but if I learn of anything I will let you know for sure." Tone said.

- -

Back on earth, PS arrived back at the outpost. He met with Coil, Ravage, Webb, Blasthole, and Squid inside the data chamber.

"We saw what happened on the surveillance monitor. So what's next?" Ravage asked.

"What's next is to prepare the boy." PS said.

170

"Prepare the boy! What?" Webb said.

"I'm with him on this one, 74. It's too dangerous." Ravage interjected.

"It is of no consequence and it is why he is here." PS said.

"None of us except Blasthole and Ravage have played these games, and we don't know how Raven has the games rigged." Coil said.

"Speak for yourself, lady." Webb quipped.

"But the boy, how will he compete against machines?" Squid inquired.

"How will you fight against them?" PS asked

"I can fight against them because I am a machine," Squid said.

PS didn't say another word as if Squid had answered his own question. PS stood up and walked out of the room. The others looked at each other miffed by the riddle.

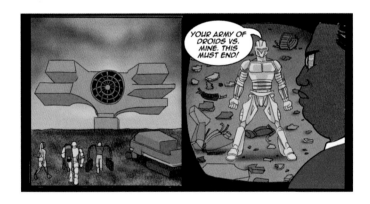

CHAPTER 23 – HELLO AND GOODBYE

I woke up shaken and startled, peeling my face up from the keyboard. I couldn't believe that I had fallen asleep in the study at the computer desk. I got up from the chair and walked over to peek in on Grandpa. He was resting on the couch just as I left him last night. I walked back to the study and opened the portal interface. The screen was dark and fuzzy. I put the microphone headset on, but I wasn't quite sure what to say.

"Missy to Grandpa. Missy to Grandpa, come in Grandpa, send a reply if you can hear me."

There was silence in the headset.

"Missy to Grandpa." A deep woman's muddy voice interrupted me. I was startled.

"Missy. Your signal was transferred to me. My name is Coil. My location is the year 3010."

"Where is my Grandfather?" I asked.

Coil could not see me, and I could not see her. I felt like I was talking to a voice in my head. All of a sudden, the visual simulator of the portal monitor activated.

"Welcome to the future." Coil said.

I jumped back from the screen. I was horrified at the woman-like robot glaring at me through the screen. Her long white hair and dark skin, and the lights and modules bolted to her face and neck scared me.

"Don't be alarmed." Coil said.

The room looked like a laboratory with computers, lights, and robot parts that I couldn't envision in my imagination. Coil was pacing the room.

"Much has happened while you slept. Your Grandfather is a noble Shell Dweller who has aided our missions across time." Coil said. "He assigned me to you, and your mission is to help us change outcomes in our future world."

"Grandpa explained this to me. But how?" I asked.

"Open the user interface," Coil said. "From here I will be able to load mission commands to you in real time. The trick is that the commands come in scratch code. Are you able to decipher our coding sequences?"

"Yes. I got plenty of practice with my Grandfather building this portal monitor. By the way, you still have not told me about Grandpa. Where is he, and what about my brother Jason?"

"The shell that was your Grandfather is gone. He is dead, Missy, as you know him," Coil said, and a tear fell from her eye.

"No!" I screamed. Then I hushed my voice, and I was fighting back my tears. Mama was in the house.

"I'm sorry, Missy," Coil said, "I did not know that Jason is your brother. So it seems he's a traveller too, who is just beginning to learn who he truly is. This is too much to explain to you now Missy, but if you want to help your brother, you will have to be focused and prepared. You will see my world through my eyes. Trust me. We will fight to keep your brother safe from harm. Now be strong, and stand-by."

Coil de-activated her visual simulator, and the monitor fizzled to black. Mama walked into the study.

"Missy, who are you talking to?" Mama requested.

"Umm, I was playing a game on-line," I muttered. I had no idea how long she was standing behind me.

"I'm worried about you child," She said. "It's too early in the morning for that don't you think?"

"Yes, Mama," I conceded.

"I'm going to the hospital to check on your brother, and then I'm going to work."

"Ok," I said. I couldn't look at her because I was crying.

"Has your Grandfather been asleep all morning or was he up earlier?" Mama asked.

I said nothing as she walked over and gave him a kiss on the forehead. Mama noticed he was not breathing. She ran to the phone screaming.

"Oh my God, No! No! Don't die now, Daddy! No!"

Mama was frantically dialing for an ambulance. I walked over and held Grandpa's hand and it was cold as ice. It was too late. Grandpa was gone and, now, I could let it all out. I stood there and cried, helplessly. I regret every time I questioned Grandpa and doubted his stories. I was crying because he taught me to dream. I always wanted to believe him. Now, there was no doubt his stories were true, and how his story ends is in my hands.

Chapter 24 – Become the Machine

PS walked into my pressurized chamber and gave me a helmet with a built-in respirator.

"Jason, here. Put this on. You're coming with me." PS ordered.

"Where are we going?" I asked.

"Training." He replied.

"Training for what?"

"The game of your life." PS said, as we walked out and hopped into the hovercraft.

We traveled through the long tunnel, deep, under the mountain that housed the Cauldron arena. We parked the hovercraft and walked to an elevator. We took the elevator up and when the doors opened, there were exoskeleton prototypes hanging from the ceiling overhead.

"Before we try any of these, how many push-ups can you do?" PS asked.

"At least fifty," I said.

"Well let's see," PS said.

I had seen a push-up, but had never really done a push-up. They looked simple, and fifty seemed like a good, round number. I got in position and began. 1, 2, 3, 4, ... I didn't make it past seven-teen.

"Was that fifteen, or fifty?" PS taunted. "If it was fifteen, I think you just hit a new personal best."

I was a little embarrassed.

PS waved his hands as the armored suits came down from the ceiling one at a time. He examined me for size utilizing a three-dimensional laser. If he didn't like a suit, he waved his hand and the suit returned to its storage place. Then he got to a suit marked A7. It didn't look like an exoskeleton at all. There was a sleek helmet with a glass mask and respirator, and a set of armored plates attached to a seat. It confused me.

"Considering we're looking for extra strength, try this on?" PS said.

"Well how do I do that? What is it?"

"Your battle suit, A7. Are you ready?"

"I guess so," I said.

I took off my jacket and stepped into the seat in the middle of the contraption. I sat down, and put on the helmet. Suddenly, the seat folded up like metal underwear. I tried to jump up out of the seat. I was terrified. Then, the attached plates transformed into limb covers and clamped to my body like a suit of armor. Lights and monitors flickered on inside of my helmet.

I turned and looked at my father, gasping, and relieved that the suit didn't kill me.

"Perfect fit." He nodded.

We walked back to the hovercraft. I was laboring just to walk in the suit. It felt bulky and awkward. I managed to lumber into the craft and we raced back to the outpost.

"So what now?" I asked.

"There is a simulator in the lower level of the outpost. It is small, and it has its limitations, but it will do. You've got to get used to the new gear."

I was quiet, and thought to myself that I have really jumped head first into the deep end.

"I can sense that you are afraid." My father said.

"I am not afraid." I chirped back.

"Well, I must admit that I am afraid for you," he said, as he brought the hovercraft to a stop.

We had arrived at the training chamber. The doors slid open and we walked into the vast chamber.

"Walk to the center, and I will activate the controls," PS said.

I lumbered in the suit to the center of the room and looked around. The lights began to dim as my father activated the control panel. Three dimensional hologram images of six Locksmith Units appeared, surrounding me. I know I said I wasn't afraid, but I was scared now!

"What am I supposed to do?" I clamored.

"Just think and react. Don't fight the suit. Become one with it."

The Locksmiths took a fighting stance. I backed away and turned in a circle slowly. The droid holograms crept closer. Suddenly, they attacked. I just covered my face with my fore arms and took the blows backing away from the droids as they punched and hammered me. The next thing I knew I was being tossed across the room. I crashed, and the A7 sparked as it screeched across the floor.

"And I thought I was bad at lacrosse." I stammered. "This is mad!"

I stood up and another Locksmith unit tripped me. Again, I

175

fell to the floor. Then, the droid hologram collared me and tossed me across the chamber. I smashed against the wall. PS reset the simulator and the lights flickered on.

"I can't move this thing! Where is the control panel?" I yelled. I was frustrated.

"There are no controls. Whatever you think, the suit can become." PS said.

It seemed impossible to me. Was the suit just going to read my mind? I was really beginning to doubt that I would be any help in this duel.

The simulator restarted. The hologram droids again came closer in measured steps.

"Think and move!" my father said.

"I am not strong enough to move this thing. It weighs a ton!" I replied.

"I doesn't matter how strong you are! The machine responds to your thoughts. It can sense that you feel like you can't do it, and that is why the machine is disabled. In the Cauldron, these won't be holograms, and the enemy won't wait for you to be ready!"

The hologram machines attacked again, and I just wanted to go into a shell. The A7 transfigured into a porcupine like shell. The spikes pierced one of the Locksmiths. I stood up and the exoskeleton collapsed back to my body. I jumped over another Locksmith as it lunged for me from behind. I thought about blasting him with a ray gun, but I then I realized that I didn't have one. Then all of a sudden, a ray canon popped out of my forearms and blasted the two Locksmiths with a fatal strike and their holograms fizzled to black.

I didn't see the droid coming from behind, and it slashed me with a plasma blade and blasted me against the wall with a ray cannon. I was thrown to the wall as the blast barely missed. I couldn't stand. I was too tired. The simulator stopped, the lights flickered on. I was bent to one knee in the center fatigued and out of breath.

PS5674 walked toward the door.

"There is much for you to learn, and very little time son. But enough for today."

He walked out of the chamber to the hovercraft. I slowly gathered myself to stand and hobble to the door. I was happy this day was over.

177

CHAPTER 25 - A DISH SERVED COLD

Dr. Raven was in his Tronics Inc. office sitting at his desk. Silas entered with two Locksmith units and Kara. Her hands and feet were bound and her mouth was muzzled. The Locksmiths slammed Kara into the chair.

"Seriously, is all this necessary for a little girl?" Raven said.

The Locksmith unit removed the muzzle from Kara's mouth. Kara launched a wad of spit that landed on Raven's tie.

"You jerk! Let me go!" she screamed.

"Forget I asked." Raven said.

"The Locksmith put the muzzle back on Kara's face. One of Raven's mini bots flew over to wipe the spit off of Raven's tie. Raven brushed the machine away, annoyed, and grabbed a handkerchief from his desk. He stood up.

"Do you know who I am little lady?" Raven said as he wiped his tie clean. "I am the mastermind of this floatation device in which the world spins. And you're trying to bankrupt my wheel of fortune. But it won't happen."

Raven flicked on a hologram of the earth and the Life Ring appeared hovering in the air. The model spins then stops at one small section of the Life Ring that is incomplete.

"You can't build things this big without a workforce. You need an army of advanced machine intelligence! How else do you think we can live inside this thing! How was it built so quickly? You kids take so much for granted." Raven said.

Then, the hologram showed a man on the table. His legs were being replaced with jackhammers. Other droids floated around the man as he is fused with machine parts. The man is screaming in agony.

"Anyone who dissented against our vision was quarantined on earth and relegated to the slum lands of the Rings. From there, we harvest them. And while they wait their fate, they live marginalized, and forgotten, blind to the reality of the world growing on top of them. They wait to die or to join my machine candidate pool, while we assimilate their children – allowing only a few each cycle to enter the Ring Sustainability Project to create an illusion of hope. This is what has happened to anyone who opposes me!" Raven screamed.

Raven walked over to Kara and looked her in her eyes as she struggled to peer over the top of the muzzle.

"Let him blow a hole in this space station." He said. "More construction means more suffering for those people and more money for me. I thought of doing it myself, too risky. But soon they will all die out, their technology obsolete. Their sad story will be forgotten and the slums rebuilt. Your meddling SCAM loving friends should feel lucky to make it into the R.S.P. to have a way out. This is the thanks I get!"

"What does this have to do with me?" Kara mumbled through the muzzle.

"What did you say? I can't hear you." Raven mocked sarcastically.

"What does this have to do with me?" Kara mumbled louder.

"I heard you the first time!" Raven laughed. "Your little boyfriend's father created the juice primer that I used to make my machine army, and now, he's a little upset about it. But he knows not to come near me because I have the power to destroy him!"

Raven pulled a small blinking orb from his pocket and angrily waved the grenade-like device in Kara's face.

"These sonic cannons would make him rot before your eyes!" Raven teased. "He stole my machines and I'm going to make him pay."

"But they are real people!" Kara said.

"It's not about people. Just like it wasn't about your deadbeat, lying, mother that we took from you! It's about money! I made them, and they are mine!" Raven screamed.

"I hate you! You're crazy!" Kara said defiantly.

"I am, and I guess this really has nothing to do with you. Your little boyfriend didn't tell you he was a rogue droid? Not something you'd want to mention on a first date. He will be another one of his father's failed experiments! Somehow he plans to use the boy! I know it!" Raven snickered. "And to catch a mouse you need a little bait!"

- -

Back on earth, my father and I ventured back to the simulator at the underground outpost for our second day of training. I stood in the middle of the simulator as the lights began to dim.

"To become the machine, you cannot be afraid," PS said.

An aero bike, almost exactly like the bikes we ride back home in the Life Ring appeared next to me. I climbed on the aero bike and five other Xenotrons were lined up with me on similar cycles. The simulator screens came to life all around us, and the start line flashed green. The other riders darted ahead, leaving me behind in their trails of wind.

"A machine does not hesitate to process code," PS said.

I zoomed off on my bike, speeding up to catch up with the pack. We entered a tube and the bikers were weaving in and out of the fray from side to side and upside down on the ceiling.

"A machines code is ordered, and you must order your steps," PS said.

Bikes zoomed around trying to knock me off the floating cycle.

"Your mind is the most powerful processing unit. Your thoughts are wireless electronic transmissions," PS said.

I swerved as two bikes were coming down from the ceiling of the tunnel. One bike clipped the front of the other causing them both to crash. I stopped my bike on the dime and the bike behind me swerved, and crashed into the mesh. I sped off and caught up with the last two racers. The tunnel was beginning to narrow and there was no room to turn or time to stop.

One of the bikes crashed, trying to pass as the tunnel shrank. There was only enough space for one bike to pass. I barely missed hitting the crashing bike and rider as I raced by. The tunnel closed behind me swallowing the rider left in my wake.

I was closing in behind the leader. I leaned in, and the bike was speeding so fast that the heat inside the A7 was becoming unbearable. I was moving faster and faster, struggling to breathe, and finally, I cleared the line just behind the leader.

The simulator lights flickered on and I heard my father applauding. I was exhausted and struggling to gather my composure.

"Almost there son, we're almost there," PS encouraged.

"Your spouting off the machine proverbs over the intercom like the voice of God was not helping." I said, panting. "I'm not going to remember any of that. I was trying to drive."

"And you did well." PS said. "Tomorrow we'll see to it that you get some additional upgrades and programming for the equipment, and increase the oxygen input for the A7."

"How do we do that?" I asked, as we walked back to the hovercraft. "Can't you just take the suit to the lab and plug it in."

"It's not what you think."

"Well, why can't you just tell me?" I asked.

"Well that would ruin the surprise, and also because I'm not a master programming module," PS said. "Are you going to ask the enemy questions in battle?"

I cracked a smile and laughed.

"I wouldn't advise it," PS said.

Later that night, I couldn't sleep. I felt like I was ready. How could I not be? I have been training against Locksmiths. I was getting the hang of the A7 and my movements were smooth. But what was on my mind was my mother. I wondered if she was safe. I thought about Kara, Mike, and Tone. I wished there was a way to let them know that I was ok. Then, I asked myself, well, am I ok? This talk of being a Shell Dweller, I had no idea what it meant. I guess I was waiting for the right moment to ask. I felt that my search for answers had only led to more questions.

- -

Back at the outpost, Coil reached out to her friend from the past.

"Missy. Come in, Missy," Coil said into her intercom.

Missy was standing on the counter in the kitchen scavenging through the top shelf of the cabinets looking for cookies, when she heard the call. She climbed down from the counter, scrambled into the den, and cued up the computer interface.

"What? Do you think I'm just standing here all the time?" You need to learn to text," Missy said.

"The time has come. We know now that Jason's final competition will be in two moons," Coil said. "The wait is over."

"I'll be here, and I'll be ready," Missy said. "If Jason is there with you, why can't I just see him?"

"Jason has to reconcile his realities on his own, and I believe he will," Coil said.

- -

The next day, PS5674 took me to a deep trench that looked like it had been quarried. I stood at the edge of the trench and looked down into the giant hole.

"It's a challenge to make it across the trench," PS said. "All I can tell you is that you have to make it to the other side, and place your hand on the stone. Are you ready?"

"Your magic stone, I don't see anything over there," I said.

"It's there. You will see," PS said.

"Seriously, this is the final exam?" I mocked. "So I can just fly

181

over there right?"

"Yes, you can try that if you want to," PS said. "Don't let me stand in your way."

PS placed a data chip in the card slot of the A7, keyed a series of commands on the forearm code pad of the battle suit, and he stood off to the side.

"You may begin whenever you are ready." He said.

I ran up to the edge and leaped out over the vast darkness of the trench. The wings popped out of the A7, and the winds swirled, viscously. I was swept up in the turbulence. I was flying out of control. I crashed into the cliff wall on the opposite side. I was holding on, by just one hand, and my fingers were slipping. My wing was damaged and the winds were still swirling. I reached my other hand up on the edge and pulled myself up to the top. My father was standing there.

"How am I supposed to get over there with that kind of wind? And now my wing is broken. You said I could just fly over there," I said. "And what is this? I crashed and landed on the other cliff wall. Why am I climbing back up to you?"

"You said that, not me. The result you achieve is a reflection of your doubt versus your desire. If you don't believe you can make it across, you won't." My father said.

"Well how am I supposed to get there now with a broken wing? That's a small canyon you're asking me to cross."

"You said it was a canyon, not me." PS said.

"This is impossible," I said "I'm supposed to be getting upgrades and we're here tearing up the suit!"

"You said it was impossible, not me." PS replied.

I took a deep breath and sprinted towards the edge of the cliff. When I reached the edge, I leaped into the air. I could feel the winds pick up as I neared the center of the chasm. I was getting closer to the other side, approaching in descent, and I slammed into the edge of the cliff. As I scratched and clawed to pull myself up to the top, crumbling rock broke away and fell endlessly into the abyss below.

Then, pieces of the A7 detached and flung up to the top of the canyon. The small pieces configured themselves into a tiny pulley. A metal cable shot down into the canyon and affixed itself to the A7 and the tiny machine yanked me up to the top of the cliff.

I picked myself up off the ground, and standing before me on

182

a platform carved out of the canyon wall was a large pyramid-like stone with mysterious text and carvings. The stone's face was split down the center like the seams of double doors. I placed my hand on the stone, and the stone opened. I was startled, and stepped back, as an ancient robot - an automaton - was glowing inside.

The automaton sat perfectly still on a throne with a golden rod, as I gazed into its lifelike eyes. All of a sudden it took its golden rod and began to solder processors and circuits onto the small chipboard in its lap. When the old machine's work was done, it lifted its hand and gave me the chip. Engraved on its reverse side were three mysterious symbols. I recognized the symbols from the walls of the script temple in the Life Ring gutters. A light sparked from the chip as it began to heat up in the palm of my hand. The chip dissolved, burning a hole in the armored glove of the A7. I was zapped into a trance.

I saw visions of a distant time. I saw a young man who looked like me. He lay dead on the grass. I heard a voice screaming. I saw an old man, and a little girl. These felt like people I'm supposed to know. I was frightened. I saw a droid. It was feminine. It came thrashing at me with a flamed whip. I saw myself trapped inside a box, and suddenly, I was pulled out of the trance. I was shaken. The automaton had disappeared and the stone was sealed shut.

The winds blowing across the canyon had ceased, and land bridges that were not there before appeared spanning the open chasm behind me. I raced back across to the other side of the square canyon and PS was there to meet me at the edge. He put his hand on my shoulder and looked me in the eyes.

"You're ready." He said.

"What?" I screamed. "What is this? That thing burned a hole in my hand!"

I looked at my hand and the hole in the A7 was gone.

"The creepy old machine? I mean," I said confused. "What's this all about? I saw me dead somewhere in the past. Who was that? "Is this some kind of sick joke?"

"You have laid hands on the Benben, and it has read your traveler's spirit. It will give you clarity from mission to mission, as you move from shell to shell to etch your destiny." PS said. "And you have been given the mark of hope."

"Wait. My destiny is on some disappearing chip? There was

nothing about the future in that vision." I said angrily. "What is that supposed to mean, huh? There is nothing clear about this. I'm not getting the clarity."

"Jason, you are going to walk into some answers along the way." PS said without acknowledging my frustration.

I'm scared! I don't know what I'm doing!"

"Pull it together!" PS said. "Nobody cares that you are scared! We've got to win. You've got to win." Raven will try to destroy you! Use all you've learned to fuel you in this moment. Use your past to help us atone this future."

The time had come. In his office, Raven stood looking out his window at the planet. Thousands were gathering at the GRID complex. The anticipation was thick like mountain fog.

Inside the GRID Complex, Cain stepped into his game cube for the final competition. He looked at Jason's game station. It was empty.

"Chicken. This game is mine," Cain said to himself, laughing, as he prepared his control panel.

Mrs. McKinney was at her usual spot in the stadium looking at Jason's empty game cube. Another boy entered Jason's cube and flicked on the controls. The arena announcer echoed over the loudspeaker.

"Replacing player 76 Jason McKinney is player 54 Vassar Kilgore."

Mrs. McKinney sat down trying to hide her eyes as the fans around her were stirring a ruckus. She was crying.

Tone and Mike were trying to inch through the crowd to get to her.

"Mrs. McKinney, Still no word from Jay?" Tone asked.

"Nothing Anthony, I'm sorry. I just don't know boys." She was trying to hold back tears, wiping her eyes and face. "I'm sorry boys, but I don't know, and what I do know, I cannot say."

She got up from her seat, squeezed out of the row, and ran up the stairs disappearing into the crowd.

"That can't be good," Tone said, and Mike agreed.

"I think you're right."

Silas and others joined Raven in his office. Raven's Chief Scientist was chatting loudly with his colleagues, and Raven hushed the men to silence as he reached for the control panel on his desk.

"Ladies and gentlemen, it is time." Raven said.

Above the players' game cubes in the GRID Complex, a hologram of the empty Cauldron arena on earth appeared. The restless chatter in the crowd quieted to an anxious whisper.

Footsteps echoed in the arena as the first Xenotrons entered the Cauldron. The crowd roared frantically, as over fifty Xenotrons, a smattering of other droids, and Locksmiths entered the Cauldron. SoNite was the last of machines to enter the field from the right tunnel and the crowd erupted.

Inside his office Raven cracked a sinister grin.

The flickering light of the Ventrosphere glowed behind Webb, Ravage, Squid, Coil, and Blasthole casting their long shadows before them. They walked to the end of the tunnel and entered the arena. The crowd at the GRID was jubilant, but it suddenly began to murmur with a groan of confusion.

"What is that?" one of the fans yelled.

I walked out of the dark tunnel into the Cauldron. I was sweating inside the A7 battle suit already. There was no turning back now I thought.

At the GRID Complex another spectator shouted out in disbelief.

"That's a kid! There's a boy in that battle suit! I can see his face."

"Hey that *is* a kid! How'd a kid get in there?" Another fan screamed.

Tone and Mike looked confused at the arena hologram monitor. They couldn't believe their eyes.

"Is that Jason?" Tone said.

"That is Jason! What the? What's he?" Mike stuttered. "How did he get into the game?"

"Game! How did he get to earth?" Tone shouted. "He's taken this a bit too far."

Mrs. McKinney came out of a GRID Complex restroom fixing her hair, looking visibly shaken. She looked up at the concourse monitor.

"What's that kid doing? He's going to get himself killed," she thought.

She walked closer to the monitor, covering her mouth and crying in disbelief. She could see that the boy was Jason.

Tone and Mike were adjusting their wrist units to plug into the fan interactive system.

"There's no way he's going to get himself out of this one. He's got to fight the machines on earth and the machines being remote controlled from the Life Ring." Tone said.

Milan Cain looked at the monitor and saw Jason standing in the Cauldron. Cain slammed his hand against his control panel.

"You will not steal this show from me!" Cain shouted angrily. "You're going to pay!"

Tone and Mike were entering disrupt codes into the fan interactive keypads at their seats.

"Someone has to get him out of there." Tone said.

Raven's voice echoed over the loudspeaker.

"Begin!"

Inside The Cauldron on earth, the lights began to flicker as the rock walls around us rose like a stage curtain, shaking the earth, and revealing the arena's finished aluminum panels.

Coil tapped the control panel on her forearm and the portal monitor in Missy's study opened up. Missy could now see into the Cauldron as if she was there.

"Missy. This show's begun. Are you ready?" Coil said."

Missy raced to the headset in the study and rushed to put it on.

"Coil, I'm here." I'm ready.

"Coil, who are you talking to?" Ravage asked.

"Missy. That's just my little ghost in the machine, a gift from Ratchet." Coil said.

"Missy? Who's Missy?" I said confused. "That name sounds familiar."

I was snatched right back into the moment when Ravage grabbed me by the shoulders and screamed through my visor.

"Focus boy!"

I shook myself out of it to gather myself, and the Cauldron's flickering light stopped and went dark.

Then, the center of the arena was illuminated with a green glow, and suddenly, I saw Blasthole slip and fall into the pool of water that was spreading towards us. We ran and leaped towards a nearby rock ledge.

It's a Hydro-Flair!" Ravage warned.

I had no idea what a Hydro-Flair was. I was in a bit of a panic and the A7 jerked unsteadily as I climbed up the rock wall to reach the ledge. Squid reached down to pull Blasthole up from the water, extending his retractable arm several feet. He could see Blasthole's hand reaching up from the pool. Squid grabbed the hand, but it was detached from the rest of Blasthole's body, and his head bobbed up from the water. What was left of his body was limp and sparking, and floated away. Squid released the hand back into the water. The liquid splashed onto Squid's forearm and hand. He felt a burning sensation in his hand.

"Goodness. It's some kind of acid!" Squid shouted. "We've got to stay above the water."

The pool was quickly rising. We watched two more Xenotrons succumb to the rising pool of bubbling acid. Their hands were reaching up for help as they sank to the bottom, but there was no one there for their relief.

Small rocket jets extended from Ravage's boots that allowed him to hydroplane above the acid. As the pool spread near the edge of the plateau, it crested. Rocket jets shot out from the heels of the A7.

"So, you're a copycat?" Ravage asked jokingly.

"What am I supposed to say?" I said. "I've got nothing."

"This cannot be true. This was supposed to be a trip to Utopia. I don't have those things in my boots so I'll stay right here on this ledge," Squid said.

Ravage and I leaped into the fray. In the center of the Cauldron, a thin metal disk descended from above and hovered about three feet above the pool's surface. From an adjacent plateau, a fleet of droids and Xenotrons controlled by players in Raven's GRID appeared. Each of Raven's droids was riding a small hovercraft called a water walker, and they zoomed onto the pond to join the fight. Two water walkers broke away from the swarm and raced toward the disk. I tried to stay out of the mix until I could figure out what the heck was going on. It felt like the simulator was making the game up as it went along.

As the water walkers raced towards the disk, SoNite's liquefied body began to form underneath the disk skimming on the water's surface, unaffected by the acid. SoNite's body completely coalesced under the disk. He leaped up from the water, sweeping up the disk. The converging riders crashed into each other and sank into the bubbling pool.

Coil leaped from the safety of the ledge leaving Squid behind. She landed right on top of an enemy droid's water walker. Coil ignited her plasma drill, severed the droid's arms, and kicked it off the craft, before taking it for her own.

SoNite ran across surface of the acid pool with the metal disk in hand. He was manipulating his liquid change-form body and the acid pool as if they were one in the same. Small plasma netted targets rose randomly from underneath the surface at the ends of the arena. SoNite slid to a stop to avoid a challenger and pushed a wave of acid on the droid that melted its components. It crashed and sank while SoNite threw the disk. It skipped across the water like a rock in between two machines and hit the electrified target for a score.

SoNite looked at Ravage.

"Your move, Coach," SoNite taunted.

Meanwhile, on the Life Ring, inside the GRID Complex, the frenzied crowd cheered excitedly at what they witnessed SoNite do over the arena hologram monitor. SoNite badgered the crowd more.

Tone was still frantically clicking keys to crack fan interaction codes to influence the game. He was trying to override and hack into a game cube control panel, get control of an avatar, and help Jason. Mike was distracted, focused in on the main monitor.

"Come on, Man, Jay needs us!" Tone growled. "We can get one of these goons, I know it!"

"I'm trying," Mike said.

"I got it! I got a goon!" Tone said.

"There's Cain." Mike shouted. "He's not controlling the change-from avatar. He has a different one."

"I got this!" Tone exclaimed.

Tone's stolen avatar was severed in two by a disk thrown from Cain and the avatar he hacked sank into the bottom of the acid pool.

"What! How could he do that? I put the auto block on just like you said. But it didn't work."

"It didn't?" Mike said.

"No, it didn't," Tone said. "These codes are from the same files you had me give to Jason."

Tone paused, and then he grabbed Mike, punched him, and threw him to the ground. People around them tried to pull Tone off of Mike. They grabbed his arms and hands before he could strike Mike again. Tone was kicking and screaming.

"Let me go! Get off me. You ratted Jay out! How could you? You gave Cain his codes, and you planted the encryption code on the chip!"

"I'm sorry. I'm sorry! How was I supposed to know he was going to be in the game for real?" Mike said.

Tone walked back to his control panel, fixing his jacket, and tried to hack into another avatar. Frustrated and angry, he slammed his hand on the control panel.

Mike stood up and dusted his clothes off. He looked at Tone, walked away, and disappeared into the crowd.

- -

Down on the dark planet, three more disks descended and hovered above the surface of the acid pool. The water walkers again raced and jockeyed to grab the disks. Now, it was time for me to get into the game. I grabbed a disk and charged towards the moving target. I was forced to leap over one droid riding a water walker that came barreling at me. I looked back at the droid and zoomed my sights on it. Coil was racing by, when she saw me getting ready to throw the disk. As soon as I let it go, Coil blasted the disk with her ray cannon and it exploded.

"No!" Coil screamed as she zipped her craft to a halt.

"What are you doing? The droid on that water walker just tried to kill me!" I screamed.

Missy gazed closely at her monitor. "Is that Jason?" Missy asked Coil anxiously.

"Missy, I need you to concentrate." Coil said. "It's not the time."

At that moment, the droid circled back on its water walker and charged towards Coil.

Coil kicked her craft into gear and a high stakes game of chicken had begun.

"Missy, take control of the water walker!" When I say, *now*, swerve to the right." Coil said. "I'm a little bit crazy, but I'm not as crazy as you think."

"You've got to be crazy, Lady, to be doing this." Missy said. "I've got the controls."

"Faster." Coil said focusing her eyes on the droid rider. "Now!" She screamed just before the two craft would certainly collide.

Missy swerved at the last second, and Coil reached out and snatched the rugged control crown from the head of the droid playing chicken. The droid immediately transformed into a metal jaguar and leaped from one water walker onto another, where a droid had Ravage in the crosshairs of its blaster cannons. Alerted by the foray, Ravage took cover from the careening craft and cannon fire.

"Jagg!" Ravage said.

"The metal jaguar quickly ripped the droid in three pieces and tossed the limbs into the pool. The careening water walker crashed and exploded, but not before the metallic big cat leaped up to the rocky plateau and clawed its way up to the landing. Squid was standing on the ledge, and he was startled and jumped back as Jagg transformed into her human form.

The game quickly reset. Ravage grabbed a disk, threw it across the pool, and it cut off the legs of two machines. The legless droids sank into the acid. Ravage's disk skipped all the way around the circular perimeter wall to the other side of the pond where I caught it. I was hovering above the acid pool with the disk, and two droids were closing in from behind.

All of a sudden, small whirlpools formed all over the acid pond's surface in front of me. I blasted the jets, leapt into the air, and front flipped over the whirlpools. The droids on their water walkers trailing me were swallowed up.

I landed, hovering above the pond's surface as if the air was concrete. I saw a Xenotron standing at the shallow edge of the pool. I guess he wasn't affected by the acid. His arm was a massive anvil. He used the anvil to splash a large wave in the pond. The wave threw acid everywhere, and knocked several droids off their flying water walkers. The machines were swallowed by the wave of acid.

I flicked on the A7's jets, and I rode the wave until I was rammed by a droid riding a water walker that seemed to appear out of nowhere, and I lost the disk.

It was Milan Cain's avatar that rammed the A7. Cain was giddy inside his game cube.

"Take that!" Cain mocked.

Cain's blow knocked me backwards. I was falling into the acid pool, when jets flamed up from the back of the A7 and stopped me from plunging to my death. The jets lifted me to my feet.

Coil caught a disk, locked it into her machine drill arm, and launched it. The disk flung through the air like a flipping coin. The hurtling disk burrowed into the chest of a machine and slammed the machine into the electrified target - frying the droid while recording a score.

Missy watched from the study desk through the portal monitor both amazed and horrified.

Coil turned around and a disk was approaching her from behind. Webb used the machine nets that webbed his fingers together to catch the disk and saved Coil from getting creamed.

"Missy, I'm going to need you to watch my back," Coil requested, sending scratch code file request for shields to stop blaster fire.

The code file popped up on Missy's visual monitor.

"Got it! Working on it right away" Missy said.

Webb slid to a stop on his stolen water walker, hovering above the pond, facing Coil, and a disk struck him in the hip, from behind rendering his legs useless. Webb fell off the craft and into the bubbling acid. Coil leaned back swiftly, so far back that her hair sizzled as it touched the acid water. The disk flew right over her chest. She sat back up. Distraught, she screamed.

Webb!

A whirlpool opened and sucked down Webb's outstretched hand.

Missy turned away from the screen. She couldn't bear to watch the carnage. She was processing code, typing with her eyes closed.

"Missy I need those shields!" Coil yelled. "We need cover."

There was no time to contemplate Webb's fate. Cain was hunting Coil down.

Inside his GRID game cube, Cain was rocking back and forth aggressively manipulating his control panel. He blasted cannons toward Coil.

"Shield's up!" Missy said.

A plasma force field enveloped Coil and deflected Cain's blaster rays. Then, Cain saw me out of the corner of his eye. Cain quickly turned his water walker around, locked the A7 in his sights, and threw a disk as he grunted.

"You are mine." Cain said.

I turned to speed away, but right in front of me SoNite emerged from the acid water. His head and torso fully formed, but below his waist his body was liquid. I couldn't tell where the acid pool began or his body ended. They were one. I stopped and ducked. The disc Cain threw at me went over my head and straight through SoNite's body. But SoNite lunged his liquid arm behind his back and caught the disc. He threw it right back at me. I back-flipped into the air, and the disk flew right into Cain's avatar nearly slicing him in half. But Cain's avatar survived the blow.

I was trapped between them - Cain and SoNite. Suddenly, the pool rumbled a tsunami-like wave, and from the water beneath Cain's avatar arose a giant scaled head with its eyes, like two giant domes of black glass, gleaming at us all. It was the head of a dragon. I was frozen with fear, as the dragon snared and chomped Cain's avatar in two, and the droid's pieces splashed into the acid pool. The dragon emerged fully from the water exposing its wings, vicious claws, and massive spiked tail. It turned in flight toward the pool of helpless droids scattering to escape and vomited flames and plasma all over them. Carnage was left in the wake of the onslaught of heat. The dragon roared defiantly, turned, and flew away into the dark sky.

"No! No!" Cain screamed. Cain slammed his control panel, took his helmet off, and threw it.

The crowd was going wild, transfixed by what they were seeing on the hologram monitor.

"Was that real?" A fan questioned in disbelief.

"Cain just went down." Tone exclaimed. "And earth has dragons!"

The Cauldron went dark. I could see the acid pool underneath us receding. I was relieved. I had survived the first challenge, but this battle was far from over.

On the Life Ring, everyone in the GRID complex was watching the hologram monitor anxiously.

Back on earth, inside The Cauldron, the lights flicked back on. Now, I was standing with my team of machine gladiators at the edge of a large ringed-platform that laced the middle of a giant egg-shaped chamber. Just above us, was a second platform with four rectangular doors carved into the walls of the egg. Two of the doors were huge, much larger than the others. In front of us were several jet-powered boards floating inches above the ground. Blue flames burst from the engines as they hummed and zinged.

"We'll have to use the volplanes. Have you ever used one of these before?" Ravage asked, as he and Coil stood up on their craft and their feet clamped in place.

"No!" I said

"Stand on the board. Stick your boots in the slots. And well, you're a smart kid. You'll figure it out," Ravage said.

SoNite stood at the opposite side of the egg-shaped chamber with several dozen of his goon droids.

We were outnumbered. Ravage and Coil were the only others to survive the Hydro-flair, and now I was faced with another game I had never seen before.

"I didn't see this in the simulator package in training." I said.

"Doesn't matter," Ravage said. "See those square holes in

the side walls?"

"Yes."

"One of us has to get through there. The corridors lead to the Final Challenge Chamber."

"Sounds easy." Coil said.

"But, there is an electric force field that fuels on and off. Better time your jump or you'll get fried. And, they don't call this oversized egg "The Tumbler" for nothing. The egg will rotate like a mixing drum, and by the way, watch out for the carob pellets shooting from the flat wall muskets." Ravage said.

"Well, I take it back." Coil said. "Maybe it doesn't sound easy."

SoNite glared his eyes at us from the other side of the bowl.

"Do you really think you're going to win?" SoNite mocked.

SoNite and his gang of machines mounted their volplanes. They dove into the egg's bottom and swooshed back up to the sidewalls riding a thin sheet of air.

I stepped onto the volplane, and I was having trouble standing steady. But I quickly gained my balance and dipped into the Tumbler. I was gaining speed when I was hit by a carob pellet that split the volplane in two. The acid inside the carob pellet was eating a chunk of metal and wires out of the ankle of the A7. I slid to the bottom of the egg.

"Excellent!" Raven said, as he watched in his office.

All of a sudden the Tumbler began to turn like a cement mixer. As the Xenotron gladiators surfed the surface, the egg split in two at its center. The top of the egg-shaped chamber rose higher and stopped. After a short pause, the top of the chamber began moving again, slowly descending to the bottom half of the egg, and blocking the exit doors.

I was scrambling at the bottom of the egg. It was like trying to climb out of a giant bowl. Finally, the egg stopped turning. I tried again to scale the wall, but vacuum tubes at the bottom of the egg-shaped chamber opened up. The power of the suction was relentless. I held on tight to one of the open wall musket doors. Four machines slid past me and were sucked in through the bottom of the Tumbler. Another fallen droid knocked me down and we were both sliding fast to the bottom.

The top half of the giant egg-shaped chamber rose up and locked into place exposing the exit doors. Coil leaped for the square door and was shocked by the force field. She fell toward the hole at the bottom of the Tumbler. The force of the shock was so powerful, that the blast sent her sliding past me. She activated her plasma drill and rammed it into the chamber wall to stop her slide. Then, she reached out her hand and grabbed me as I came careening past her.

Coil looked me in my eyes like she was looking with the eyes of someone else.

Missy jumped up from the study table.

"Jason!" she screamed

"Focus, Missy!" Coil screamed.

"What was that? I heard a little girl's voice!" I said panicked. The voice echoed in my head.

Missy scrambled back to the study desk. She wiped away tears, as she gazed into the portal monitor at her brother.

"We can't hang on here forever!" Coil yelled.

A headless droid carcass was falling toward us, and we swung out of its way. I ripped the droid's volplane away as it careened by and fell into the hole. I clipped the volplane under my feet and darted off, barely dodging a blazing hot carob pellet.

Coil scaled up the wall.

SoNite leaped from his volplane and morphed into liquid to avoid being hit by a carob pellet. He landed safely on the ledge. The force field protecting the door receded, and he walked through the tunnel into the darkness.

I was speeding on a volplane, and the Tumbler began to turn again. Two droids were chasing me. Ravage was coming at me head on, and the droids were gaining from behind.

When Ravage and I met, we hooked our arms together and spun each other around in a half circle. We launched each other in the opposite direction.

The droids chasing me were now chasing Ravage. The droids turned their heads to look at me. When they turned back to find Ravage, the two droids were hit by carob pellets and exploded.

I raced the volplane toward the middle ledge as the top half of the egg was beginning to descend to block the entrance to the final challenge chamber. The protective force field was charging up, and getting ready to eject a fierce burst of plasma. I zipped through the gate narrowly missing the force field blast, and the Tumbler door slammed shut behind me. I dismounted the volplane and entered the dark tunnel that stood before me.

When I exited the tunnel, I was in a round chamber with jagged stone walls. I could hear the buzzing, crackling sound of electrical sparks over my head. I looked up and the light from the Ventrosphere was blinding. I adjusted the lens on the A7 visor and through the shadows I saw a person with a respirator, a young lady tied up by her feet, with her hands tied behind her back. Cables suspended her. Beneath her, spikes lay at the base of the chamber. It was Kara, and she was dangling high above a live electrical field.

"Kara!"

"Jason! Help me!"

Then I heard Raven's voice.

"The world is watching? But they can't see what's at stake. Sound familiar?"

"There's nothing to gain Raven! She has nothing to do with this. Let her go!"

"They can't hear you! There's everything to gain! I'll send you a prospectus! I have already doubled my profits from the losses suffered at the hands of your daddy's sticky fingers. Now we will give truth to the old adage that children bear the sins of their fathers!"

"SoNite entered the chamber and without warning he threw a spear at me that just missed. I watched it pass by and split the stone wall. I turned around and another spear pierced the A7. My shoulder was bleeding. I used my other arm to pull the spear from my shoulder. The spear tip was still stuck in the flesh. The A7 was sparking. SoNite leaped into the air and slammed down on me feet first, pinning me to the ground. SoNite pulled out a round sonic grenade from inside his liquid metal body.

"You're finished!"

I configured the right arm of the A7 into a propeller blade that rammed through SoNite's midsection spinning a hole in SoNite's belly. I jumped up right through the hole in SoNite's liquefied body, and landed on the ground behind him. I watched his body morph back together. The sonic bomb landed on the ground and rolled to a stop, perfectly splitting the distance between us.

Inside the GRID complex, the crowd gasped with anticipation. All the players who were eliminated from competition sat on top of their game cubes watching the hologram monitor, mesmerized by what was unfolding.

I charged toward the orb. SoNite, too, raced to the orb. We

dove after it, and it slithered out from underneath us. The orb rolled across the room. SoNite changed his arms to double bladed swords and he thrashed them at the A7. I blocked the blows with the forearm guards of the exoskeleton. I was backing up toward the stone wall. SoNite lunged with his double blades and I dodged the blow. He rammed the blades into the wall and he was stuck.

I snatched SoNite from the wall and pinned him to the ground. His body began to liquefy, and I lost my grip on him. I smashed my fist into his chest and it went straight through to the ground. A small piece of SoNite rolled over to capture the orb and his whole body reformed standing above me. My hand was stuck in the floor. He threw the orb at me and it exploded. My arm was freed, but the blast sent me clear across the chamber and I slammed up against the wall. I looked up and Kara's rope inched closer to the electrical field. The shock wave from the sonic grenade blast caused the anchors holding her up to shift.

"Jason No! Help me!" she screamed.

SoNite pulled another orb from inside his body, surprised that the blast had no effect.

Tone looked on at the GRID Complex monitor.

"What, does this guy poop bombs or something?" Tone said.

"Get up Jay!"

SoNite threw the orb at me.

"It is finished!" SoNite boasted.

I stood up and configured the arm of the A7 into a lacrosse stick. I caught the orb in the plasma net and threw the orb at SoNite. The orb stuck inside SoNite's lucid body and exploded him to pieces. The small liquid metal blobs tried to come back together as they fell from the air, but they hardened and fell to the ground like raindrops of volcanic rocks.

The shockwave from the blast caused the anchors holding Kara to break. As she was falling towards the electrical field, I leaped into air and burst through the arching bolts of electricity. I caught Kara in my arms as her body passed through the powerful currents. I could feel her body grimacing and shaking in pain. I was too late. I flicked out the A7's wings as we exited Raven's trap, but I forgot that the wings were damaged. Now we were both falling toward the ground. Just before we hit the A7 ejected a shielded air bag that enveloped us both and we crashed to the ground crushing the spikes below.

The airbag deflated and released from the A7. There was smoke and sparks spewing from the A7. I tried to get up, but I was woozy. The pain from the spearhead in my shoulder was draining my strength. I was losing blood. I stood up holding Kara in my arms. Her body was limp and her respirator was broken. She was not breathing.

Everyone in the GRID complex was cheering. Cain was stone-faced standing on top of his game cube. Mrs. McKinney was horrified, looking on in fear, while the people around her were clapping. Her face was mute with concern.

Back inside the Cauldron, SoNite was destroyed. His chards were scattered about.

"She's dead!" I said as I walked out of Raven's spiked death trap holding Kara in my arms. "Look what you've done!" I kneeled down and rested Kara's body on the ground. Then I collapsed beside her.

"Jason!" PS said as his cruiser zoomed to a halt and he ran over to us. "No! Jason, no!" He lamented.

I was again having flashbacks of my life in a distant past. I saw a little girl and an old man. Then I saw myself lying in a field of grass. A woman was screaming "No! Jason No!" I saw myself playing the games from the old world, and then I saw Raven.

In the Life Ring, inside the GRID Complex, The crowd was stunned to a deafening silence. Mrs. McKinney screamed at the monitor. "Get up Jason!" A woman next to her embraced her, trying to console her.

Tone looked at the screen, expressionless.

Back on the desolate earth, as PS5674 kneeled over me, he looked into the hidden camera in the ground.

"No more games." PS said.

He pressed the detonator and the hologram monitor in the arena went blank.

Crowds gathered in pedestrian malls throughout the Life Ring stood staring at blank screens in silence.

Then, there was a huge explosion that ruptured a giant cavity in the side of the Life Ring. People inside of the Life Ring were running and screaming. Thousands were sucked out into the freezing vacuum of space.

The security monitors and systems were deactivated in Raven's laboratory with its rows of human bodies floating in glass chambers. The human specimens were awakened. The fluid drained from their chambers and the capsules opened. The Locksmiths guarding the lab didn't know what to do as the mob of naked humans came running and stumbling out of the lab. The laboratory exploded and Raven's tools for converting humans into droids were destroyed.

Raven stood up from his desk and walked solemnly to the door. He opened the door and walked out without saying a word.

I was slowly getting my wits about me. I tried to stand again. There were hundreds of wires attached to my hands, my arms, and my head connecting me to the A7. Those wires were not there before. I looked to the sky as the Ventrosphere blazed and flickered above.

PS walked over and slapped an emergency facemask on Kara and began assessing her vitals.

"She has a very weak pulse." PS said. "Once you got a hold of her in the electrical field, I think the A7 allowed the electricity to arch around you. There may still be time to save her. Let's get her to the outpost."

"How did you know that would work son?" PS asked.

"She's not breathing! She's dead! Raven killed her, and what have you done to me?" I shouted. I was angered and confused by the wires and electrical components fused to my body, connecting me to the A7.

"We need to get her to a pressurized chamber." PS said. "I believe there is time if we hurry, and your suit has taken damage. You could be going delirious losing clean oxygen."

"What about Raven?" I asked, as tears flowed from my eyes. "I loved her!" I screamed in anger.

"I believe the girl can be saved. The colony is secure. We can rebuild from here. We've won. You won. It's over. Getting Raven proves nothing!"

"I'm going after Raven." I said. "I'm going to make him pay, for all of this!"

"Jason no!" PS pleaded.

I converted the A7 into a wheeled cycle and raced toward the bottom of the mountain where Raven's droids had set up camp. My father knew he couldn't come after me and leave Kara. I didn't share the hope he had of saving her. If he believed she could be saved, he would have to work that out. I wasn't feeling that. Kara was dead. I felt her body limp in my arms. I wanted Raven.

Coil and Ravage pulled up in a transport, before the dust from my cycle could clear.

"PS, where is the kid going?" Coil asked.

"He's going after Raven."

"Can't you catch him?" Ravage said.

"I can't. We've got to get this girl back to the outpost." PS said. "I've got to try to save her."

"Why not? Stop him!" Coil said. "You know who he is."

"They are coming!" PS said. "This war has just begun. I know who Jason is and he is about to learn who he is too."

As I closed in on Raven's droid camp, I initiated the A7's heat seeking targeting system. I locked in, and I destroyed the exposed guards and Locksmiths with a barrage of plasma cannon bursts. The droid camp was caught off guard. While they scrambled through the smoke and carnage to decipher what happened, I climbed into a fighter ship. The A7 overrode the controls and the shuttle blasted off into space headed toward the Rings.

- -

In the Life Ring, a fleet of Raven's destroyer ships loaded with Locksmith Units was closing its hulls and readying for takeoff. Smaller fighter planes accompanied these destroyers. They were armed for a battle and their destination was earth.

I flew the stolen shuttle cruiser right through the hole that was blown in the Life Ring. I landed, exited the shuttle, and configured the A7 into a wheeled cycle. I raced towards Tronics Inc.

Spikes came out of the toe and forearms of the A7 as I ran toward the Tronics Inc. building. I slammed the spikes into the wall, and scaled up the side of the building. As I neared the top, I looked down and I could see the glass atrium below. Just as I reached the top - the shuttle port - Raven was walking out of the doors to board his shuttle.

"What are you doing here? How did you get up here?" Raven said startled.

I ran over and pinned him up against the wall. Raven held on tightly to his cane. I looked him in his eyes.

"You've got some explaining to do." I said.

"We're more alike than you know." Raven said.

"You were building it all along. They couldn't see it because of the canopy. I know the truth. You kidnapped people and made them slaves.

"Nonsense, we saved those people and their children!" Raven said.

"You stole my father's gene code, the knowledge of the stone, brainwashed him and the others, and after the asteroid impact you forced them to work to complete the Rings!"

"Naive little boy! Your father stole my machines! They are mine! For all you know your father is a lie! He's a con! He's a thief!"

Raven slipped the sheath from his cane that exposed a metallic digital key.

"I've gotten my payback! I hope you get yours." Raven said.

He stabbed his cane into my chest and the blade-tipped digital key made me shake violently. In a flash, I saw a vision from a time long ago – three men ran out of a building wearing masks. The three men were surprised and apprehended by authorities. A fourth man exited the building, and he was gunned down.

I was zapped back into the moment, standing before Raven, and I was burning under my skin. I fell to the ground.

"So, tell me! Who is the fool?" Raven taunted. "It's nothing personal. It's called big business. I have more of it to take care of, and you're in the way."

The A7 was locked up. I couldn't move. Raven pulled the blade out of my chest, put the cane back in its sheath, and kicked me over the edge of the shuttle port.

"Tell Daddy I said hello!" Raven shouted as I was falling. He climbed into his ship and blasted off.

I had always had a fear of falling. But now that I was falling, I was not afraid.

I came crashing through a glass ceiling. People were running and screaming. I smashed into three floating tables that were now mangled and smoking. Racks of droid parts tumbled to the ground. Alarms were ringing. Glass and debris was scattered about. I could feel a metal battle suit attached to my body, but it was damaged. It would not respond to my thought commands and I could not free my arms or legs. The fixed hologram monitor inside the mask was flickering in and out. My peripheral sound was spotty at best. I could see three droids hovering over me.

"We should remove him from the exo-shell." The droid said. I heard a random voice. "He just fell from the sky right after the explosion! They're calling for an evacuation!"

"Help me! Help me!" I screamed. "Get this thing off of me, I'm still alive!"

The droids were ignoring me, talking about me as if I wasn't there.

"Hey can't you hear me! Get me out of here!" I yelled.

I felt like I was trapped inside a box. The three droids zoomed abruptly towards me; one of the droids was trying to peer through the cracked glass in the facemask of my battle suit. Another droid inserted a needle in between the bars of the metal frame and into my thigh. The needle pierced my skin injecting me with a tranquilizer. I screamed in pain. The medicine immediately made me feel drowsy.

"It appears that the shell is permanently affixed to the human," I heard the last of the droids say. "There is no registered serial number for this droid, and no record of it in our catalog."

One of the robots stammered as it turned toward me, "Our protocol is to inform the Locksmiths, and he is to be examined and purged."

"Wait! No, you can't send me back to him," I slurred.

A small door opened from the side of the droid and a long arm with three plugs at the tip extended towards me. It was trying to access and override my battle suit's power system. I was still trying to free myself. The other droids circled behind me extending large vices to restrain my arms. I was thinking that maybe the droid is right. Maybe I am stuck in this machine. I mean, maybe I am a machine, and if that's the case these droids have agreed that it's best if I'm destroyed. Sparks were flying from the suit as I resisted with the last bit of my strength. The droid's plugs were inches from ramming into my chest and the droids suddenly stopped.

"We've been instructed by Missy to report to the nearest Locksmith outpost." The droids said.

"Missy! Mesi! Mesi! The ghost in the machine! Is that you?" I said. "Mesi, help! Get me out of here!"

Missy turned away from the computers in the study as she noticed that Grandpa's old footlocker was trembling. The magazines were shaken to the floor as the tarnished brass latches clanked. Missy walked slowly toward the footlocker. She flicked the latch and opened it. She jumped back, as the metallic droid hand reached up from inside the footlocker and she saw a face through the mask of the helmet.

I climbed up out of the footlocker and stood there before her – a living, breathing cyborg.

"Missy, I'm sorry." I said. "Everything he said was true. I should have believed him. I should have listened when it was easier."

"I love you Jay!" Missy said hugging the cold steel of the A7.

"Now, let's get to the computer." I said. "You've got to figure out how to send me back before mama get's home."

204

Made in the USA
Middletown, DE
07 January 2022

58038394R00115